By Peter David

Knight Life
One Knight Only
Fall of Knight

Sir Apropos of Nothing
The Woad to Wuin
Tong Lashing

Howling Mad

Darkness of the Light

Spider-Man
Spider-Man 2
Spider-Man 3

Hulk

Iron Man

Batman Forever

BABYLON 5
In the Beginning
Armies of Light and Dark
Out of the Darkness
The Long Night of Centauri Prime
Thirdspace

STAR TREK
The Next Generation: Before Dishonor
The Next Generation: Imzadi Forever
New Frontier: House of Cards
New Frontier: Missing in Action

FALLEN ANGEL
To Rule in Hell
To Serve in Heaven
Back in Noir

Tigerheart

And many more

IRON MAN

PETER DAVID

BALLANTINE BOOKS • NEW YORK

Iron Man is a work of fiction. Names, places, and incidents either are products of the author's imagination or are used fictitiously.

A Del Rey Books Mass Market Original

Copyright © 2008 by MVL Film Finance LLC. & ® or ™ where indicated.
All Rights Reserved. Used under authorization.

Iron Man, the Movie © 2008 MVL Film Finance LLC. Marvel, Iron Man, all character names and their distinctive likenesses: ™ & © 2008 Marvel Entertainment, Inc. and its subsidiaries. All Rights Reserved.

Published in the United States by Del Rey Books, an imprint of The Random House Publishing Group, a division of Random House, Inc., New York.

Del Rey is a registered trademark and the Del Rey colophon is a trademark of Random House, Inc.

ISBN 978-0-345-50609-2

Printed in the United States of America

www.delreybooks.com

OPM   9   8   7   6   5   4   3   2   1

To Stan—
The original Iron Man
of comics

IRON MAN

Anthony Stark is bored.

On some level, he supposes that boredom is a good thing. Considering his present environment, the opposite of boredom could well be life threatening. Perhaps he should be grateful. Perhaps . . .

Nope. Nope, still bored. Impossible to be grateful for being bored. There are simply too many interesting things going on in the world to tolerate boredom for even a moment.

It's probably his mind that is to blame. His mind is always racing, always thinking, always conceiving new ideas, new concepts. His mind chafes against boredom, rages against the very notion of tedium. He thinks about a friend of his who was a drug addict, claiming that the reason he regularly put junk up his nose or into his veins was that he was bored, and taking drugs helped to counteract the threat of impending tedium.

Idiot, thinks Stark. Why would someone like that threaten the safety of his brain by introducing something so dangerous into his system? He shakes his head at such foolishness as he sips Scotch from the metal tumbler in his hand, wondering why some people would engage in self-destructive behavior.

He glances out the window, hoping that there will be something to break up the monotony of the view. Nope. It's the same sort of rocky, arid vista that he's been witnessing steadily as they truck across the heart of Afghanistan, about two hundred miles northwest of

Kabul. Not for the first time, he wonders why in the world anyone would willingly live there, to say nothing of using vicious terrorist tactics to defend the right to do so. There is nothing but flat emptiness, broken up by pebbles, rocks, and a distant mountain range with a large flattened area smack in the middle from which smoke is steadily rising. Stark glances at that vast emptiness with considerable pride and then goes back to his musings about the oddity of terrorists fighting for their brutal tribal existence. If anything, people should be fighting for the opportunity to get the hell out of there. He wonders, just for a moment, if blowing up the terrorists is the wrong way to go. Instead just offer the lot of them beachfront condos in Santa Monica and see how quickly they abandon this hellhole they call home.

It is, of course, a ridiculous position to take. So ridiculous, in fact, that Stark considers the notion of saying it with a straight face in front of a bevy of reporters just to see the reaction it will get. Stark enjoys doing that now and then: saying things that he knows will drive people berserk. When one's profession involves coming up with new and exciting ways to take lives, sometimes it's fun to do something just to feel alive.

The airmen riding with him in the Humvee would very likely not laugh at the notion. They are deathly serious. Stark studies them. They come across to him as children who are wearing their big brothers' G.I. Joe helmets and doing their damnedest to look like real, true, genuine soldiers. Kids with battle-worn faces. When other kids their age are busy trying to find friends with benefits, these guys have seen . . . what? Friends of theirs blown apart?

What the hell are they doing here? He understands intellectually the obvious fact: They are here because they were assigned here. They signed on for a job and they're doing it, no questions asked. Still, there's the cosmic "whyness" of their presence here. He wonders if they're asking themselves that very same question. Maybe that's why they appear so humorless: In pondering the question, they're not wild about the answer they're coming to.

Stark looks and feels out of place. Unlike the soldiers, he's there because he chose to be there. He felt the need to prove a point, and Afghanistan was the best place to do it. But he has made no concessions to the formidable environment in which he now finds himself. His suit is dapper and pressed. His one acknowledgment of the heat has been to loosen the knot on his designer tie and open the top button on his shirt. His black hair is properly coiffed, his van dyke beard is trimmed, and he would be perfectly suited for a GQ cover photo, which is the effect that a five-hundred-dollar haircut will get you.

The airman sitting across from him to the right is the oldest of the three. He maintains a grim, determined expression. His dog tags say "Pratt, Adam" on them. Next to him is a younger man who is trying not to look at Stark directly, but keeps stealing sidelong glances just the same. His ID pegs him as "Ryan, James." Jimmy to his friends. Stark met Jimmy earlier; he'd been assigned to help Stark set up his weapons array for the demonstration that he had completed only minutes earlier. Good kid. Eager to talk but determined to be all business, especially since top military brass had been present. Seated next to Stark is Ramirez comma Pedro. Their helmets and the manner in which they're hunkered down give the three of them a sort of sameness. The only distinguishing feature is that Jimmy is wearing a wristwatch with the distinctive orange and blue colors of the Mets. A New York boy, obviously. Stark smiles, despite the fact that he is a die-hard Yankees fan.

"So," Stark says finally, determined to do something to break up the tedium. "Show of hands: How many of you are from out of town?" No response, although Jimmy does allow the slightest signs of a grin to tweak the edges of his mouth.

"Oh, I get it. You guys aren't allowed to talk. Is that it? Are you not allowed to talk?" Now Jimmy's grin is unstoppable, reaching from one side of his face to the other. He fiddles with his Mets watch.

"No, we're allowed to talk," says Jimmy. Pratt fires him an annoyed look, but remains silent.

"Oh. I see. So it's personal," says Stark.

Ramirez leans over slightly. "I think they're intimidated," says Ramirez. He speaks with the telltale confidence of the streetwise kid. Stark believes that, from that one sentence, he's got a bead on Ramirez. Tough, savvy, maybe ran with gangs, then sought a way out of his tough neighborhood. Then again, what the hell did Stark know? It was entirely possible that Ramirez grew up in a privileged section of Long Island and enlisted as part of a grand family tradition. No point in making assumptions based on ethnicity.

"Good God, you're a woman," Stark says with a mock chiding tone to Jimmy. "I honestly . . . I couldn't have called that."

The airmen are desperately trying not to laugh. Stark remains relentless. "I would apologize, but isn't that what we're going for here? I saw you as a soldier first. But hey, if you won't ask, I won't tell." He bats his eyes for comic effect and all attempts by the soldiers to maintain their professional demeanor is shattered. Laughter fills the back of the Humvee.

"I have a question, sir," says Jimmy.

"Please."

"Is it true you're twelve for twelve with last year's Maxim cover girls?"

"*Excellent question,*" says Stark, looking wistful. "*Yes and no. March and I had a schedule conflict but, thankfully, the Christmas cover was twins. Anyone else? You, with the hand up,*" he says to Pratt, who appears to have given up on the notion of being the one who was setting an example of how to behave.

"*It's a little embarrassing,*" says Pratt.

"*Join the club.*"

"*Is it cool if I have my picture taken with you?*"

"*Yes. It's very cool,*" Stark says. "*Are you aware that Native Americans believe photographs steal a little piece of your soul?*" He grins and adds, "*Not to worry, mine's long gone. Fire away.*"

Pratt and Ramirez exchange places as Jimmy brings up a small digital camera. "*Now I don't want to see this on your Myspace page,*" Stark says. *Pratt gets in close to Stark and raises his fingers in a "V"-for-Victory gesture.* "*Please, no gang signs,*" Stark tells him sternly, and then when a startled Pratt quickly lowers his hand, Stark admits, "*No, throw that up there, I'm kidding.*" Relief visibly floods through Pratt's body as he raises his fingers in the "*V*" once more.

Jimmy snaps the picture, and it makes a sound.

These digital cameras, *thinks Stark.* It's not enough that they make this sound effect of a shutter snapping as if they even have shutters. Now they have sound effects of explosions?

It is at that moment that Stark realizes his brain has essentially disconnected from what's happening around him, trying to shield him from the reality of what's going on.

It is not a sound effect from the camera. It is an explosion, an actual explosion. It is impossible to determine just how close it is, but the Humvee rocks wildly. Everyone is shouting, Pratt barking orders, and suddenly

Stark's jaw drops at what he sees through the windshield.

They had not been the lone Humvee moving down the road; instead they had been part of a convoy. Now Stark sees the Humvee in front of them erupt in a ball of flame and flip over.

Tony Stark has never witnessed death. He was halfway around the world when his father died, although he'd returned home immediately upon learning of his father's passing. The weapons that the billionaire industrialist has built are designed to deliver death, but it has always been an abstract notion for him. Death has never gotten up close and personal with him.

That is no longer the case as he witnesses the lead Humvee ripped apart by some sort of missile. He has a brief glimpse of the men within, illuminated by the fireball. Then they are gone, enveloped in a blast of yellow and orange and red. Horrifically, as if his thoughts have bifurcated, he recoils at the carnage while at the same time admiring the quality of the weapon that is delivering it.

The Humvee in which Stark is riding slams to a halt. The soldiers, in full battle mode, scramble out. Pratt turns to him and this is no longer the face of a young man, a misplaced kid who would be more at home hanging out at the local mall or getting some pretty young cheerleader into a world of trouble. This is a trained combat veteran as he shouts, "Stay here!"

Stark tries to figure out where the hell else he might possibly have gone, but he doesn't ask. Pratt has vanished. Soldiers are running this way and that. Stark feels as if he should be crouching on the floor of the Humvee. Instead he rolls the window partway down and peers out, trying to see what's happening. It's hard to determine who's who. Then he spots a comforting, familiar flash of blue and orange. Jimmy is standing about five feet away, holding his rifle, and trying to find a target.

And then Jimmy is gone. It happens so quickly that it makes an imprint in Stark's mind and he has to analyze it after the fact. Jimmy had taken a step forward and suddenly a mine bounded from the ground as if propelled from a spring. An M16 mine, nicknamed "Bouncing Betty" after the German mine of the same name. His weapons-designer mind runs through the specs: When tripped, the mine is ejected about three feet into the air and then detonates, spraying shrapnel everywhere. As with other tools of death, Stark has designed them, understood them . . . but never seen them in combat action. He sees it now as the mine literally rips Jimmy to shreds. The kid likely never even knew what happened.

What were his last thoughts? *Stark wonders, horrified.* Were they of the mission? Of the Mets? Of the girl he'd never see? My God . . . what have I gotten myself into?

A familiar figure sprints by. It's United States Air Force Lieutenant Colonel James Rhodes, a.k.a. Rhodey. If there is anyone that Stark wants to see in this particular situation, it's Rhodey. Square jawed, with no trace of fear in his eyes, and black skin made even darker since it's smeared with charcoal. He is firing a 50-caliber machine gun. It's impossible for Stark to determine whether he's shooting at something in specific or just laying down suppressing fire or maybe simply shooting wherever he can and hoping to God he hits an enemy. He notices Stark peering out of the window.

"Get down, Tony! Get the—"

More explosions. Smoke is billowing everywhere. Rhodey fires into the chaos, and Stark wonders how Rhodey can see what he's shooting at. Maybe he's not. Maybe he's just firing blind. It's easy to sit nice and snug at home and wonder how one's own soldiers can wind *up getting killed through friendly fire. Now Stark sees all too easily how such a thing could occur.*

Rhodey advances into the smoke and murk. Stark twists around and looks out the back window. The other Humvee is there. That gives him some small measure of comfort, right up until another explosion annihilates it as well. The windows of Stark's Humvee all blow in. Stark barely ducks in time, throwing his arms over his head, as glass and bits of metal ricochet around the contained space.

It's clear what's happening. One by one, they—whoever they are—are blowing up the vehicles. All the shouted advice to "stay put" pales next to the realization that his car is likely next. Staying put is no longer an option.

Stark shoves open the door and half steps, half tumbles out of the car. He puts his hands to his face and realizes that he is bleeding. That's to be expected; with all the debris flying around the inside of the Humvee, injury was inevitable.

Once out of the car, Stark starts to run. He has no destination in mind; all he knows is that he's got to put some distance between himself and the site of this madness. Smoke is everywhere. He covers his mouth with his designer necktie, trying not to breathe in the smoke, fearing his lungs could collapse. Machine gun fire is all around. Tracers zip past him. The ground erupts directly in front of him; if it had detonated even a second later, he would have been right in the middle of it and would be in a million pieces by now.

He shields his eyes, trying to see Rhodey or anybody. He catches fleeting glimpses of running forms. Then he spots an M16 rifle lying on the ground. There are small tufts of fire all around it. Stark runs up to it, kicking dirt on the flames to extinguish them so that he can get to the M16. He manages to do so and pats himself on the back for his cleverness, right up until he actually endeavors to pick the gun up. Then he lets out a startled yelp and drops the weapon, his fingers reflexively curling in pain. The gun had been red hot, its surface temperature increased near to the melting point thanks to the fires all around it.

He hears an explosion behind him and to the left. Naturally he moves forward and to the right. I'm being herded, he thinks, and then a voice comes floating to him, uncalled for. A female, teasing voice that says lazily, Not everything is about you.

Just for a moment he remembers what it was like, looking up at Christine as she smiled down at him. She had been half joking, half serious. The truth was that Tony Stark knew the entire world didn't revolve around him. He preferred to think that it rotated around him.

He finds himself back near the Humvees. One is sitting there, smoldering, the interior blackened. He wonders if any of the occupants managed to get out. He wonders if any of them are still alive. He wonders if anyone besides him is still alive.

Rhodey had tried to talk him out of coming here. Why the hell didn't he listen? What in the name of God was he thinking . . . ?

He realizes with a sinking heart that his is a study in hubris. He had been convinced that, because he was Tony Stark, billionaire munitions mogul, he was invulnerable to all harm. Death was the poor man's concern.

He is looking away from the Humvee when he hears something thunk off it. He turns, half wondering if it's going to be a random body part that was hurled in his direction courtesy of an explosion. Instead he sees a rocket-propelled grenade—an RPG—ricochet off the burned-out Humvee and fall practically at his feet. His eyes widen as he sees its pedigree stamped across the side: USM 11676 Stark Munitions.

Having designed the damned thing, Stark knows precisely what the blast range is (one kilometer). He knows the amount of time to detonate (four seconds). He knows how close he is standing to it. Those three numbers collide in his mind and he comes to the realization that there is simply no way he's going to be able to get far enough away from it.

His mind unaccountably spins away to an old Frankenstein movie. His oncoming monster is confronting the beleaguered scientist, and he is shouting with equal mixture of anger and terror, "Keep back! I'm your creator! You cannot hurt me! You cannot!"

This thing, this RPG, owes its existence to Tony Stark. Now it lies at his feet, ready to annihilate him. This is the thanks I get?

The grenade appears to sense its lack of gratitude. It sits there, as dangerous as a piece of fruit.

Stark fights back the urge to laugh. A dud. *He's heard all the running jokes in the military about what one can expect from having munitions provided by the manufacturer who puts in the lowest bid. He'd always taken offense at such jibes. He never thought that he would have reason to be grateful over—*

The RPG explodes.

Stark is lifted off his feet by the power of the detonation. The barrage of fragments shreds his suit. He is wearing body armor beneath his suit, a precaution that he had considered ridiculous, but that had been insisted upon by military personnel. Now it appears that it is going to save his life . . .

. . . or maybe not.

He hits the ground, tries to get up, can't. He lies face down on the ground, his mouth filled with blood and dirt. His ears are ringing, making it almost impossible for him to hear anything. He thinks he can hear distant voices shouting, and somewhere far away is the chatter of small-arms fire.

The world begins to fade out around him. He waits to see if his life is about to pass before his eyes. It doesn't. He's not certain if that's a good thing or not.

A word floats across his consciousness. Not a word: a name.

Pepper.

He has no idea why in the world that name would creep into his mind during what might well be the very last moment of his life, and before he can give it further consideration, the world fuzzes out around him.

i.

"December 7, 1941: The day the world changed forever."

James Rhodes—"Rhodey," as his friends called him—was seated to the right of a large screen, mounted on a wall behind a podium. He acted as if being on stage was the most comfortable and natural thing in the world for him, rather than being what it was: incredibly nerve-racking. But Rhodey was far too accomplished a military man to let any display of nerves be evident. Besides, someone who had faced enemy fire should be able to deal with this stupid fear he had about public speaking. Still, he would have felt a little more comfortable if at least a couple of people in the audience were aiming weapons at him.

He was at the front of a huge ballroom, one of the larger meeting facilities in Caesars Palace in Las Vegas. The lighting in the room was dimmed, with the recorded voice of a narrator who sounded suspiciously like James Earl Jones coming through the PA system. There were about a hundred people seated at a dozen tables, the remains of their rubber-chicken dinners being collected by waiters and waitresses. On the screen was footage of President Franklin Delano Roosevelt seated in front of a radio microphone, delivering quite possibly the most famous radio address in history. The narrator continued portentously, "President Roosevelt declares the United States will build fifty thousand planes to fight the armies of Hirohito and Hitler . . ."

The image on the screen shifted. Invading Nazis were goose-stepping their way through the streets of Paris.

"Although no such capacity to build existed, Howard Stark, founder of the fledgling Stark Industries, answers his call to duty."

The screen depicted a hangar in a small rural airfield. The landing strip that was visible was barely more than a dirt road. The words "Los Angeles" were superimposed over the picture just to establish a place. A man dressed in a 1940s-style suit was standing proudly in front of the hangar, arms akimbo. He had a pencil thin mustache and was wearing a fedora pushed back on his head. He was pointing proudly at the sign that read "Stark Industries."

". . . and builds not fifty, but a hundred thousand planes."

Howard Stark, grinning ear to ear, was standing in the Oval Office. He was shaking hands with FDR. He looked like the happiest man in the world. FDR looked as if he were working to keep the smile on his face; perhaps, Rhodey thought, he'd just had an argument with Eleanor.

The image on the screen returned to Stark Industries, and it was obvious that time had passed. The forest that had been visible in the background was gone, razed to the ground. In its place was a row of hangars rather than the one, and the name "Stark" was spelled out via huge raised letters atop the hangars, like the "Hollywood" sign. The small, unimpressive runway had been replaced by smooth, endless vistas of concrete. It was a genuine airfield rather than just some small start-up endeavor, and it was covered with B-29 bombers just off the assembly line. They were rolling forward, gleaming in the sun, ready to fight for democracy around the world and—ideally—bomb Hitler and Hiro back to the Stone Age.

The image of them on the ground dissolved to the bombers in flight. This was not promotional footage taken by Stark Industries back in the day; this was newsreel footage, showing Stark bombers airborne. Their versatility in battle was clearly depicted as some of them were shown dropping bombs while others were spitting out paratroopers, cracking silk and descending upon the enemy.

All of them old men now, Rhodey thought as he saw young examples of the Greatest Generation hurling themselves into combat. *Old men or young dead men, immortalized on film.*

A mushroom cloud erupted in a New Mexico desert. The narrator said, "Later, Stark's work on the Manhattan Project makes the end of the war possible." There was Howard Stark again, observing the explosion alongside Robert Oppenheimer. One hoped that they were a sufficient distance to avoid getting their chromosomes scrambled courtesy of radiation.

Then again, that might go a long way toward explaining Tony, he thought, and then decided that that was a rather uncharitable attitude to have. Certainly it was unworthy of an Air Force officer.

"Stark Industries would go on to contribute to every major weapons system through the Cold War." The visuals were now coming so quickly that they were almost a blur. The mind's eye barely had time to register B-52s, ICBMs, nuclear subs gliding through the ocean, F-16s launching from carriers. A series of presidents flew by: Harry Truman, Dwight Eisenhower, John F. Kennedy, Lyndon Johnson, Richard Nixon. And next to every one of them was Howard Stark. It almost reminded Rhodey of that Woody Allen film, *Zelig,* in which the actor/director was visually inserted into great moments of history. The difference, of course, was that Howard Stark was really there.

"But Howard Stark's greatest achievement would come in 1973 with the birth of his son, Tony, who—barely a year later—met his very first president," said the possible James Earl Jones. There was President Gerald Ford, standing next to Howard Stark while cradling baby Tony. Howard Stark was looking slightly nervous; perhaps he was concerned that Ford, who occasionally garnered a reputation for clumsiness, might drop the infant. Moments later, as years subjectively whizzed by, four-year-old Tony was shown building a massive city entirely of Lego blocks. Already one could see the gleam of determination and the excitement of discovery in his eyes. And then, just like that, Tony Stark was twelve years old, working alongside Howard to assemble a hot rod engine. A gleaming-red hot rod, the obvious eventual recipient of the engine, was visible in the background with its hood open.

"From early on, it was clear that Tony Stark had a unique gift. At seventeen he graduated at the top of his class from MIT."

Tony Stark, looking unconscionably young, was shown in a hangar full of F-18s. He was climbing around inside a turbine engine while other workers were looking on in unfeigned amazement.

"Four years later, tragedy would pass the Stark mantle from father to son," said the narrator. At Howard Stark's funeral, Tony was shown alongside U.S. presidents both past and present. "The loss of a titan. But Tony did not let personal grief distract him from his duty. At twenty-one, he became the youngest-ever CEO of a Fortune 500 company."

Tony was shown cutting the ribbon on a brand-new Arc reactor at Stark Industries West Coast headquarters. He was smiling, posing effortlessly for cameras. The difference between father and son was instantly evident. Whereas Howard Stark was stiff, even slightly uncom-

fortable on camera, making an effort to look at ease and
not quite succeeding, Tony Stark was born to have a lens
aimed in his direction. His body language was relaxed,
his smile so perfect that Rhodey wondered if he didn't
practice it in the mirror.

"And with it came a new mandate: smarter weapons.
Fewer casualties. A dedication to preserving life."

A laser-guided bomb was shown hitting its target with
a precision that previous generations of missiles could
not even begin to achieve. Other examples of Stark
weaponry flashed across the screen, a visual cascade of
America's modern military might. Rhodey's voice became louder, building toward the climax of the pre-
sentation. "Today Tony Stark's ingenuity continues to
protect freedom and American interests around the
globe."

When Rhodey had seen the next visual in advance, he
had winced inwardly. He had thought it was, frankly, a
bit much. But Tony Stark had sat next to him, viewing
the video when it had first been cut together, and personally approved the image that was now on the screen: a
waving American flag superimposed with an Annie
Liebovitz portrait of Tony.

The crowd, somewhat to Rhodey's surprise, cheered
in approval. Well, Stark had been right when he made
that call, obviously. Nothing stirred a room full of top
corporate executives and movers and shakers who were
thriving on consumerism—not to mention military officers who revered the American flag—quite like an in-
your-face symbol of the American way of life.

As the image on the screen faded out, the applause
continued to swell. A light shined down on Rhodey,
who blinked uncomfortably against the glare but tried
to take it in stride. "As program manager and liaison to
Stark Industries, I've had the honor of serving with a
real patriot, a man whose life has been dedicated to pro-

tecting our troops on the front lines," said Rhodey.
"He's a friend and a great mentor. A man who has always been there for his friends and his country. Ladies
and gentlemen, this year's Apogee Award winner, Mr.
Tony Stark."

Rhodey wouldn't have thought it possible, but the applause actually kicked up a few notches. A spotlight
swept across the darkened room and came to rest on
Tony Stark's chair.

Unfortunately, Tony Stark was not occupying it.

The applause slowly trailed off and the lights began to
come up. There was a confused and clearly annoyed
buzz from the occupants of the room. Rhodey felt his
stomach clench, as it typically did when Tony Stark did
something pigheaded.

A figure was making its way up toward the podium
now. Rhodey squinted to make out who it was, and realized that it was Obadiah Stane. Stane, the chief financial officer of Stark Industries, was clearly about to try
to do some damage control.

Stane had a shaved head and a salt-and-pepper beard
that made him look older than he was, but he never
seemed to mind. He was also one of the most personable
people that Rhodey had ever met. Very little seemed to
throw him off his game; he was, to use an overused
word, unflappable. Rhodey supposed that when one
had to deal with Tony Stark on a daily basis, it was either cultivate that attitude or lose one's mind. Stane had
obviously opted for the former.

"Thank you," said Stane, as if the audience was expecting him and genuinely pleased to see him. "I, uhhhh,
I'm not Tony Stark, but if I were Tony, I'd tell you how
honored I am and . . . what a joy it is to receive this
award." He held the plaque, which had an image of the
sun on it. "The best thing about Tony is also the worst
thing. He's always working."

There were tentative nods of understanding from the men and women in the room. They were, for the most part, all type A personalities and could totally relate to the notion that Tony Stark was so work-obsessed that he couldn't even cut himself loose to attend an award ceremony being given in his honor. Rhodey had to hand it to Stane. He knew just what to say to finesse delicate situations.

Rhodey just wished that what Stane had said had an ounce of truth to it. In this instance, however, Rhodey had a very good idea of exactly where Tony Stark was, and it sure wasn't at work.

The red dice bounded across the green felt of the dice table. Tony Stark leaned forward, watching the dice bounce, his gaze never wavering. They rolled, ricocheted off the far end of the table, and came to a halt.

The crowd erupted in cheers. Stark had hit his number, and since he had taken it upon himself to lay down bets for everyone around him, naturally they all had a stake in it. A massive pile of chips was slid across the table to land in front of him, while smaller piles were doled out to the people immediately surrounding him.

Gorgeous women—"lucky ladies," as Stark liked to call them—stood on either side of him. One was a blonde, the other a brunette. Stark glanced around, hoping that he could find a worthwhile redhead in order to complete the set, but none appeared to be presenting herself.

Stark sensed, before he saw, Rhodey heading his way. He had to figure that was what happened when you worked with someone long enough: You become aware of their presence before you actually see them.

The thing was, he wasn't expecting to see Rhodey there at all. The last he'd heard, Rhodey was in Washington, D.C., not Las Vegas. "My God, what are you—?"

he started to say. Then he considered the timing, and the lack of likelihood that it was all a coincidence, and Stark came to a conclusion that he couldn't say enthused him.

"They roped you into this thing, too?" he said.

"They said you'd be deeply honored if I presented you with this award." With that, Rhodey unceremoniously dumped the plaque on the felt surface of the table.

"Lots of people would consider that award a serious honor," said Rhodey.

Stark looked at the plaque with undisguised distaste. "It belongs to my old man," he said and looked back to the dice as if that pronouncement settled the entire matter. He shook the dice, trying to force positive karma into them. All around, people were holding their collective breath. He rolled the dice and watched them bounce across the table.

Moans erupted as the dice crapped out.

Stark looked at Rhodey in a scolding manner. "You cooled my table," he said as a stack of the chips moved away from him and back into the house's pot. Stark didn't even give it a glance, but losers around him looked stricken as they lost their money.

"You cooled your own table, pal. Good luck runs out, remember that."

Stark decided not to remember it at all. "Color me up," he said to the boxman.

The boxman happily collected Stark's lower-denomination chips and exchanged them for differently colored chips of a higher denomination. Casinos liked when gamblers chose to "color up": It made the gamblers more likely to drop larger amounts impulsively. Not that Tony Stark needed all that much prompting.

Seeing that Stark was making a chip exchange, his security entourage—which had made itself nicely invisible while he was at the table—correctly took that as their cue that the boss was about to go into motion. Three security men, identically dressed in dark suits and nearly indistinguishable from one another, moved in to surround Stark. A fourth man joined them, taking point. He was a different sort from the guards. He was dressed in a chauffeur's uniform that didn't fit him particularly well. It wasn't the uniform as much as it was the man wearing it: He just wasn't comfortable in suits no matter how well they were tailored. Periodically he would pull at the front of the jacket, or the shoulders, or the back. He was always hitching up his pants even though they didn't require it. Stark would, from time to time, watch him go through his countless little struggles with the chauffeur's uniform and always be amused by it. This was a man who was clearly far more comfortable wearing sweat pants and a T-shirt.

He had a lantern jaw, cauliflower ears, and a mashed-in nose, all of which cried out that this was a man who had spent a considerable portion of his life in a boxing ring. His mouth was turned in a permanent downward frown that cast his entire face in a perpetual hangdog manner. Little surprise that the man, Harold Hogan, had been tagged with the shamelessly ironic nickname of "Happy."

Stark, Rhodey, Happy Hogan, and the entourage of security men moved through the casino and created the same stir as if Stark were a rock star. People gawked, snapped pictures with their cameras or their telephones, and attempted to whisper to one another—in voices that carried—"Is that him?" "I think so." "Couldn't be." "I thought he'd be taller?" "I thought he'd be shorter." Stark was used to it, and yet it never failed to entertain him. His escorts simply seemed resigned to enduring it. To the guards, it was a job. To Rhodey and Hogan, it was one of the burdens of being out in public with Tony Stark.

Stark passed a roulette wheel and stopped. Rhodey

plucked at his arm, trying to keep him moving, but Stark shook it off. He knew that there was some risk to that. When he was in public, Tony Stark had to be like a shark: Keep moving or else, the "or else" being to be surrounded by autograph seekers or picture takers. Still, what was the purpose of living if one couldn't take small risks every now and then?

Deciding to place an even-money bet, he set all the chips he had on the black square of the board. The croupier's face turned ashen when he saw the amount. Seeing the croupier's expression, Rhodey said in a low tone, "How much is that?"

Stark honestly wasn't sure. He hadn't been paying attention. He looked down at the stack, did fast mental calculations, and said carelessly, "Three million dollars."

Rhodey make a small choking noise in his throat. Hogan just rolled his eyes.

"Sorry, sir," said the croupier, who had found his voice. "That exceeds the table limit."

"Come on, I thought this was Caesars Palace?" Stark said challengingly. "I bet the MGM Grand would cover it. Come on, kid: no guts, no glory."

The croupier, clearly out of his depth, turned to the pit boss, searching for guidance. The pit boss looked at Stark, looked at the bet. An older, more seasoned hand, the pit boss didn't let any hint of uncertainty cross his face. Instead he simply nodded, as if the possibility of Stark doubling his money to six million didn't bother him at all . . . which was pretty impressive, considering his job might well be on the line should that happen.

"Ha!" said Stark approvingly. "A man with guts. A man after my own heart."

"You have a heart?" said Rhodey.

"Well, the jury's still out on that. Depends who you talk to."

Rhodey looked nervously at the bet. "Red. I'm telling you, it's going to be red. I just have a feeling," he said.

"Sometimes you gotta live on the edge. I want it all on black."

This prompted half a dozen other people to immediately put their own bets entirely on black . . . and one scuzzy-looking guy to place his on red, looking defiantly and contemptuously at Stark. Stark knew his kind immediately: He was the type who was jealous of Stark's acclaim and wealth, and was hoping to take the opportunity to show up the great Tony Stark. Stark would have felt sorry for him, but that would have required him to give a damn one way or the other, and so he didn't.

"No more bets, please, no more bets," said the croupier as he sent the wheel spinning. After a few moments he dropped in the ball. It clattered around the wheel, bounding from one pocket to the next to the next. Stark watched it. He was waiting for the excitement to build. To his disappointment, it didn't happen. At most, he was somewhat interested, and even that was married to a degree of detachment.

As he watched the ball ricochet relentlessly, Rhodey said, "Listen, about tomorrow. We should be doing the test here in Vegas, not in a hot zone."

"The system has to be demonstrated in true field conditions," said Stark.

"But there's safety issues . . ."

"Come on," said Stark. "Are you telling me that the army's best can't protect one guy? What's that say about us?"

"It's just that anything can happen."

"Then we'll just have to be ready for anything, won't we?"

Their attention was grabbed by the sudden lack of

noise from the wheel. They looked back and saw that the ball had indeed stopped bouncing around and nestled into a spot. The spot was the number twelve; the color was red.

The croupier tried not to let out a sigh of relief and utterly failed as he hauled forward Stark's winnings for the evening. There were moans from the others who had followed Stark's lead and also lost their money. The only one who was chuckling was the envious jerk that had bet on red and had managed to pick up a quick one hundred dollars. Stark had no doubt he'd dump it all into the slot machine inside of ten minutes.

Stark shrugged, signed a couple of autographs, and then turned away. His entourage fell into step behind and around him.

"Don't know what was more exciting," said Stark. "The fact that I won it, or the fact that I don't care I just lost it."

Rhodey shook his head. It was clear that, no matter how long he knew Tony Stark, he would never understand him. That was fine. There were times when Stark felt exactly the same way. "Try not to be late tomorrow," Rhodey warned him. Then he turned and walked away before Stark could say anything else.

Rhodey's miffed with me. Ah well. He'll get over it. He always does. Who could possibly stay mad at me?

Hogan, with his customary efficiency, had arranged to have the limo waiting. As they approached it, an attractive young blonde insinuated herself between Stark and the limo. She was holding a tape recorder. Everything about her fairly screamed that she was a reporter. "Mr. Stark!" she called.

The security men immediately went into action. Two of them moved around Stark and came in on either side of her, taking her firmly by either arm. Despite the fact that the security men were in the process of dragging her away, she continued to speak as quickly as she could. "Christine Everhart, *Vanity Fair* magazine. Can I ask you a few questions?"

Stark put up a hand, the gesture halting the security guards. "Can I ask a few back?"

She gave him a disarming smile.

Within earshot of Stark, Hogan muttered, "Awwww, here we go again." Stark didn't acknowledge the comment. Instead he indicated to the security guards that they should let her pass. They were clearly not happy about it, but nevertheless they stood to either side and allowed her through. Hogan shook his head. Then, choosing not to say anything since he no doubt figured—correctly—that it would be ignored, he headed for the limo to climb into the driver's side.

She held up the tape recorder and said, "Do you mind?" When he shook his head, she clicked it on and then, all business, said, "You've been called the Da Vinci of our time. What do you say to that?"

"Absolutely ridiculous. I don't paint."

Her tone changed, and Stark read volumes into it before she spoke another word. Clearly she thought she'd set him up with a puffball question, and now she figured she was going to bring in the high heat. Sure enough: "And what do you say to your other nickname: 'The Merchant of Death'?" she said challengingly.

Stark considered it a moment. "That's not bad."

Her attitude immediately turned icy toward him.

Stark smiled. It was clearly not the answer she had wanted or anticipated. She had probably figured he'd stammer or deny it or bleat how it was unfair. As if he cared what sort of heartless nicknames were attributed to him by people who condemned him on the one hand, but on the other hand depended upon his weaponry to help keep America and her interests safe.

"Let me guess. Berkeley?" he said.

"Brown."

"Well, Miss Brown," he said, "it's an imperfect world and I assure you, the day weapons are no longer needed to keep the peace, I'll start manufacturing bricks and beams to make baby hospitals."

She tilted her head slightly. "Rehearse that much, Mr. Stark?"

In spite of himself, he liked her. This one had a bit of fire to her, as opposed to many of the mindless sheep that were calling themselves journalists these days. "Every night in front of the mirror. Call me Tony."

"I'm sorry, Tony. I was hoping for a serious answer."

"You want serious? Here's serious," said Stark, and much to his own surprise, he really was being serious. "Remember the old Teddy Roosevelt line regarding diplomacy? 'Speak softly and carry a big stick?' My old man had a philosophy: Peace means having a bigger stick than the other guy."

"Good line, coming from the guy selling the sticks."

Oh, she's good. She's very good. This is turning into a fencing match. "My father helped defeat Hitler. He was on the Manhattan Project. A lot of people—including your professors at Brown—might call that being a hero."

"Others might call it war profiteering."

He had to smile at that. She was relentless. Other reporters usually felt they had their story after his first couple of comments. The line about his father being a hero was usually a showstopper. This girl was making him dig deep. She was trying to get through the invisible armor he wore that typically shielded him in such confrontations, and he wasn't entirely sure that she wasn't succeeding.

Deciding that the best defense was a solid offense, he removed the sunglasses that he'd been wearing, took a step toward her, and said, "Tell me: Do you plan to report on the millions whom we've saved by advancing medical technology? Or kept from starving with our inteli-crops? All were breakthroughs spawned from, that's right, military funding."

"Wow," she said. "You ever lose an hour of sleep your whole life?"

He laughed. "You," he said, "are tough to impress. I mean, this is my 'A' material. My best stuff."

"I'm not like other reporters you may have met," she said. "I tend to do my homework. I've gone over every interview you've done in the past three years. Any canned responses you toss at somebody else? They're all up here." She tapped the side of her head. "So if you want to impress me, as you clearly are desperately trying to do, then you're going to have to come up with something new. Because the stuff that works on the schmos from the *New York Times* isn't going to fly with me."

"And what if I don't care about impressing you?"

"Ohhh," and she smiled, "I think we both know that you do. Your psychological makeup won't have it any other way."

"Wow. You really have done your homework, haven't you?"

"Mr. Stark?"

It was Hogan, standing by the passenger side of the limo and holding the door open. Traffic was starting to stack up behind them.

"Tell you what," said Stark. "Just how in-depth are you interested in going here?"

"As in-depth as you're willing to take me."

"Well then," and he gestured toward the limo. "Get in. And I guarantee you that you'll see sides of me that no schmo from the *Times* has ever seen. Consider that an iron-clad promise."

ii.

Light filtered through the windows into Tony Stark's bedroom. Naked under the covers, Christine Everhart—alone in Stark's bed—stretched and opened her eyes a slit. She saw that the clock had just gone from 5:59 to 6 AM, and the change in time appeared to have triggered alterations in the bedroom. The light that was coming in through the windows was being permitted to do so courtesy of the darkened windows turning translucent. *He can't just have shutters like a normal person,* she thought.

The television flickered to life automatically, which startled her slightly. A CNN anchor was staring right at her, speaking to her. Automatically she raised the sheets slightly to cover herself, and then—feeling a bit silly for having done so—allowed the sheets to slip away as she slid out of bed.

She stepped to the window and gazed out. It was a hell of a view. Tony Stark's estate was perched atop a cliff that looked out upon the Pacific Ocean. She couldn't begin to guess how in the world the house managed to cling to the cliff, but it did. She even suspected that if they were hit with a major earthquake, the house wouldn't budge from its foundations.

She glanced around and didn't see her clothes. How typical for Tony Stark: Keep 'em naked in the bedroom. That was how he liked his women, obviously.

And she had fallen right into it.

Even as she had writhed atop him last night, attacking

him with such fierce abandon that she could scarcely recognize herself in retrospect, she had been chiding herself for falling for his undeniable charm, for his looks, for the quiet power that he exuded. How the hell was she supposed to write a story with any sort of objectivity when she had just become romantically involved with her subject?

Well, that was easy to justify. There was no romance here, no relationship. She already knew what she was going to write, and her . . . dalliance . . . with Tony Stark wasn't going to change one word of that. For all the impact that this assignation was going to have on her doing her job, she might just as well have been shaking hands with him for an extended period of time.

Oh my God, you're pathetic . . .

She shoved her after-the-fact remonstrations from her mind as she rummaged through his closet. She pulled out a shirt of his and threw it on, buttoning it. It went down to about mid-thigh, which would suffice for her needs.

She padded over to the doorway and called downstairs, "Tony? Tony?"

No sign of him. She emerged from the bedroom. There was a long, curved stairway ahead of her. She descended the stairs, which wound past an indoor waterfall. She stared at it in wonderment. What kind of mind looks at a living room and decides what it really needs is a waterfall? She didn't know whether to be struck with awe or amusement, and decided for a combination of the two.

She entered the living room, calling, "Tony? Where are you?"

Although they had come through the living room when they'd entered last night, everything had been such a whirlwind that she hadn't taken any time to notice things around her. Plus the room had been fairly dark:

mood lighting, no doubt. Now in the full light of day, she was able to see the place fully for the first time.

It was hard to believe anyone actually lived there. It looked like someplace designed specifically for a photo shoot. There was an elaborate-freeform sculpture dead center of the room. Her eyes widened: Unless she was completely wrong, she was looking at a piece by Alexander Calder.

She reached a single finger toward it, giving in to the childish impulse to touch something so valuable.

"Please refrain from touching the sculpture."

She jumped a foot in the air. The voice that had spoken was crisp, British, no-nonsense. And it had seemed to come from everywhere.

When she landed she almost lost her footing and fell over. There was no one in front of her, no one to the side. She turned and there was, indeed, someone behind her. It was a young woman with strawberry blond hair and a wry, patient smile on her face. She was holding Christine's clothes; they were neatly hung and surrounded by plastic covering from a dry cleaner.

The limo driver from last night was standing next to her. But she had heard him speak last night and knew he wasn't the one who had addressed her. Which left the woman . . .

Christine stared at her, trying to reconcile the voice she had just heard with the face she was looking at.

The woman spoke and her voice sounded nothing like the voice that had startled Christine. As if intuiting what was going through Christine's mind, the woman said, "That's just Jarvis. He runs the house."

"You mean there's a man watching everything that—?"

"No, not a man. A computer system."

"A machine?"

"No, a computer system," the woman said again as if

addressing a child. "Just a really very intelligent system."

"Named Jarvis?"

"It's an acronym, actually."

"What does it stand for?"

The woman smiled thinly. "Just. A. Really. Very. Intelligent. System."

"Oh. Heh. Guess I should have seen that coming, huh?"

"Here. Your clothes cleaned and pressed. Hogan?"

Hogan took the clothes from the woman and walked them over to Christine. She took them, still trying to get herself oriented. "Who . . . ?"

"Virginia Potts. They call me Pepper. I'm Mr. Stark's personal assistant. Anything else I can get you?"

Christine cleared her throat, trying to cling to some degree of normalcy in what had become a very abnormal situation. "Tony wanted me to stay for breakfast, but I've got to get a jump on the day. Call me a cab, would you?"

"A car is waiting outside," said Pepper.

"And a coffee, hon. Black. One Splenda."

"I'll have it waiting in the car." Pepper smiled sweetly. "Should I tell Mr. Stark that you were satisfied with the interview?"

Christine winced, all the excuses that she'd come up with to pardon her behavior suddenly sounding very hollow, even in her own mind. She skulked up the steps, holding her clean clothes tightly to her.

"Might want to pull the shirt down in the back, dear," Pepper called after her.

Christine swung the clothes around so they covered her backside.

The first time that Pepper Potts had entered Tony Stark's massive workshop, she had felt as if she were walking into a real-world representation of the inside of Stark's head. Although she had become accustomed to the barely controlled chaos that the workshop represented, that initial impression had never left her.

The amazing thing was that Tony Stark was never able to find—for example—a particular memo, even if it was in the correct file drawer in the proper file. That was the kind of thing that Pepper attended to with such efficiency that he had stopped noticing when she attended to it. In Stark's workshop, however, Pepper would have had no chance; she would have been too overwhelmed by the mess. Yet Stark could locate whatever tool he needed or part he required within seconds, typically pulling it out from under a pile of half a dozen other assorted things. It was uncanny.

Someone had once said that time was what kept everything from happening at once. Pepper had decided that Stark's workshop was the place that time forgot, because every moment of Stark's life seemed to be unfolding simultaneously in that one space. It was nothing short of miraculous that he was able to keep it all straight.

Ultramodern drones and missile parts shared space with sports cars and long-abandoned prototypes. There were framed photos of Tony and his dad. There were no famous people standing next to them, as seemed typically to be the case whenever there were photos of Howard Stark on display. There was nothing posed about these photos: They showed Stark father and son in the midst of working on a variety of automobiles, Tony becoming progressively older through the array of pictures. Pepper's favorite was the two of them refurbishing a classic 1932 Ford. She knew it was the one they'd been working on when Tony's father had passed away, so it had a touch of melancholy to it.

On several computer screens there were various CAD

images of a flathead engine, and then Pepper smiled as she saw Stark dressed in slacks and a grime-colored undershirt, working on the very same 1932 Ford. He had been working on it on and off for as long as she had known him. Someone of his caliber of genius would certainly have been able to finish by now if he had desired to. The fact that he was still working on it, still fine-tuning it, told Pepper a great deal. It wasn't that Stark hadn't finished it, or wasn't capable of finishing it. It was that he hadn't wanted to finish it. He had come near to completing the engine rebuild any number of times and then always felt compelled to find something wrong and take apart the entire thing to get back to it again. It was obvious to Pepper why: If he completed the engine, it would be the finish of the last job that he and his father had ever worked on. It would close a door to his past that he wasn't ready to shut.

All that went through Pepper's head in a matter of seconds. Then the warm smile on her face was replaced by an all-business expression as she consulted her PDA. "You still owe me five minutes," she said.

"Five? I'll need a bit longer than that—"

He sat up, displaying the sort of wry grin he always wore when he was using a line on Pepper that he fancied was a come-on. It meant nothing; they both knew it.

"Focus," she said briskly. "I need to leave on time today."

"You're rushing me." He'd been holding a wrench, but now he put it down and regarded her thoughtfully. "What, you have plans tonight?"

"The MIT commencement," she said, refusing to give in to his prurient interest in her social life. "Yes or no?"

"Maybe. Tell me your plans."

"I'll tell them 'yes,' " she said, tapping a waiting e-mail on her PDA and sending it winging to the dean of MIT before Stark could countermand her. Moving on, she said, "You want to buy the Jackson Pollock? He's got another buyer in the wings—"

Apparently giving up for a moment on trying to discern her evening plans, Stark said, "What's it look like?"

"It's a minor work in his late Springs Period; it's ludicrously overpriced."

"Buy it."

She sighed. She couldn't tell whether he was buying it because it was of genuine interest to him, or because she had recommended against it and he was purchasing it just to torque her. She had a feeling it was probably the latter. She supposed that on some level she should be flattered by the fact that he was willing to spend an insane amount of money just to get a reaction out of her. She'd be damned, though, if she gave it to him. With perfect timing, her phone rang. She tapped her Bluetooth headset and listened.

"He's there, isn't he," came Rhodey's voice without preamble. "He's fiddling with his damned car or something and he's going to leave us all standing here waiting for him to show up in his own sweet time. Isn't that right."

"He left an hour ago," she said.

"You're covering for him. I get that. You're doing your job. Just so I know, though, and can try to cover his ass on this end: If you're lying, just say 'Okay' and hang up."

"Okay," she said, and hung up. "It's Rhodey again. He said to remind you the plane's scheduled departure time is five minutes from now."

"Wow. Sounds like I'm going to miss it. Oh, wait," he said as if suddenly remembering. "I own the plane. Don't I?"

"Last I checked, yes."

"Kind of undercuts the merit of owning a plane if I have to worry about it taking off without me, doesn't it?" Without waiting for a reply, he returned relentlessly to the topic of her evening. "You have plans, don't you—?"

Seeing that Stark wasn't going to let this go, Pepper said, "I'm allowed to have plans on my birthday."

"It's your birthday again?"

"Yep. Funny . . . same day as last year."

Stark seemed a little startled. Small wonder. The man had absolutely no sense of time. "Well, get yourself something from me. Something nice."

"Already did."

"And—?" he prompted.

"It was very tasteful, very elegant. Thank you, Mr. Stark."

He inclined his head slightly. "You're welcome, Miss Potts." He walked away from the car and pulled out wipes from a box to clean his hands. "Rhodey knows you were lying, doesn't he."

"Yup."

"Well then, I guess I'd better leave an hour ago, hadn't I?"

"If you could make it an hour and a half ago, that would be even better."

"Done. Consider it an early birthday present for next year."

He walked out of his workshop. Pepper couldn't help but notice that he'd never once asked about the girl he'd brought home. She might still be there eating breakfast, or she could have gone home, or she might still have been sleeping. Obviously he hadn't cared enough to ask.

iii.

Rhodey watched the sun rising in the sky and took it as a personal affront. How dare the sun continue to climb, thus making him later and later. Why was he focusing his ire upon the sun? Because Tony Stark wasn't there; otherwise he would have been more than happy to let Stark know just how royally pissed off he was.

The Stark aviation hangar at Santa Monica airport bustled with activity, which was pretty impressive considering that not a thing was happening. Rhodey paced past the Boeing business jet that had the words "Stark Industries: Tomorrow Today" etched on the side. He pondered the irony of those words: At any given time when Tony Stark was supposed to arrive someplace today, there was every chance that he wouldn't show up until tomorrow.

He pulled out his cell phone and started to dial Pepper again. Then he heard a low rumble in the distance. Roaring toward them was an Audi R8, glinting in the sunlight. It screeched up and stopped about two feet short of Rhodey. Rhodey didn't take so much as a single step backward; he'd be damned if he gave Stark the satisfaction. He knew perfectly well that Stark was at the wheel; he wouldn't let anyone else touch the Audi, not even Hogan.

Seconds later, a Rolls-Royce limo pulled up. Hogan clambered out, popped the trunk, and removed a single overnight suitcase. The Audi's scissor door swung open and Stark stepped out of it. Hogan was at his side with the suitcase, handing it to him. Stark took it without a backward glance and headed straight for the plane. "Sorry, pal. Car trouble," he said carelessly.

Rhodey looked to Hogan. "Car trouble?"

Hogan shrugged. "He couldn't decide whether to take the Audi out for a spin or arrive in the Rolls because it was fancier."

"Oh, for the love of—"

"Be thankful," said Happy with his customary mournful expression. "If I hadn't suggested this, we'd still be back home trying to sort it out."

Rhodey groaned, shook his head, and then trotted up the ramp two stairs at a time into the plane. Seconds later the jets fired up and the plane pulled back from the hangar area.

Stark was already settling in to his seat, clicking the lap belt into place. Rhodey dropped into the seat opposite. "I was standing out there three hours! What the hell—?"

"I had car trouble," Stark told him again serenely.

"Trouble deciding which car to take?"

"That's trouble of a sort."

A flight attendant walked up to them carrying a tray with small, rolled-up steamy towels on it. She was holding a pair of tongs. "Hot towel?" she offered.

"Thanks, maybe later."

"Right, always good to have hot towels later," said Stark. "Gives them plenty of time to cool off." He extended his hands. The flight attendant picked up one of the towels with the tongs and dropped it into his palms. Rhodey, with a sigh of aggravation that he seemed to use a lot whenever he was around Tony Stark, grabbed the towel with his bare hands. He flipped the towel from one hand to the other to cool it slightly. Stark grinned while the whine of the engines built up.

The pilot's voice came on, issuing the standard cautions for any departing flight. Rhodey barely paid attention; what was some corporate jet pilot going to be able to tell him that he didn't know?

Within minutes the plane had lifted off with smoothness and precision. Rhodey had to admit to himself that the guys piloting the plane were damned good. Typically, on the rare occasions that he was a passenger in a commercial plane, he sensed dozens of little mistakes that no one else would. The flaps might not be adjusted quite right, or the take-off velocity wasn't achieved as smoothly as it might have been. But Stark's pilots were as good as it got. He supposed he shouldn't be too surprised over that.

Once the plane had reached its cruising altitude, one of the two flight attendants approached Tony. Displaying a pair of teeth so blindingly white that they bordered on incandescent, she said, "Would you like a drink, Mr. Stark?"

"Two fingers of Laphroaig," said Stark. He looked at Rhodey. "You want one?"

"Don't you ever just order a beer or something?"

Stark stared at him as if his head had just exploded.

Ignoring Stark's look, Rhodey said to the flight attendant, "No, thanks," and then he pointedly added for Stark's benefit, "We're working."

"You should have a drink," said Stark. "We've got a twelve-hour flight ahead of us."

"It's two in the afternoon."

"It's two in the morning where we're going. C'mon, ten hours 'bottle to throttle,' " Stark tried to cajole him.

"Don't start with me."

"Jeez, we're not getting hammered," said Stark, not letting it go. "Just a nightcap. We'll sleep better, arrive fresh. It's the responsible thing to do. I don't know about you, but I want to sell some weapons. Tell you what: I'll even let you get a beer without making a face."

"Why are you so determined to have me drink with you?"

"I gave you the reasons."

"No. Those are the excuses. What's the reason?"

Stark half-smiled and gestured for the flight attendant not to wait around for Rhodey's drink order. "You obviously have something in mind already. So why not just tell me what you think the reason is?"

"Okay," said Rhodey. "I think you're worried about becoming just like your old man."

"You think I'm worried about having a son named Tony?"

"He drank too much."

"Rhodey, my friend, I don't drink too much. You know how I know? Because it's impossible to have too much of the finer things in life, whether they be beautiful drink," and as the attendant brought him his Scotch whiskey, "or beautiful women." The attendant smiled as her cheeks blushed, and Stark took a sip of the whiskey. He savored it, swallowed, and made a soft "Ahhhhhh."

He looked at Rhodey expectantly.

Rhodey sighed, looked at the flight attendant and said, "Bring me one of those, would you?"

Many hours later, the airplane was hurtling through the night sky. Rhodey had lost track of how many drinks he had. He didn't think he was drunk; he'd been trying to drink responsibly. But he certainly had a comfortable buzz going in his head. As for Stark, Rhodey had no idea where the man put it all. Stark's liver had to look like a relief map of the moon.

The flight attendants hadn't exactly been sloughing off either. Thanks to Stark's wheedling, which was no less effective with them than it was with Rhodey, they'd been tossing back drinks as well. Now, with the music cranked up, the two of them were dancing in the aisle. Rhodey had a feeling that another couple of drinks, the girls might start making out with Stark . . . or with each other. Anything was possible in the world of Stark Industries: Tomorrow Today.

"You don't get it," Rhodey was saying. "I don't work for the military because they paid for my education, or my father's education. Don't cheapen it like that."

"All I said was," Stark said, trying not to slur his words, "with your smarts, your engineering background, you could write your own ticket in the private sector—on top of which, you wouldn't have to wear that straitjacket." He indicated Rhodey's uniform jacket.

He knew that Stark was kidding around. Nevertheless, Rhodey took offense, or at least as much offense as his alcohol-addled mind would permit him to take. "Straitjacket? This uniform means something. A chance to make a difference. You don't respect that because you don't understand."

Stark didn't reply immediately. When he did, he wasn't looking at Rhodey, but rather at one of the flight attendants. At that moment she was slithering against the interior bulkhead like a stripper. All she needed was a metal pole. "See that one," he said, motioning with a nod. "*Her* I understand. Croatian. Hot blooded. I'm serious," he continued when Rhodey shook his head. "Must be those winters in Zagreb . . ."

"You're not listening to a word I'm saying."

"I am listening," Stark said. "I'm changing the subject." When Rhodey grunted in response, Stark told him, "It's the same litany every time you've had a thimble of alcohol. Drink one: Reflections on the new American century and related topics . . ."

"Something's seriously wrong with you, man."

"Drink two," said Stark, "A history of World War II and the Tuskegee Flyers. Drink three . . ."

Rhodey bridled at the litany, mostly because he knew that Stark was right and he despised the notion of being that predictable. He undid the seat belt and stood up a bit more quickly than he should have, wavering before catching himself on the top of the seatback. "You know, hell with you. I'm not talking to you anymore."

Stark shrugged. "Go hang with the pilot. You'll get along. He's got a personality just like yours."

"I will."

That suited Rhodey just fine. At least another pilot might understand where he was coming from. Besides, he wanted to congratulate him on the quality of both the takeoff and the continued flight. At several points the plane had encountered turbulence, but the pilot had handled it with such aplomb that the shaking had been minimal.

Rhodey headed to the cockpit. He staggered only once, put his hand against the wall to steady himself, and then—upon reaching the cockpit—opened the door.

For a split second, he thought they were in trouble.

There were no pilots in the cockpit. Instead there were two empty pilot chairs.

In his inebriated haze, he flashed back to *Indiana Jones and the Temple of Doom,* thinking that the pilots had bailed out, leaving them to crash to their deaths. *My God, who's going to fly the plane!* Rhodey wondered before belatedly realizing that the obvious answer was: He would. He was a freaking pilot.

It took him a few seconds to realize what he was staring at: a fully automated flight system. Everything was computer controlled, right down to the occasional announcement from the pilot that they had heard.

He slammed the door to the cockpit, turned on his

heel and stomped back to Stark, with Tony's comment about the robot pilot having a personality just like his ringing in his ears. He stood there, staring at Stark, who looked up at him with wide-eyed innocence.

"That's funny," Rhodey said sarcastically.

Stark looked genuinely surprised. "You could tell?"

The Bagram Air Base in Parwan province was one of the more strategic points in Afghanistan. Most of the United States air activity went through Bagram, and this meeting with the army brass was no exception.

An array of army officers were lined up to meet Stark once the plane had landed. They were all wearing "digis," the nickname for the camouflage uniforms that had a digital array of gray squares on them. Stark trotted down the ramp looking fresh and ready to greet the day, unperturbed as his sunglasses shielded his eyes from the scorching Afghan sun.

As he greeted each of the officers by name, shaking their hands one by one, Rhodey appeared at the top of the stairway. The world tilted around him and he thought his face was about to melt from the heat. There was a dull ringing in his ears as he belatedly pulled out sunglasses and put them on. He watched Stark confidently and easily working the line of officers. He was all business, full of confidence. Rhodey could see that Stark already had the brass chuckling over some remark he'd made. Incredible. Rhodey had had a fraction of the alcohol that Stark had consumed, but Stark seemed to be completely unaffected by it.

A military transport had already arrived at Bagram, and an assortment of weapons was being off-loaded from them. The most conspicuous were three missiles, each with the world "Jericho" prominently displayed on the side, and the Stark Industries logo just below them.

All the weaponry was being escorted under heavy guard to a waiting convoy.

Time for the dog and pony show, thought Rhodey.

Tony Stark was determined to give them a good show.

The army generals were seated on folding chairs behind a safe zone of barricades and sand bags. Meanwhile, Afghan soldiers and Air Force security men patrolled the perimeter. Obviously, no one was taking any chances; the last thing anyone needed was a group of insurgents launching a successful raid and taking out a bevy of America's top brass in one shot . . . to say nothing of its top weapons manufacturer.

Stark was standing some distance away, firing an N.R.F 425 machine gun. The generals watched, their faces impassive. They'd seen machine guns before. Granted, Stark produced as good a machine gun as anyone else did, but at the end of the day, that's all it was. Stark knew that he had promised them something more impressive than standard-issue weaponry, and he also knew that they were waiting to see what he'd be presenting them.

That didn't mean he couldn't be as much of a showman as possible while he was doing it.

Stark put the gun down next to an assortment of other weapons. Then he sauntered toward the generals, hands in his pockets, his voice adopting the cadences of a carnival barker. Behind him in the distance a mountain range sat framed against a clear blue sky.

"The age-old question: Is it better to be feared or respected? I say, is it too much to ask for both?" He nodded toward the Jericho missiles, perched on their mobile launchers. "With that in mind, I humbly present the crown jewel of Stark Industries Freedom line. It's the first missile system to incorporate my proprietary Repulsor technology. They say the best weapon is one you never have to fire. I prefer the weapon you only need to fire *once*. That's how Dad did it. That's how America does it. And it's worked out pretty well so far."

One of the Jericho missiles roared into the sky with a thundering blast, fired from its mobile launcher. As the Jericho arched through the sky, Stark continued, "Find an excuse to fire off one of these and I personally guarantee the enemy is not gonna want to leave their caves."

Then Stark waited patiently for the gasp.

The generals watched as the Jericho missile continued on its course . . . and suddenly it appeared to blow apart. For half a heartbeat it seemed as if the weapon had catastrophically malfunctioned. But then they realized what they were seeing, for the Jericho had not in fact blown apart. Instead, it had subdivided into a score of mini-missiles.

The generals gasped, right on cue. Stark permitted a small smile. He raised his arms, displaying as much showmanship as possible, as he said, "For your consideration, the Jericho."

An entire section of the majestic peaks behind him blew up.

One minute there; the next, gone. They saw it before they heard it. When they did hear it, it was the astounding sound of twenty explosions all occurring at exactly the same time. And by the time that sound reached them, the shock wave had already come rolling across the vast expanse and enveloped Tony Stark. He never budged from where he was standing, even as a massive wave of dust washed over him. The generals dove behind the barriers for cover, but it didn't do them any good. The dust and debris were everywhere, inescapable, covering them from hat to boot toe.

Long moments passed until the rumble of noise and the sweeping cloud of dust subsided. As that happened, Stark loosened the knot of his tie and undid the top button of his shirt. As if blowing a mountain to bits was a casual feat that one saw every day, he brushed the dust from his suit as he said to the still-amazed army brass, "Now there's one last creation I haven't shown anyone yet. You might be interested."

There was a large silver case set near the other weapons. Stark removed a small remote control from his jacket pocket, aimed it at the case, and tapped a button. The cover of the case flipped back. White vapor seeped out of the top, the type generated by a freezer unit. Stark tapped another button and a bottle of champagne slowly rose out of the unit on a small metal platform. Champagne glasses hung from small hooks around the platform. Stark removed the champagne bottle and effortlessly popped the cork as the generals and the Afghan military officials exchanged awkward glances. He poured himself a glass of champagne, raised it, and said, "To peace, gentlemen. And with every five hundred million dollars you spend, I'll throw in a free one of these."

Some time later, Stark and Rhodey were heading toward their respective waiting Humvees. Eager to bring his CFO up to speed, he dialed up Obadiah Stane on his videophone. It rang for what seemed an unconscionably long time and finally Stane answered it, looking bleary eyed at Stark. He was bare-chested and the room behind him was dark.

"Hey, what are you doing up?" Stark said cheerfully.

"Sleeping." Stane tried to stifle a yawn and failed. "How did it go?"

"I think we got an early Christmas coming."

Stane nodded approvingly. "Sounds good."

"Hey, why aren't you wearing the pj's I got you?"

"I don't do monograms. I'm hanging up now. Bye-bye."

He clicked off the videophone and looked around at the assorted young soldiers who were part of the security force. "All right, who wants to ride with me?" His eyes rested upon a young soldier who had helped him set up the weapons display that he'd used earlier. "Jimmy?"

"Me?" said Jimmy, clearly psyched.

"Sure, you. And whoever else you want."

Jazzed, Jimmy and two other soldiers jumped into the Humvee that Stark would be riding in. He watched as the generals headed off in the other direction. No one had committed to anything yet, of course. That wasn't how they operated. But Stark could read an audience, and he knew he'd read them right when he'd seen just how eager they clearly were to get their hands on the Jericho. No more having to risk the lives of soldiers, creeping around in mountain ranges trying to find terrorists hiding in caves. Just annihilate the mountain range in one shot and send the terrorists straight to hell.

Unaccountably, he thought of the nickname that Christine had brought up: the Merchant of Death. He'd laughed it off. But the truth was that he didn't understand how people could view him that way. His actions saved lives. Yes, people died courtesy of his weaponry . . . but it was the enemy. Only the enemy. And it was enemy that would kill Americans if given the slightest opportunity. So if it came down to a choice between them and us, Stark was going to pick us every time, as his most ardent critics would most likely also do. Merchant of Death. What a crock.

As Stark prepared to climb into his Humvee, he saw Rhodey approaching. "Sorry, Rhodey, no room for my conscience in here. Or that hangdog look." His handy drink chest had also had a bottle of vodka tucked away in it, and he now raised a glass that was filled with it. "See you back at base."

Rhodey shook his head and went off toward a different Humvee. Stark clambered into the back of the Humvee and slammed the door shut.

Eight minutes later, the Humvee would be gone.

As would be Tony Stark.

He has no idea what is happening. There is dankness around him, and a coolness. Why that would be in the middle of a desert, he hasn't a clue. He snaps awake. He tries to move his arms and is unable to. He looks down and there are bloody rags covering his chest. He tries to turn his head, see what's behind him because he hears muttering. He is barely able to make out a group of armed, hooded men. Behind them, on the wall, is a red banner with ten rings in a circle and an X in the middle.

He shifts his focus back to what's in front of him. There are two more hooded men standing on either side of a digital video, or DV, camera. A third man, larger than the others, holding a curved Choori knife the size of Tony's head, is reading some sort of message. Stark doesn't know what language it's in, although if he had to guess, he'd say that it's Dari. That would seem to be the right one for the region.

Stark tries not to look into the camera. He doesn't want to come across as one of those desperate, terrified hostages one always sees in such videos. But then he's faced with the realization that he is, in fact, one of those desperate, terrified hostages, and if he's trying not to show it, it has nothing to do with his status and everything to do with his own bravado.

He starts to feel a twinging in his chest. He looks down. The blood is spreading. Whatever his condition is, it's deteriorating. The others must notice it because he hears a change in the tenor of their voices. He's starting to fade out. In his mind's eye, he sees himself not sitting in a chair but instead as a pixilated image, beginning to come apart and dissolve into white.

As the world turns to haze around him, he allows himself the smug satisfaction of knowing that, whatever ransom they were going to demand for him, whatever use they were going to put him to, is going to be thwarted by the simple act of his dying. He, Tony Stark, had the last laugh. The final thought that crosses his mind is that he hopes the first thing the military does is unleash one of his Jericho missiles on these bastards and blow them into rubble, burying them along with their beloved cave hideout. And then he is gone . . .

Except . . .

He returns . . .

He is no longer in front of a camera. Instead he is in what can only be described as a crude operating room. Stabbing lights lance into his face. He hears a rush of garbled voices, except . . . they're not all talking at once. There is one voice above the others, commanding, firm, and it sounds different from them. Differently accented, providing that Stark can make that sort of determination.

Stark sees a scalpel above him. It is tinged with red. He struggles, tries to yank himself free of the table, but restraints are holding him down.

The scalpel stops several inches above his chest. A man's face comes into Stark's field of vision. It is the face of a bespectacled man in his sixties. He looks vaguely Asian, but his skin is the hard, tanned brown of a desert dweller. Stark can't see the lower half of his face because a surgical mask obscures it. He appears surprised that Stark is conscious. He shouts something in their language, and a rag is pressed over Stark's face. Chloroform, *Stark thinks*, and at first he is determined not to inhale it. But the stabbing pain in his chest forces him to gasp for air, and instead all he inhales is chloroform. The world dissipates around him once more. He wonders if he will, *as the old joke goes, wake up dead.*

iv.

When Stark first began to awaken, he dared to hope that everything he had experienced up until now had been a dream. In his mind, he was rolling all the events back to two nights ago, and was hoping that he was going to awaken next to the still warm body of the reporter . . . *what's her name. Christine. Right. Christine.* Were that the case, he would take everything that he had "seen" in his waking mind as a prophetic warning of what could happen—not unlike *A Christmas Carol*—and the first thing he would do upon waking would be to cancel the trip to Afghanistan. If the brass wanted to see how his weapons functioned, let them make the trip to Las Vegas, where all one had to worry about was losing one's shirt in a casino rather than losing one's life in a cave.

It only took a few seconds, however, for the reality of his situation to come crashing down upon him. He was looking up and he was seeing not the ceiling of his bedroom, but instead the craggy surface of a cave. There was a tube protruding from his nose. He was lying on the hard, flat surface of a cot.

I didn't die . . . how could I not have died . . . ?

In curious contrast to his environment, he heard a distant and oddly discordant humming. He tried to lift his head and couldn't. So instead he turned it slightly and was able to make out a man standing a few feet away, humming what to Stark's ears sounded like a rather aimless tune. The man was looking into a mirror and shaving. Seeing such a mundane, ordinary action in this bizarre environment only added to Stark's total sense of disorientation.

There was a table next to Stark, and on the table was what appeared to be a jug of water. Stark tried to reach for it, but his hand wasn't coming anywhere close to it. He was parched, thirstier than he had ever been in his life, which made sense, since he couldn't remember a time in his life where he hadn't had something to drink close at hand.

He tried to say something to the shaving man, tried to ask him for the water. But he couldn't speak. Instead, all he was able to produce were faint choking sounds. It was the tubes, the damned tubes that were sticking out of his nose. Fed up, he reached up for the tube, wrapped his fingers around it, and pulled. He gagged as two feet of tubing slithered from his nostrils.

"Water," he whispered hoarsely. "Water . . ."

The shaving man didn't hear him. Instead he was continuing to hum as he shaved. *What the hell . . . ? Who concentrates that much on shaving?*

He tried to reach for the water, but there was an IV in his arm that brought his hand up short. He yanked the IV from his arm and reached once more. But he came no closer. This time he was brought up short by wires that were attached under his chest bandages. They snapped taut, bringing him thudding back onto the bed. He started to reach for the wires, reasoning that they could be dispensed with as easily as the IV and the nose tubes.

"I wouldn't do that if I were you."

The shaving man had finally spoken. He lowered his razor and looked straight at Stark. It was at that moment that Stark recognized him as the surgeon who had been cutting into him.

There was something in the surgeon's voice that caught Stark's attention and conveyed to him that there were life and death matters at stake. He focused on the wires for the first time and then craned his neck to see where they went. To his astonishment, he saw that they were attached to a car battery.

Stark began to tear at the bandages. The surgeon looked as if he were about to offer a protest or advise against it; instead, he carefully put down the razor and then watched, his arms folded across his chest.

Within seconds Stark had clawed away enough of the bandages to see what lay beneath. He didn't recognize his own chest; there was a depression in it, a vicious wound, and some sort of round device had been implanted into it.

It was too much for him. The world spun around him and Tony Stark, for the first time in his life, swooned. The last thing he saw and heard was the surgeon rolling his eyes and muttering, "I warned him not to, but did he lis—?"

When Stark came to again, an indefinite amount of time later, it was because he smelled something. He raised his head and saw that the surgeon was stirring a bubbling pot on a furnace. It smelled wonderful. Then again, considering the thirst that was still scratching at his throat and the hunger gnawing at his stomach, the surgeon could have been boiling shoes and it would have been appetizing.

He looked down at his chest once more. There were fresh bandages in place, but they were unable to hide the bulge of the bizarre device that had been inserted into him. Stark felt violated.

"What have you done to me?" he said. The words were barely intelligible; his tongue was swelling up.

"What did I do?" the surgeon said, obviously repeating it to make sure that he had understood the words. When Stark nodded, he said, "What I did . . . what I did was save your life. I removed what I could, but there's a lot left headed for your atrial septum."

Atrial septum? Oh, right. The wall between the two upper chambers of the heart. But a lot of what? What was headed toward . . . ?

"Do you want a souvenir?"

The surgeon tossed Stark a jar. Stark caught it, which wasn't a bad accomplishment, all things considered. He stared at it, fascinated in spite of himself. There were scores of bloody, Christmas-tree-like barbs within. He recognized the design immediately. No reason he shouldn't: He held the patent for it.

"I've seen many wounds like this in my village," the surgeon was saying. " 'The Walking Dead,' we called them, because it took a week for the barbs to reach vital organs."

Stark felt a chill as the surgeon spoke. There should have been anger, rancor in what he was saying. Instead, he spoke in a flat, sad voice, as if he were resigned to the horrors that he had already witnessed. The surgeon pointed at the mechanical array on Stark's chest. "I anchored a magnetic suspension system to the plate. It's holding the shrapnel in place . . . at least for now."

Stark struggled to sit up on the cot. Curiously, the pain had subsided in his chest. The rest of his body ached, though. Then he noticed something glinting against the cave wall: the lens of a camera, focused straight on him.

The surgeon noticed Stark staring at the camera. "That's right. Smile."

He rose from stirring the broth or stew or whatever it was that he was preparing and went over to the water pitcher. He poured Stark a small glass and handed it to him. To Tony Stark, who never subjected his palate to anything other than the most expensive alcohol ever manufactured, this was the best-tasting liquid he had ever consumed. He drank it so quickly that he almost choked.

The surgeon eyed him and then said, "We met once— at a technical conference in Bern."

Stark searched his memory, but the surgeon's face wasn't coming forward. "I don't remember."

"You wouldn't. If I'd been that drunk, I wouldn't have been able to stand, much less give a talk on integrated circuits."

He nodded. Now he remembered the conference. He was told the day after he'd delivered the speech that he'd been absolutely brilliant, even revelatory. He had smiled and said "Thank you" and never once admitted that he couldn't recall a single thing he'd said. It was amazing that this man had been able to discern that Stark was inebriated; typically no one could.

Stark glanced around. The cramped room—if it could be called a room—wasn't looking any better once he was fully conscious. "Where are we?"

Before the surgeon could respond, there was a *thunk* sound from off to the right. Stark repositioned himself on the cot and looked in the direction of the sound. For the first time he saw a door closing off the far end of the room. Inset into the door was a slat that had just been slid forcefully aside. That had been the source of the noise he'd just heard. A pair of bloodshot eyes was peering in.

The surgeon's reaction was instantaneous. He dropped the spoon, stood, and placed his hands upon his head. The gesture seemed ludicrous to Stark. What, did the people outside the door think this unarmed senior citizen posed a threat? What was he going to do, ladle them to death?

Clearly, however, the surgeon found no humor in the situation. Instead he shouted, "Stand up! Do as I do. Now!"

Spurred by the fear that laced the surgeon's voice, Stark struggled to get to his feet. The car battery wires had been removed from his chest; the device was clearly up and running, although there was no doubt that he'd have to be hooked up again and "recharged." So Stark was able to at least stand. But he was so exhausted that he couldn't get his arms up over his head. The surgeon moved quickly over to him and helped him do so. The absurdity of the situation continued to present itself to Stark. He was so weak that he literally could not harm a fly. If he tried to swat one, the insect would just shake it off and sneer, "Is that all you've got?" The notion, therefore, that he had to keep his hands atop his head in order not to be a threat . . . it was ridiculous. Still, he did nothing to impede the surgeon's efforts as he placed Stark's hands atop his head. Stark interlaced his fingers so that they'd remain there.

Getting in close to Stark's ear, the surgeon said in a low, intense voice, "Listen to me: I have a plan. Whatever they ask you, refuse. You understand? You must refuse." Stark did not, in fact, understand, but he nodded as if he did.

The door opened and three men entered. Even though they had no hoods, Stark instantly recognized them as the three individuals whom he'd seen grouped around the camera: The two camera operators, and the leader who had been making the pronouncements.

Stark decided he preferred them with the hoods on. Each of them had similar features: Dark, harsh, thick eyebrows, and the sorts of sneers that only bullies who had others in a weakened position could possess.

"Abu Bakar," the surgeon said in a voice so low that only Stark could hear, "is the leader, the one in the middle. To his right and left are Ahmed and Omar, two lieutenants."

Stark didn't nod or in any way indicate that he'd

heard the surgeon. He wasn't even looking at him. His gaze had been drawn directly to the wrist of the man identified as Ahmed. Ahmed was wearing a distinctive watch: the telltale blue and orange of Jimmy's Mets watch.

Tony Stark had never wanted to kill anyone before. At that moment, what would have appeared to his captors to be rapt attention on Stark's part was actually Stark trying to figure out how he could gather the strength to cover the distance between himself and Ahmed, jump him, and strangle him. He wanted to feel the man's life ebbing between his fingers. This man, whom he had known for exactly five seconds, was a man that Tony Stark hated more than any other man he'd ever known.

No. Not with your bare hands.

You'll build a weapon.

Because that's what you do.

And you will use that weapon to take him down. Take all of them down.

It was the first, fleeting notion of an idea, a mere seed. It popped into his conscious mind and then left just as quickly. But it did not depart for good, instead taking root in the back of his mind.

Abu spoke to him in Arabic, snapping Stark's attention back to the here and now. Stark stared at him blankly, not understanding a word.

The surgeon promptly translated. "He says welcome Tony Stark, the greatest mass murderer in the history of America. He is very honored."

Abu was looking Tony Stark up and down as if he were a prize racehorse that he had just acquired. Then he reached into his jacket pocket and produced a photo. He thrust it forward so that Stark could see it and spoke as he did so. The words were naturally unfamiliar, but the image in the picture was not. It was a surveillance photo of the Jericho missile.

"You will build for him the Jericho missile you were demonstrating," translated the surgeon.

Stark hesitated, then exchanged a firm look with the surgeon and said, crisply and clearly while shaking his head so Abu would understand, "I refuse."

The surgeon turned and backhanded Stark across the face as hard as he could. Stark sagged and collapsed onto the cot, his eyes wide in confusion. As his face stung from the blow, the surgeon screamed at him, so filled with ire that his face looked almost apoplectic. "You *refuse*? You will do *everything* he says. This is the great Abu Bakar. You're alive only because of his generosity. You are nothing. *Nothing*. He offers you his hospitality, and you answer only with insolence. He will *not* be refused! *You will die in a pool of your own blood.*"

As the surgeon ranted, Abu was busy spooning down some of the food that the surgeon had been preparing. When the surgeon ran out of breath, Abu nodded in smug satisfaction. He dropped the spoon back down into the mixture, and then headed out, followed by his lieutenants. Ahmed reached back in to close the door, providing Stark one last, brief glimpse of Jimmy's watch. Then the door slammed shut.

The picture of calm, the surgeon said, "Perfect. You did very well, Stark."

Stark stared at him in complete bewilderment as the surgeon returned to his cooking. He was talking to himself more than he was Stark as he nodded and said, "Good. I think they're starting to trust me."

Stark tried to talk, but his jaw was beginning to swell. *I have a plan,* the surgeon had assured him. What the hell was that about? What was this so-called plan? When was it going into operation?

"Well," said the surgeon, as if he'd read Stark's mind, "that's the end of my plan."

Stark moaned.

Stark felt as if he'd just managed to drift back to sleep when he was rudely and abruptly jolted awake. Ahmed was shoving a hood over his head. For half a second he thought, *This is it. They're going to march me out somewhere and shoot me.* But then he realized what a nonsensical concern that was. He would hardly be in a position to build a weapon for them if he was dead.

Stark was yanked to his feet. His strength had been returning, but very slowly, so he still felt off-balance as they hauled him out of the room. He tried to figure out why they would put a hood on him. What could he possibly see that could provide a danger to them?

Then he realized: They were probably taking him outside. By putting the hood over his head, he wouldn't be able to see the pathway out through what might well be a maze of tunnels. He wished there were some way that he could make a break for it, but none readily presented itself.

Even with his face covered by the hood, he could still tell that he was moving from the relative gloom of the caves toward daylight. Moments later he felt fresh air wafting toward him, and then the hood was yanked from his head. He blinked like an owl in daytime, momentarily blinded by the sun. He raised one hand to his brow to try and ward off the sun even as he squinted, and then he saw something that stunned him. Considering all that had happened to him within the last day . . . days . . . weeks . . . however the hell long it had been . . . he would have thought there was nothing more that could happen to him that could have any sort of strong emotional impact. As it turned out, he was wrong.

There were skids arrayed before him, covered with

camouflage tarp. Abu's men were standing nearby them and, once they saw that Stark could perceive what was in front of him, they unfurled the tarps.

The skids were piled with boxes and boxes of weapons. The boxes had all been meticulously labeled with the manufacturer's logo: Stark Industries. In smaller print below the logo were the specifics of what was contained in the boxes. Stark couldn't believe it: It was weaponry dating back to the 1980s. Some of the crates had printing that was faded, while others were new.

Stark took a tentative step forward. They were making no effort to prevent him from doing so. He continued to move toward them until he was standing in the midst of the crates. He touched them cautiously, as if he were in a dream and might be able to awaken from it by coming into contact with one of them. But no, they were all far too real to be so easily disposed of.

"Quite a collection, isn't it?"

It was the surgeon. He was standing next to Stark, watching impassively. Stark hadn't even realized that the old man had been there since he'd been so overwhelmed by the sight of all this weaponry, designed for American hands and American needs, in the hands of terrorists and marauders.

When he finally found his voice, he said, "How did they get all this?"

The surgeon did not reply. He didn't have the opportunity. Abu strode over to them as if he were the king of the world, and spoke in rapid-fire Arabic.

"As you can see," the surgeon translated, "they have everything you need to build the Jericho. He says make a list of materials."

Stark wasn't paying attention to Abu. He had spotted another man—heavily armed and imposing—standing a distance away, and even though no one had told him, he instantly realized that Abu wasn't the alpha male in this particular little pack. That title clearly belonged to the man who stood on an outcropping of rock while several other men, including one of Abu's lieutenants, attended to him in the same manner that pilot fish surrounded a shark. He radiated danger the way that the sun radiated heat.

"You will start work right away," the surgeon was saying, "and when you are done he will set you free."

Stark shifted his gaze to the surgeon. Keeping his head absolutely still so as not to betray the meaning of his words, Stark actually smiled as if he believed he was being given good news. What he said was: "No, he won't set me free, will he?"

The surgeon looked as if he was briefly considering another answer, but instead he simply nodded and said in English, "No. He won't."

The seed that had been planted earlier in his mind tried to start growing at that point, to prompt him to think, *They want a weapon? I'll give them a weapon, one they'll never forget.* But it was washed away by a wave of despair that swept over Tony Stark as he became convinced that no matter what happened to him, no matter what he did or did not do, this hideous hell-hole was where he was going to meet his end.

V.

Rhodey walked through the ambush site, staring at the wreckage that was strewn about the area. It had been several days since everything had gone completely off the rails, but this was the first opportunity that he'd had to get out there and survey it.

He was damned lucky to be alive. Certainly enough people had told him that. He'd had to take their word for it because he didn't remember the last moments of the assault. The last thing he had recalled was charging into a swirling cloud of smoke and mist, trying to pull together the troops and launch a counterattack on whoever the hell was assailing them. Then there had been an explosion that had knocked him off his feet, and blackness had claimed him. When he'd come to, it had been in a military hospital where he was being treated for smoke inhalation and possible concussion.

They'd advised Rhodey that he should be there for at least a week for observation. He had thanked them politely for their opinions and made sure that he was out of there within forty-eight hours.

Even after that relatively brief time, it seemed that the trail had already turned cold.

General William Gabriel was standing a few feet away from Rhodey. Gabriel had often told Rhodey that he had a wrinkle on his face for every battle that had been fought under his watch. Rhodey fancied he could see the crease forming on Gabriel's forehead to commemorate this particular disaster. A team of security men were clambering over the remainder of the wreckage, looking for clues.

"Something's not right," Rhodey finally said.

Gabriel surveyed the remains of the doomed convoy and clearly wondered if he and Rhodey were looking at the same thing. "Looks like a standard hit and run."

Rhodey shook his head. "Sir, I'm telling you, this was a snatch and grab. A perfectly executed linear ambush. As soon as they got what they wanted, they melted away."

Gabriel considered his words, but then shrugged. The gesture spoke volumes: Even if Rhodey was correct, there was nothing that he, Gabriel, could do about it. "Intel's on it," he said confidently. "We're in good hands. If he's out there, we'll get him."

"With your permission," Rhodey said, drawing himself up and squaring his shoulders, looking every inch the military man that he was. "I'd like to stay in theater and head up the search and investigation."

The general shook his head. "There's a PR firestorm brewing over this at home. Right now the best way to serve your country is to get back there and handle it." He started to walk away, clearly believing that that was the end of the discussion.

But Rhodey wasn't about to leave it there. Rather than fall into step with the general, he stayed right where he was, his body language sending a distinct message. "Tony Stark is the DOD's number one intellectual asset, and I can be of value in the field."

Gabriel stopped walking, turned and faced Rhodey. "Duly noted, but we need you back home," he said, his voice conveying the fact that he wasn't thrilled over Rhodey's making an argument of this. Then, after a moment, he relaxed both his posture and his voice ever so slightly. "Colonel," he said softly, "it's not lost on me that Stark is a lifelong friend. But as a lifelong friend, don't you think that he would respect your doing your duty?"

Probably not. He'd call me a puppet and a robot and unwilling to think for myself. And I'd be pissed off with him, and we'd argue, and at the end of the day we'd wonder why in the world we bother with each other . . . and the very next day we'd start all over again and be glad for the opportunity . . .

"Yes, sir," said Rhodey.

The general nodded in approval. Rhodey was about to follow him to the Humvee when his cell phone rang. He looked at the caller ID and moaned softly. This was not something he was looking forward to, but he couldn't let it just kick over the voice mail, if for no other reason than that he'd let the previous eleven calls from her bounce over there and his voice mail box was filling up.

He answered it with a curt, "Yeah?"

"Well?" That was all Pepper Potts said. "Well?"

"Well . . . he's alive. We know that much."

"Because you didn't find his body."

"Yeah," he admitted.

"Who's got him, Rhodey? What do they want with him? Ransom? What?"

"We don't know, Pepper. I wish to God we did, but we don't. But we have our best people on it. We'll find him."

"You'll find him." There was distinct bitterness in her voice. "Because we've done such a fantastic job finding people hiding in mountains in Afghanistan, haven't we . . ."

"Pepper . . ."

"*You were supposed to protect him, dammit! You with all your weapons and security! You were . . .*"

He had never heard her like this. She had never been anything other than in control, on top of everything.

Smiling, efficient, nothing ever threw her. To hear her like this tore him up.

He tried to respond, but before he could, Pepper had brought herself under control. "I'm sorry," she said.

"You don't have to apolo—"

"No. I do." Her voice had reacquired its detached, businesslike demeanor. "That was . . . unprofessional. You didn't ask for this to happen. You did your best. We should be grateful that you weren't killed in the attack. I have . . ." She paused, and there was a slight choke in her voice that she promptly shoved away. "I have every confidence that you'll find him. And Mr. Stark is very resourceful himself. You shouldn't count him out."

"Absolutely. He's probably building a matter transporter out of three paperclips and a toaster oven as we speak, and he'll just beam himself out."

"You'll keep me apprised."

"Absolutely. You'll be the first one to know."

"Thank you. That means a lot."

"And Pepper—"

The phone beeped at him. The person on the other end had disappeared. He couldn't tell whether it was a dropped call or if she had hung up. Either way, the conversation was over.

He pocketed his cell phone and wondered, not for the first time, if Tony Stark was aware of just how completely, totally, and madly in love with him Pepper Potts was. For that matter, he wondered if Pepper herself knew.

vi.

Tony Stark, who had nothing but designer ergonomic couches and chairs in his various homes, had taken up residence in a wheelbarrow.

Tony Stark, who slept under a goose-down comforter on chilly nights, had wrapped himself in an army-surplus blanket for warmth.

Tony Stark, who had been in control of his life for as long as he could remember, was convinced that his life was going to be ending in short order and there was nothing he could do about it.

His passing thoughts over taking revenge, of building a weapon that would annihilate his captors before they even realized it, had been just that: passing. Then they had given way to self-pity and a bleak conviction that nothing mattered.

His heart device had been hooked up to the car battery to recharge it, but Stark wasn't stupid. He knew the car battery was hardly an infinite power source. Hell, if a car battery could be drained dry just by leaving on the headlights for a few hours, how much juice could it possibly possess to power a magnetic suspension system? Once it ran out, there would be nothing to prevent the shrapnel from piercing his heart, and that would be that.

The insurgents had brought a generator into the room. It was small, but more than powerful enough to keep Stark's heart safe for days after a single charge. However, the generator was run on gasoline, and the insurgents hadn't filled it. So it stood over in a corner, little more than an oversized paperweight. At the other end of the room was a fuel drum, but it was secured in a cage under lock and key. It might as well have been on the moon.

The surgeon had been watching him, his face inscrutable. Perhaps he had been waiting for Stark to come out of the depression that had paralyzed him all on his own, but it didn't appear to be happening. Finally he spoke.

"Hoping to hold out, are you, Stark?"

Stark's gaze flickered toward the surgeon, a mildly questioning look in his eyes.

"You're figuring that if you simply shut down, refuse to cooperate, they won't kill you because they need you, and perhaps it will provide your friends with enough time to find you and come to your rescue."

The surgeon could not have been more wrong. Stark wasn't thinking anything like that. He was, in fact, convinced that they wouldn't find him, and further convinced that his captors would indeed kill him if they decided that he wasn't going to cooperate. There was no grand stalling tactic involved here; Stark was simply positive that there was no way out.

Unaware of that, the surgeon continued, "I'm sure they're looking for you, Stark, but they will never find you here. That car battery is running out, and they won't turn on the generator until you start to work."

Stark knew all of that. That was what was contributing to his disengaged attitude.

The surgeon approached Stark and crouched so that they were on eye level. His voice became soft, even understanding. "You didn't like what you saw out there, did you." It was not a question. Stark shook his head, despondent. "I didn't like it either when those weapons destroyed my village. What you just saw . . . that's your legacy. Your life's work in the hands of these murderers.

Is that how you want to go out? Is this"—he gestured at the pathetic, wretched creature that Stark had become—"the last act of defiance of the great Tony Stark? Or are you going to try to do something about it?"

Stark shook his head. "Why should I do anything? They're going to kill me, you . . . and if they don't, I'll be dead in a week."

"Then," said the surgeon, "this is a very important week for you."

Slowly Stark looked at the surgeon as if truly focusing upon him for the first time. "Why do you care what happens to me?"

The surgeon shrugged. "Someone has to."

Stark leaned back in the wheelbarrow. For the first time in ages, it seemed, his thoughts moved away from his own predicament, spurred by what the surgeon had just said.

Someone has to.

If he died here, now, forgotten in some cave—*would* anyone really care? Anyone besides the army brass who would be devastated that Tony Stark wasn't developing new and more exciting ways to kill.

Rhodey. Rhodey would care. And Hogan. Happy Hogan, the former boxer whom Tony had always promised would never be out of a job because once, many years earlier, Hogan had saved Stark's life. Tony Stark never forgot debts such as that.

And Pepper.

How was she handling all of this? She must be worried sick, out of her mind with fear. How would it be for her if her boss never turned up again . . . or worse, was depicted on a video tape screaming in agony while they severed his head with a rusty saw?

And his father.

Yes, Howard Stark was long gone. But he had counted on his son to carry on the family name, the tradition of devoted service to the safety of his country. With Stark gone, and no heir to the Stark name around, the company would be vulnerable. It might well be sold off, absorbed. The Stark name, the Stark legacy, all vanishing into the mists of history and eventually forgotten.

And Jimmy.

He'd known him for a few minutes, but the recollection of his watch on that bastard's wrist . . .

All of that went through Stark's head, and as it did so, the sheer anger that it generated began to energize him, to scrape away the misery and self-pity like barnacles being scraped from the hull of a vessel.

And not just any vessel, but a warship.

A great armored warship.

Slowly he eased himself from the wheelbarrow. His voice flat and even, he said, "The next time Abu shows up, tell him I'm ready to cooperate as soon as he fills the generator. If he's got me being powered by a car battery, the most I'm going to whip up for him is antilock brakes. He gets the generator going as a show of good faith, I get going on his weapons."

The surgeon looked surprised at the sudden turnaround in Stark's demeanor. When Abu showed up half an hour later, flanked by his lieutenants, the surgeon conveyed Stark's sentiments. Abu nodded to Omar, who left only to return a few moments later with an empty can. He walked over to the cage, unlocked it, and then drained some fuel from the drum into the can. Without a word he carried the can over to the generator and filled it. Abu's gaze moved from the generator to Stark, back and forth until the generator was fully gassed and ready to go. Then Omar took the can, shoved it into the cage along with the fuel, and locked them both up tight.

Ahmed, meantime, fired up the generator. After a couple of false starts, it roared to life. The lights in the cave lab flickered and then shone brightly.

Abu looked at Stark expectantly, as if Tony were capable of pulling a Jericho missile out of his sock.

"Okay, here's what I need," said Stark. The surgeon translated quickly, and he had quite a chore ahead of him because despite the complexity of his requirements, Stark wasn't slowing down in the least as he rattled off his shopping list.

"S-category missiles. Lot 7043. The S-30 explosive tritonal. And a dozen of the S-76s. Mortars: M-category #1, 4, 8, 20, and 60. M-229's, I need eleven of those. Mines: The pre-1990s AP 5s and AP 16s."

Abu's men were already in motion. As Stark continued to speak, they were running in with the armament, that he was requesting. Stark, meantime, assessed his work area with clinical efficiency. The surgeon continued to translate. "This area free of clutter with good light." He indicated a workbench. "I want it positioned at 12 o'clock to the door to avoid logjams." He turned away from the workbench then and proceeded to count off on his fingers the rest of the equipment he'd be requiring. "I need welding gear: acetylene or propane, helmets, a soldering set-up with goggles, and smelting cups. Two full sets of precision tools."

The never-ending list was beginning to exasperate Abu. One of his men had pulled out a notebook and was scribbling as fast as he possibly could.

Stark didn't slow down. "Finally I want three pairs of tube socks, white, a toothbrush, protein powder, spices, sugar, five pounds of tea, cards." Before Abu could question the litany, Stark added the final insanity: "And a washing machine. Top load."

Abu's eyes bulged. His aide who was scribbling down the requests, was muttering to himself in Arabic, and Stark assumed that he was simply repeating the list over to himself so that he could get everything right. This approach did not endear him to Abu, though, who took a second's break from being angry with Tony to cuff his quickly scribbling aide in the head.

That attended to, Abu was in front of Stark in a mere three quick steps. He bellowed at him in Arabic, with the surgeon providing the translation: "A washing machine? Do you think he's a fool!?"

Stark didn't look away. Instead he thrived on Abu's reaction. This entire situation was a struggle for control for who would be in charge of whom. Thus far, Abu had been running the table. But now the balance of power had tilted in Stark's direction. Clearly Abu had no real idea what Stark needed and didn't need. He couldn't really know for sure if Stark was messing with him or if he truly required everything that he claimed he did. That was an advantage that Stark had every intention of pushing as far as he could.

Tony leaned in toward Abu, his face drawing within an inch of Abu's. Abu reflexively pulled back as his personal space was invaded. This was enough to give Stark the emotional upper hand, if only for a moment. As if he were a missionary endeavoring to communicate with an island native, Stark spoke slowly, one word at a time: "Must have everything. Great Satan make big boom— kill for powerful Abu Bakar. Big boom kill."

Abu snarled in disgust but did not press the subject. He snapped at his subordinates, shouting at them because at least them he could control. Then he headed out the door without waiting for them to flank him as he usually did. They hurried out after him, the door slamming shut.

The surgeon stared at him, clearly not knowing what to make of what had just happened.

Stark spoke very softly, touching the area of his chest. "I should be dead already. But I'm not, and I have to think that the fact that I'm not . . . I have to think it's for a reason."

He left it there.

For the first time in ages, Stark stopped thinking of the door as a prison door and instead as nothing more than an obstacle. Tony Stark thrived on overcoming obstacles, and that door would be no different. It would be overcome.

Stark wasted no time getting his lab in working order. He pulled open the housing of an S-category missile and within minutes the missile's innards were as exposed as the guts of a surgical patient on the operating table. Using a pair of needle-nose pliers, he extracted a glass ring from its inner workings. He placed it delicately upon the workspace and then set it aside.

The surgeon proved to be a valuable and willing co-worker. With the surgeon's help, he pulled open one of the M-229 crates and removed the chip-rack cylinder from one of the larger warheads.

"You do know they've removed all the explosives before they brought this to us," the scientist told him cautiously.

"I know. They're crazy, not stupid."

Grunting slightly under the weight, Stark walked the heavy chip-rack to the workbench. He set to work and minutes later had removed a tiny palladium strip. "This," he said, sounding so pleased with himself one would have thought he'd just cracked the code for DNA, "is what we're looking for. I need eleven of these."

"Eleven?"

The surgeon didn't pretend to understand, but that didn't slow him. Over the next hour, carefully and methodically, the two of them extracted the palladium strips from the remainder of the chip-rack cylinders.

Stark then set the surgeon in front of the furnace while he set the palladium into a crucible. He brought them over to the surgeon and instructed, "Heat the palladium to 1825 kelvin."

"How will I know when it reaches that temperature?"

"The palladium will melt," Stark said in a matter-of-fact manner.

While the surgeon attended to that, Stark didn't slow in his efforts. Up until now, time had lost meaning to Stark because life had lost meaning. Now it was different: Time continued to mean nothing to Stark, but it wasn't because of a sense of hopelessness. It was for the same reason it usually happened: He was in the throes of creativity. Tony Stark was perfectly capable of getting up first thing in the morning, heading down to his workshop, and working until he finally noticed the hunger pangs in his stomach screaming at him. Taking a break, he would head to the kitchen to grab some breakfast only to discover that it was dinnertime.

That same focus of energy and effort was present now. Over the past days, Stark's life had seemed a long, bleak tunnel of nothingness. Now his life was broken down into a series of tasks: He was wrapping a copper coil around the glass ring.

He was dropping palladium strips into a crucible on the fire. He was sculpting a sand mold for the palladium ring. One thing after the next after the next, and for the first time since his captivity began, Tony Stark was truly alive.

The surgeon brought the crucible of melted palladium to Tony. "Careful. Careful," said Stark.

"Relax. I always had steady hands. It's why you're still alive."

"Oh yeah, thanks." Stark looked with curiosity at the surgeon and realized that he didn't have the faintest idea what the man's real name was. First he'd been so steeped in helplessness and self-pity that he hadn't cared, then he'd been so caught up in his endeavors that he'd simply forgotten to be inquisitive. "What do I call you?"

The surgeon looked confused at the question, but then he understood and smiled. "My name is Yinsen."

"Nice to meet you."

"Nice to meet you, too."

The individual strips had melted together into a single ring. Stark allowed time for it to cool and, once he was satisfied it was ready, he lifted the ring out of the mold with a pair of tweezers.

"What are you building?"

"The ring of power," said Stark. "Just wait until you see me start carving elvish lettering on it. As soon as it cools, I slip this puppy on my finger, turn invisible, and walk right out."

Yinsen stared at him a moment. "Tell you what: I will ask you the question again, and perhaps this time you will give me an answer that I actually understand. Now: What are you building?"

"Something big." He smiled. "A better mousetrap."

As Tony Stark plugged a cable into the generator, he noticed that Yinsen was shaving again. He had to commend the man on his meticulousness: During the entire time of their imprisonment, Yinsen had somehow managed to keep his pin-stripped suit pressed, his vest buttoned, his tie fastidiously knotted. It seemed that he was refusing to acknowledge the uncivilized nature of his surroundings. Knowing that he could not elevate them to his level, he refused to permit them to drag him down to theirs.

As Tony plugged a cable into the generator, he said over his shoulder, "What are you shaving for? We're almost done."

"Look like an animal, and soon you'll start behaving

like one." Yinsen spoke primly. Stark considered the possibility that when (not if, but when) he got out of this place, he'd buy a network just so he could provide Yinsen his own self-help talk show.

Stark threw a switch on the generator. The lights in the cave flickered, went out completely, and then came back on, but at a much lower output than before. There was only so much power to go around in the place and Stark was the primary consumer. Mirthlessly he envisioned the terrorists receiving an inflated power bill in the mail and cursing out Stark in colorful Arabic phrases.

The device over which he had been laboring all this time lay upon the workbench. It was round, about two inches in depth and the width of Stark's palm. It softly glowed to life on the workbench. Stark monitored the cable that was jacked into it, holding his hand over it to make certain that no heat was radiating from it. The last thing he needed was for it to overheat.

Yinsen said nothing as the device continued to charge. Instead he meticulously wiped the last bits of stray shaving cream from his face. Then he washed off his shaving implements and placed them back in their proper cases with so much care that he might have been handling surgical implements. During all that time, however, he never took his gaze off the device.

Watching the gauges, Stark finally nodded in approval. He shut down the generator and detached the device from the wires.

"That doesn't look like a Jericho missile," Yinsen said quietly with the reserved understatement he so commonly employed.

"That's because it's an Arc reactor," Stark said. "A miniature version of a much larger generator first developed by Stark tech—" He stopped and smiled to himself. How hard did old habits die, that he was automatically slipping into the showman, hucksterish mode that he employed when addressing the army brass. He didn't have to impress anyone here, nor was he out to try to sell someone an order of missiles. Indeed, his whole purpose was to avoid supplying missiles to an interested customer. It was like fighting muscle memory. His voice becoming softer, he continued, "It should suspend the shrapnel in my chest and keep it from entering my heart."

"What an original invention."

"Yeah," Stark said, nodding, "but this one is going to last a bit longer than a week."

"It's pretty small. What can it generate?"

"Three gigajoules," Stark paused and then added with satisfaction, "per second."

Stark was pleased to see that, for once, he had managed to pierce Yinsen's reserve. "That's . . . three thousand megawatts," said Yinsen. "You can't be serious. That's the equivalent of . . . of an entire power station. Or Hoover Dam. That's on par with the maximum output of the world's largest nuclear generator."

"You're right and wrong."

"What am I wrong about?"

"That I can't be serious. Everything else, you're on target."

Astonishment in his voice, Yinsen said, "That could run your heart for fifty lifetimes."

"Or something very big for fifteen minutes."

"The output you're discussing could power a small city for a lot longer than fifteen minutes. How big are you talking about?"

"Well," said Stark softly, "I don't like to brag."

They exchanged a long look. For the first time, Yinsen seemed as if he was beginning to understand exactly what Stark had in mind.

"You're talking about grafting something on par with

a nuclear reactor to your chest, Stark. Aren't you afraid of what could happen?"

"Well," said Stark thoughtfully, "considering how violently some people oppose nuclear power, I'm figuring the greatest threat I need to worry about is picketers. But I'm willing to take the chance if you are."

In spite of himself, Yinsen smiled.

"Let's put it in," said Stark.

A pair of suspicious eyes watched Stark on the monitor.

Stark was lying on the workbench, with Yinsen crouched over him. Because of the way Yinsen's body was positioned, a clear view of Stark was not possible.

The man watched, his feet propped up on an instrument console. In as mundane a manner as could be, he was spooning peanut butter into his mouth. He was scooping it from a jar that had arrived courtesy of a military airdrop. It would have been impossible to tell if he was inclined to give a moment's thought to the starving children for whom the peanut butter and half ton of other food was intended.

He considered what he is seeing. He had plenty of military knowledge, but knew nothing of science. He tried to determine the significance of what he was witnessing, and finally decided that Yinsen was endeavoring to keep Stark's heart going so that Stark, in turn, could live long enough to provide them the weapons they desired. There was nothing here to be concerned about. An old man and a crippled, spoiled American. They posed no threat, their spirits sufficiently broken that they would do whatever was required in order to keep on living.

How pathetic, he mused, the lengths to which such godless, soulless beings would go to cling to their little lives. How sad it must be to lack any confidence or faith in the justness and inevitability of final reward that awaited them. As long as he and his followers were happy to die for a cause while Stark and his ilk were unhappy to die for any cause, triumph could and would be his.

He allowed his tongue to slide lovingly over his lips, savoring the taste of the peanut butter. They may be godless, soulless, and hopeless, but those Americans could produce tasty snacks. Perhaps when he sent Stark's head back to the American president, he would include a complimentary note to that effect.

vii.

The bloody chest plate that had once been implanted in Stark's chest—the only thing that had kept him going—lay in a corner, gathering dust. Several smaller components had been stripped from it to be used in other applications; otherwise it was tossed aside. The car battery to which the chest plate was attached was in the same condition: cannibalized and forgotten, the coat of dust upon it underscoring how much time had passed since Stark had given it even a second look.

Although Yinsen had remained vigorous with his ablutions, Stark had let himself go. This had nothing to do with any sense of giving in to misery or despair, as might have once been the case. Instead, for Tony Stark, this was business as usual. In the normal course of his normal life, once Stark became caught up in the throes of creation, personal hygiene went out the window. It usually fell to the disembodied promptings of Jarvis or, failing that, the corporeal prodding from Pepper, to remind Stark that he should think about changing the clothes he'd been wearing for three days or maybe run a razor across the bushy growth that was accruing on his face. After the first day or so, Yinsen had simply taken to staying the hell out of Stark's way. He had even stopped asking Stark if he was hungry since he tended not to receive answers. Instead, every so often, he would just put out food for Stark, who would—sooner or later—eat it without looking at it or even noticing that he was doing so.

Now Stark was in the midst of cutting metal flat-stock with a torch. The room was littered with what he had described as "missile components" to his captors when they had periodically entered the cave. He had even rattled off names for specific pieces. They responded by nodding and trying to look as if they understood what he was talking about. Their insufferable pride was turning out to be one of the most useful weapons against them that he could have hoped for.

His shirt was hanging open, and the glowing device was visible implanted in his chest. The terrorists had demanded to know why he had installed it. Maintaining a completely straight face and acting as if it was the most sensible and natural thing in the world, Stark had claimed it was a personal night-light and that he'd developed it so that it would provide him illumination any time, even in the event of a power failure. That way he could keep on working on the missile technology and meet their needs. They had scratched their heads or stroked their beards thoughtfully and then, best of all, had praised him on his ingenuity and determination. Either that or they were just starting to become concerned that he was losing his mind and felt it best not to press him on it.

"Stark! Tell me what you're doing and I'll tell you what I'm doing."

Somehow Yinsen's innocuous comment managed to penetrate Stark's work-centric mindset. He glanced over and saw that Yinsen was carving something out of a flat piece of wood. His computer of a mind analyzed the design and determined what it was going to look like in its final form. As he started filling a cylinder with gas from the torch (making certain to angle his body so that the perpetual monitor would not be able to determine what he was doing) he said, "Looks to me like you're making a crappy backgammon board."

Yinsen reacted with horror to the notion. "Crappy? This is Lebanese cedar."

The response prompted Stark, once he had finished filling the cylinder, to focus his attention on Yinsen even as he continued to cradle the cylinder in his palm. "Is that where you're from? Lebanon?"

Yinsen didn't acknowledge the question. Instead, he continued shaping the board as he said, "I'm impressed you even know what this is. How about we play, and if I win, you tell me what you're really making?"

Stark didn't reply immediately. He simply stared at Yinsen impassively. "A: I don't know what you're talking about," he said after a time. "B: I was the backgammon champ at MIT four years running."

"Interesting," and Yinsen's reaction really did underscore his very genuine interest. "I was the champion at Cambridge."

"Please don't use 'interesting' and Cambridge in the same sentence," Stark said dismissively. "Is that still a school?"

"It's a university," Yinsen correctly him gently, taking pains to sound regretful for having to point out Stark's error. With a mock consoling tone, he added, "You probably haven't heard about it since Americans can't get in."

"Unless they're teaching."

This prompted a wry grin from Yinsen, the first such that Stark could recall in the entirety of their weeks shared in this pit.

Before the good-natured jibing could continue, the familiar sound of the door slat thumped behind them. Typically this was the signal for them to assume their submissive poses, but Abu—defying procedure—yanked open the door without waiting for them to do as was expected of them. Clearly, he was in an even fouler mood than he typically was.

Unfortunately because he was so startled by Abu's abrupt entrance, not to mention the unexpected turn of events, Stark dropped the cylinder he'd been clandestinely filling. It clattered to the floor. The sound was lost in the noise of Abu's entrance, since Ahmed and Omar followed him as always. Yinsen, however, did notice, and he and Tony exchanged nervous glances. Stark knew that if he bent down and picked it up, tried to conceal it, the motion alone would be enough to draw Abu's attention to it.

To add to Stark's confusion and hesitation, more men were pouring in behind Abu. He didn't recognize them at first, but then he realized they were vaguely familiar. He just wasn't sure why until he recalled: They'd been standing near that larger, dangerous individual he'd seen from a distance all those weeks ago.

And here was the individual now. He strode in, his head swiveling like a spotlight. He moved past his personal guards, who were standing there with backs stiff and shoulders squared.

Even Abu looked apprehensive about the bigger man's presence. No, not just the bigger man. The Boss Man. This just reaffirmed Stark's earlier assessment: This guy was clearly running things.

Yinsen and Stark had raised their hands as the newcomers stomped into their cell. Now the Boss Man looked them over and, incongruously, a smile spread across his swarthy face. In perfect English, he said, "Relax."

The word startled Stark. It seemed ages since he had heard anyone besides Yinsen speak Stark's native tongue.

Still, out of reflex, their hands remained in the air. He gestured for them to lower them and slowly they did so. The Boss Man meandered about the lab, picking things up, putting them down. This guy was better at playing his cards close to the vest than their other captors. Stark couldn't determine whether he was genuinely inspecting and understanding what he was looking at, or was just picking everything up and putting it back down so that he appeared to comprehend the purpose of it all.

His foot came dangerously near the cylinder that Stark had been filling. Just before his boot could come down upon it, the washing machine caught his eye.

He turned toward it, leaving the cylinder unmolested. Stark tried not to let out a sigh of relief lest that tip him off. The Boss Man looked the washing machine over slowly, with growing disbelief. Finally he switched his gaze to Abu and stared at him, obviously looking for some sort of explanation. Abu shrugged and smiled wanly. The Boss Man's cold glare indicated that he hardly considered that an adequate explanation.

Then he turned to the workbench. Stark's onion-paper schematics of the missile lay spread across it. He studied them with what might have only been vague interest . . . or perhaps something more. The longer this guy was here, the less good Stark was feeling about it.

"The bow and arrow was once the pinnacle of weapons technology," he said finally. His voice was polished, educated. "It allowed the great Genghis Khan to rule from the Pacific to the Ukraine." He turned the schematics around, and instantly Stark knew that he'd overplayed his hand. The schematics had already been right side up. It was like watching someone with a fifth-grade education trying to decipher the Rosetta stone. Nevertheless, not letting up on his act for even an instant, the Boss Man went on. "Today, whoever has the latest Stark weapons rules these lands. Soon it will be my turn."

Then he glanced back and forth between Yinsen and Tony. Something in his voice changed, something that seemed to indicate that he knew Stark was trying to pull a fast one. He said something to Yinsen. It sounded very soft and very dangerous.

"Nothing," Yinsen said quickly. "Nothing is 'really going on here.' We're working."

The Boss Man spoke again. It was significant to Stark that Yinsen kept responding in English. Obviously he was doing it for Stark's benefit, to keep him apprised of precisely what was being said and what sort of threat they were facing. "I know it's been a long time, but the weapon is right here," he said, gesturing around the lab. "He is working very hard. It's very complex."

Yinsen glanced toward Tony then, as if looking for back-up. Stark nodded numbly, but he didn't think he was being especially convincing.

The Boss Man's next actions indicated that Stark had made the correct assessment. He snapped something at Abu while gesturing toward Yinsen. Yinsen paled as Abu and Ahmed stepped forward, grabbing Yinsen by the shoulders, and forcing him to his knees. As they did so, the Boss Man used a pair of tongs to extract a single hot coal from the furnace. It glowed threateningly in the dimness of the room.

He walked—strolled—toward Yinsen, keeping the coal out in front of him. This time he spoke in English, obviously for Stark's benefit. "Tell me what is going on?"

"Nothing! *Nothing* is going on!" said Yinsen.

"Open your mouth."

Yinsen did not do so. Stark stood paralyzed, wanting to make some sort of move to intervene, but knowing that the Boss Man's guards would cut him down before he took two steps. Abu and Ahmed, meantime, gripped Yinsen's face and forced his mouth open. He struggled fiercely but in futility.

The coal came closer to Yinsen's open mouth. "Tell

me now!" said the Boss Man, with the implicit threat in his voice that Yinsen was running out of time.

Stark braced himself for Yinsen to spill everything he knew. It wouldn't be much, but it would be enough to save him. *Something big! Something to break out of here! He's playing you all for fools! You might as well kill him now before he kills all of you!* All this and more was what Stark was expecting.

Instead, in a pitiful but last-ditch effort to convince them, Yinsen bellowed, *"He's building your bomb!"*

The desperate lie hung in the air for a long moment. The Boss Man stared as if he were studying the words, floating invisibly, considering them, and giving them weight. Then he dropped the coal on the floor in front of Yinsen. It bounced away, cooling as it rolled. Without having to be told that the moment had passed, Abu and Ahmed released Yinsen, although they didn't do so without an added shove for good measure.

Seconds later they had exited, the door slamming shut behind them. Stark quickly went to Yinsen, who was still on his knees. "Who the hell was that?" Stark said in a low voice.

"Raza. A tribal warlord. They answer to him."

"I could see that," Stark said grimly. "Are you okay?"

Yinsen looked at him in a way that indicated that was quite possibly the dumbest thing Stark could possibly have asked him. Stark nodded in tacit, silent acknowledgment of that truth.

He helped Yinsen to his feet and Yinsen said, "That's twice I saved your life. *Now* are you going to tell me what the hell you're really building?"

This time Stark did not hesitate. He walked over to the light board and flicked it on, then he lifted it up. It was a simple hiding place, so obvious that no one had tumbled to it. From under the board he pulled out a sheaf of schematics and started laying them out on the board, keeping his body between himself and the ever-present camera to make certain they had no clear view of what he was doing. He gestured for Yinsen to come over and take a look. Yinsen did so, his eyes widening in wonderment as Stark produced sheet after sheet of designs.

Yinsen studied them, whistled softly, and then said approvingly, "Finally, an idea of your own."

"Unless you count ancient knights."

"I think the bravest of those knights would have taken one look at this walking toward them and fled the battlefield. Let us hope that Abu and his men have at least that much wisdom."

Stark's eyes were cold. "Honestly," he said, "Part of me is hoping they don't."

Stark stood in front of the sink, using Yinsen's shaving implements. Yinsen, all unknowing, had stepped into the role that Pepper traditionally played, thrusting the utensils at him and insisting that it was time to attend to certain matters of personal hygiene and deportment. That included both washing and shaving. As Stark shaved, he heard the door slat slam aside. He tensed, nicking himself slightly as he did so, and—courtesy of the mirror into which he was gazing—was able to cast a glance in the direction of the door. Abu's eyes, which he could recognize from across the room by now, glared in at him. There had been no accompanying stomping of feet, however, which signaled to Stark that they weren't about to have intruders. Every so often, Abu just looked in on them, scowling, presumably to serve as a reminder that he was not a man of infinite patience.

Now that Stark had encountered Raza, however, the experience had diminished Abu in his eyes, transforming the terrorist from dominating figure to just another nervous flunky who was watching over his shoulder. It didn't make him any less dangerous. But it enabled Stark to acquire a bit more mental distance when it came to how he thought of him.

Perhaps annoyed that he wasn't getting any sort of reaction out of Stark, Abu closed the slat and went on about his business . . . frightening children, kicking puppies, whatever the hell it was he did to pass the time. Stark, meanwhile, wiped the remains of the runny shaving lather from his face. Then he returned the shaving tools to their place and pulled on a pair of thick gloves as he moved toward the furnace.

Using oversized tongs, he removed a white-hot piece of metal from the furnace. He lay it down on a makeshift anvil and started hammering at it with a mallet. Across the room, Yinsen was busy soldering a bit of complex circuitry. He looked up and stared at the image of Tony Stark, strong and resolute, pounding away on the metal.

"My people have a tale," said Yinsen slowly, distantly, as if he were speaking from a place far in the future, "about a prince, much hated by his king, who was banished to the underworld and jailed there. The evil king gave him the most difficult labor, working the iron pits."

Stark didn't turn his attention away from his work, but his gaze flickered over to Yinsen just enough to convey that he was listening.

Yinsen went on. "Year after year the prince mined the heavy ore, becoming so strong he could crush pieces of it together with his bare hands. Too late, the king realized his mistake. When he struck at the prince with his finest sword—it broke in two. The prince himself had become strong as iron."

Stark held up the metal that he'd been working on. A

crude iron mask stared back at him. He lay it down carefully and it sat on the ground, cooling. Stark stared at it.

A man as strong as iron. An iron man.

He liked the sound of that. He liked it a lot.

viii.

Rhodey walked into the visitor's reception area of Edwards Air Force Base, making no attempt to keep the surprise from his face. He hadn't been expecting anyone to come by this evening, much less this individual.

Happy Hogan stood leaning against the wall. He was holding his chauffeur's hat uncomfortably in his hands, looking about as out of place as a human being could possibly look. "Rhodes," he said with a nod.

"Hey, Hogan," said Rhodey, putting out a hand as he walked across the room. Hogan shook it firmly and Rhodey tried not to grunt. Hogan might not have been any good as a boxer, but his strength was still considerable. "You should have given me a heads-up. I could have left word at the gate and you wouldn't have gotten all that hassle."

Hogan released his grip and shrugged. "Hassle don't bother me."

"Okay, so," and Rhodey folded his arms across his chest, flexing his fingers slightly to restore circulation, "what can I do for you?"

"Just wondering if there's been anything going on with the boss."

"They're still looking. Narrowing down leads. They're—"

"That's a lot of talk that means nothing's going on, ain't it?"

Rhodey pursed his lips and then said, "Hogan, truth

to tell, it's all classified. Much as I'd like to tell you, I really can't."

"Yeah, 'cept you already told me tons. Look, Rhodes," and Happy tried his best to force a smile. His best, unfortunately, was none too convincing. "I'm just a palooka, okay? I know that."

"You're more than that and I think we're both aware of it, Hogan," Rhodey said. "Any man who saves Tony Stark's life and gets a permanent job because of it . . ."

"Just the right guy in the wrong place. Point is, there's tons of guys like me. There's not a lot of guys like you."

"What are you saying?"

"I'm saying," said Hogan, and there was challenge in his voice, "what the hell is a guy like you doing over here when a guy like him is stuck over there?"

Rhodey studied him for a moment and then said softly, "Pepper put you up to this?"

He watched carefully to see Hogan's reaction. Hogan, by nature, wasn't gifted with the ability to hide his thoughts. "Not in so many words . . ."

"How many words, then?"

"Not any," Hogan said firmly. "But, I seen her. Every day. I see what she's like. I see how this is getting to her. And I . . ." He looked down, turning his hat over and over in his hands. "It just kills me, y'know? I want it to go back to the way it was. I want her to go back to being the way she was. And I feel like I should be doing something, and this is the only thing that I could think of."

"That's . . . very considerate of you, Hogan. You're a good friend to her."

"Yeah. Good friend."

The way he said it spoke volumes to Rhodey. It suggested someone who wanted to be a great deal more, but believed for whatever reason that he didn't have a chance in hell with her. Rhodey felt as if, between what he was certain Pepper felt for Stark and what Hogan felt for Pepper, he had a ground-floor view of a love triangle that rivaled anything one might see on a weekday soap opera.

"Look, Hogan," he said slowly, "bottom line is, I'm under orders. There's only so much I can do."

"Yeah, well, funny thing," said Hogan. "Guy like you, I'd think that if you run into something where there's only so much you can do, you find a way to do more. Then again," and he shrugged, "I could be wrong. Been wrong a lotta times before. Probably been wrong more than I been right."

He put his hat atop his head, tipping it slightly to Rhodey as he did so. "Thanks for taking the time, Rhodes."

"You too, Hogan. You too."

He stayed in the visitor's reception center long after Hogan had departed. By the time the sun was crawling up over the horizon, he had decided what he was going to do.

The sun had reached its zenith as a line of special operations forces, or SOF soldiers—Snake eaters, as they were nicknamed in this instance—were assembled and entering a troop transport bound for Afghanistan. Rhodey was aware of the puzzled looks he was receiving from the Snake eaters as he headed over to join them, a duffel bag slung over his shoulder and a C-17 rifle strapped across his chest.

He studied the transport as he got closer. He was familiar with this type; he could probably fly it in his sleep. Considering how little slumber he'd gotten the previous night, that was probably fortunate.

He heard a familiar sound drawing closer and didn't look in its direction, hoping against hope that maybe it wasn't coming his way. He was destined for disappointment, however, for the golf cart (which he had correctly identified by sound) rolled up next to him. General Gabriel was at the wheel.

The soldiers promptly stopped, snapped to attention, and saluted. Rhodey did so as well. The general returned the salute in an absentminded manner and, stepping out of his jeep, pulled Rhodey aside.

"What do you think you're doing, Rhodes?"

Rhodey took a deep breath. "Going back there, sir."

Gabriel looked as if he couldn't decide whether or not to laugh. He opted for the latter. In a patient voice, he said, "Listen, son—it's been three months without a single indication that Stark is still alive. We can't keep risking assets, least of all you."

Rhodey had rolled dice and apparently had crapped out. He'd filled out the reassignment request first thing in the morning and handed it to Gabriel's aide, an attractive young lieutenant whom Rhodey had dated for six months. The split had been amicable and they were still good friends, or at least so Rhodey had thought when he'd asked her to try and slide the paperwork past Gabriel, ideally with him signing off on it without paying close attention to what he was doing. Clearly she had not done so, which meant one of two things: Either Gabriel was far more observant than Rhodey had thought, or else the split hadn't been quite as amicable as Rhodey had believed it to be and this was a little payback.

There was no point in trying to finesse his way around it. "Are you blocking my transfer, sir?" he said stiffly.

Gabriel didn't answer immediately. Instead, he chucked a thumb over his shoulder in the direction of the line of soldiers standing at attention. "Any one of these guys would kill for your career. Are you telling me you're willing to sacrifice that to fly a bunch of Snake eaters on a desert patrol half way around the world?"

"I am, sir."

"Then I have one thing to say to you," he informed him stiffly. Rhodey braced himself, prepared for an order to return to station—an order that he was not looking forward to fighting or even, heaven help him, disobeying.

Instead, to his utter astonishment, General Gabriel said, "Godspeed."

Rhodey tried not to look startled and was only partly successful. Gabriel brought his hand up in a salute and Rhodey promptly snapped a salute back. Gabriel smiled and nodded with what actually appeared to be approval. Then he climbed back into his golf cart, turned it around, and drove off, calling "As you were!" to the soldiers as he motored past.

Feeling as if he'd dodged a bullet—certainly not for the first time in his life—Rhodey turned and headed up the ramp into the loading bay. Minutes later, under Rhodey's careful and firm hand, the plane was heading into the sky on its way to try to rescue America's foremost military asset.

ix.

Stark had become skilled at working in such a way that he was capable of blocking out from the video camera's view something that he didn't want them to see. He couldn't do it with anything large, but something smaller than, say, his chest, he could keep hidden by body positioning for the duration. Besides, he suspected that even when they had a perfect view of him, they didn't have the faintest idea of what he was working on at any given moment or what they were looking at.

They certainly wouldn't have a clue what he was up to in this instance.

Carefully he put the finishing touches on a small box. It contained a laser pointer, a fan, and tinsel. He taped it shut, then peeked through a tiny hole in its side to make certain that the final effect was what he was looking for. Satisfied that it was, he tucked it under his arm and stepped away from the workbench.

Stark then casually, as if it were of no importance, strolled straight toward the video camera. He kept going until he was standing directly under it, out of range of the lens. Then, as quickly as he could, he placed the box directly over the lens, making certain that the hole he'd created was properly positioned. With a piece of tape that he'd secured to his finger, he affixed the box to the camera. Then he stepped back and waited to see if there was a pounding at the door in response.

He knew that not only was the timing of making the

switch all-important, but it was the one thing that he had no control over. If whoever was watching the monitor was staring straight at it when he made the switch, they would realize that he had done something. If, however, they were looking away for any reason—distracted by a conversation, in the middle of a card game, dozing, whatever—then the next time they glanced back at the monitor, they would think they were looking at the furnace flames glowing in the dark. At least that's what Stark's low-tech illusionary box was designed to accomplish.

He allowed ten minutes for a reaction of some sort from their observers. It was ten of the longest minutes of his life. When there was no response, he let out a long, relieved sigh and then, all business, turned to Yinsen. No words were required; a brief nod was all that was necessary.

Minutes later, Stark and Yinsen were by the workbench. Stark had taped a small, round sensor patch to his leg. A thin wire ran through a crusty-looking laptop computer, and the computer in turn was attached to a miniature armature on the workbench. It looked like a small replica of a human leg that a child could have constructed with metal Tinkertoys. But Stark wasn't interested in aesthetics. He just needed to know that what he had been planning in theory was going to function in fact. What he was creating was going to be too heavy for sheer human muscle power to manipulate. Without the help of servos or mechanisms that would respond to the actions of his muscles, he wouldn't be able to budge the contraption. It wouldn't do him a damned bit of good to be all-powerful but stationary.

Plus, of course, there was the question of powering the whole thing. As Stark prepared to plug the entire setup into the small Arc reactor that was protecting his heart, he told himself that he had anticipated every possible thing that could go wrong. But he knew that that wasn't really the case, that it was impossible to allow for every eventuality. There could be some small, obvious thing that he had overlooked, and as he lay there dying upon the floor he'd be mentally kicking himself over having failed to foresee whatever it was. It would be a little late for regrets though.

He shrugged mentally, thought *Here goes nothing,* and plugged the setup into his chest reactor.

Nothing happened for a couple of seconds, which was just long enough for a finger of doubt to brush across Stark's consciousness, and then the laptop's screen lit up. Data flooded the screen and Stark watched it intently. Everything looked exactly the way he expected it to. Then slowly, carefully, since he had no desire to have the armature overreact and throw itself off the table, Stark moved the leg to which the sensor was attached.

The armature promptly responded in kind. He moved; it moved. Yinsen gasped in amazement. Stark thrust his knee upward and the armature did so as well. He turned his leg to the right, then to the left, and the armature continued to mirror his movements. He checked the readouts in relation to the reactor and saw to his satisfaction that the energy required to accomplish what he was doing didn't make so much as a blip. For all the energy his movements were expending, he might well have been just standing there. There was a brief dimming from the reactor, yes, but it instantly powered right back up again.

His gaze drifted over to Yinsen's. The two men looked triumphantly at each other and both nodded simultaneously.

"We're ready," said Stark briskly, unplugging himself from the setup. There was no telling when one of their captors might show up, so he disassembled the rig as quickly as possible, lest he have to provide answers that he wasn't enthused about giving. "A week of assembly and we're a go."

"Then perhaps it's time we settle another matter," said Yinsen with such gravity that Stark wondered what could possibly be hanging over him. Then the older man's gaze shifted to the backgammon table he had constructed. Stark laughed.

A half hour later they were deep in the midst of a hard-fought game. Food, hardly touched, sat to either side of them. Yinsen watched Stark's next move and nodded in approval. "Ah, anchoring with 13-7," he said. He could not have sounded more proud if Stark were his son or if he'd made the move himself. "You know, I have never met anyone who understands the nuances of this game like you."

"Right back at ya," said Stark. "You know, you never told me where you're from."

Yinsen hesitated, although Stark believed it was more from habit than reluctance to speak. "I come from a small village called Gulmira. It was a good place . . . before these men ravaged it." He nodded in the direction of the door unnecessarily; Stark knew to whom he was referring.

"Do you have a family?"

Yinsen smiled. "When I get out of here, I am going to see them again." He had been studying the board, but then he looked up at Tony. "Do you have family, Stark?"

"No." Stark didn't sound regretful. He didn't sound any particular way; just detached, even indifferent. His tone might have been exactly the same if someone had asked if he had the latest U2 CD.

For the first time that Stark could recall, Yinsen regarded him with something akin to pity. "You're a man who has everything and nothing."

Stark tried to determine what Yinsen meant by that,

but before he could give it much thought, Abu's voice shouted in Arabic from behind the door slat. A moment later he strode in and Stark thought, *Oh God, what now?*

But he saw that Yinsen was the picture of calm, and then he smiled to himself as the scientist informed Abu, "Your laundry's over there." That was simply the way of things around here. One never knew from one moment to the next if one's life was endangered or if something utterly mundane was going to transpire. And the occurrence of the latter never seemed to make the threat of the former any less impending.

Abu went to the basket where his laundry had been neatly folded. Stark found it amusing: Abu had ranted and raved about Stark's request for a clothes washer. Stark's asking for the washer had been for a far more significant reason than cleaning clothes. He hadn't wanted Abu to scrutinize too closely his other requests, most of which wouldn't provide him anything he required in terms of constructing the Jericho missile. By tossing in something as random as a washing machine, he had correctly guessed that Abu would be distracted from thinking too much about the specifics of Stark's other demands. The ploy had worked well—almost too well, in fact, as Abu continued to rant about it right up until the point that Yinsen had coolly offered to attend to Abu's laundry. Then he had calmed down. Who knew that terrorists despised the chore of washing their own clothes? Stark supposed he shouldn't have been surprised at that: Cleaning one's clothing didn't afford the opportunity to kill, maim, or blow up innocent people, so obviously it wasn't fun.

Abu went over to the basket where his laundry lay neatly folded. He lifted the basket it and smelled it. He smiled. The smile looked strangely out of place on him. Then his far more customary scowl returned as he slung the basket under one arm and headed for the door. He said something in Arabic and Stark looked questioningly at Yinsen. In a low voice, Yinsen translated, "You idiots don't know what you're doing with that game."

Stark shrugged and called after Abu, "Yeah, yeah, enjoy your laundry."

Abu yanked open the door, about to head out, and suddenly froze in place. Stark instantly sensed a change in the atmosphere of the room. Danger was present where it had not been before. Even before he clearly saw what Abu was reacting to, he had a suspicion that was moments later borne out as Raza strode slowly in. His gaze wandered over Stark and Yinsen, and then to Abu, and then, finally, to Abu's laundry.

Abu forced a smile and started to say something.

Raza pulled his gun out of his holster and swung it viciously. The butt of the gun slammed into Abu's head, snapping it back. Blood flew from his crushed nose, splattering all over his newly laundered clothing. He collapsed into the hallway, the clothing spilling all over the floor.

Stark and Yinsen did not move. They were terrified to, not knowing whether this was a warning or a precursor to their immediate demise.

That was clarified the next moment as Raza said with no trace of emotion, "You have until tomorrow to assemble my missile."

He turned on his heel and walked out. Two of his henchmen stepped in, grabbed the groaning Abu and hauled him out. The door slammed shut behind him.

Stark was still trying to process what he'd just seen. Part of him was trying to convince himself that it was some sort of trick to scare the crap out of them. But he knew perfectly well that there was no trick involved. Raza had made absolutely clear, if it were not already so, who was running things.

Silence hung between them.

And then Stark mouthed three words to Yinsen: *Time to go*.

Yinsen nodded.

A leisurely completion of Stark's plan was no longer an option. It meant that corners were going to be cut, that systems checks were not going to be possible. He was going to have to get everything right the first time, and if he failed to do so, then it wasn't going to work and they were dead. On the other hand, if he did nothing, they were dead anyway.

A thin red trail of Abu's blood trickled under the door, a mute commentary on what awaited them if they failed.

X.

There was no question in Raza's mind that Stark was going to meet the deadline. His study of Americans had been detailed and thorough. They talked a good game. They were skilled at swaggering displays of machismo. But ultimately they were overstuffed, overfed, and over-confident. All one had to do was remove them from their comfort zone and subject them to pressure and they would inevitably fold. Stark had lasted longer than most, probably due to the influence of Yinsen. Raza knew that, realistically, he should have disposed of Yinsen so that Stark would break that much faster. But Yinsen had been a necessary evil just in case Stark's medical situation took a downward turn. So Yinsen had been permitted to live. It made little difference in the long run; Yinsen's fate would remain the same, as would Stark's.

Abu had been far too generous in his overseeing of Stark and Yinsen and far too lax in keeping them working. Raza had decided to attend to both problems with a single blow. Mildly regrettable, mostly because Raza was going to have to inform his sister that her idiot son was injured, and he wasn't looking forward to that. Naturally he would blame the incident on Stark, claiming it had happened during an attempted breakout, and that Raza had then killed Stark in retaliation. She would accept that and wind up unknowingly offering thanks to her son's assailant. Such were the accommodations one had to make where family was involved.

Morning had come and Raza strode into his control room, annoyed that the fans seemed to be operating at far below their normal capacity. He wiped his sweating brow with a towel, determined to find out what was causing this unacceptable dip in the power output. He walked in to discover his lieutenants embroiled in an argument as they poured over a map of a local village they had targeted. They were trying to determine when and where would be the best opportunity to attack. The main point of contention seemed to be whether to wait for U.S. troops to show up in the town, since there were known troop movements in the general area. There were arguments for both sides. If the troops showed up to discover a demolished village, it would be a blow to the ego of the soldiers who would realize they had arrived too late. Plus, it presented minimal risk to the terrorists. On the other hand, if their assault on the village was held until the soldiers were present, it offered a chance to kill Americans, albeit naturally at a higher risk to Raza's forces.

As this arguing continued, others of Raza's men were busy assembling and cleaning various weapons. Raza cast a quick look over their activities and nodded approval. His bickering lieutenants hadn't noticed his presence yet. Not bothering to alert them, he shifted his attention to the monitor. Khalid, one of his more trusted lieutenants, was watching them closely, paying particular attention—as he'd been instructed to do—to Stark and Yinsen.

Yinsen was visible, working with furious intensity on the jig, which was the part of the metalworking machine that held an object in place. But Raza couldn't see from this angle just what the object was, although sparks were flying everywhere. Yinsen's face was smeared with dirt while perspiration seeped down, leaving little tracks in the filth.

Even more troubling was the fact that Raza couldn't see Tony Stark at all. He wasn't next to Yinsen or behind him. The only other places he might be standing would be under the camera, which meant he was planning something, or up on the metalworking table, which was also out of camera range. But that made no sense at all. Why in the world would Stark be up *on* the metalworking table?

"Khalid. Where is Stark?" said Raza.

Khalid shook his head.

"Well? Go look!" Raza said impatiently.

Khalid nodded and jumped up from behind the monitor. "With me!" he called and the men who had been doing the weapons inspections quickly followed him out the door, guns cocked and ready for use. Raza slid into the place Khalid had vacated. His lieutenants now realized he was there and quickly started offering their arguments about when to attack the village, but Raza waved them off. His attention was elsewhere.

The lab was not the only place where cameras were keeping surveillance. They were set up throughout the cave-bound complex, including directly outside the door that led into the lab. There was still a smear of blood on the floor that had yet to be cleaned up. Raza wasn't concerned about that. Instead he was watching Khalid closely as Khalid arrived at the door, slid aside the slat and peeked inside. "Yinsen!" he called through the slat. "Yinsen!"

Raza's gaze shifted to Yinsen. The old man was ignoring Khalid's shouts, or perhaps he simply couldn't hear them over the racket he was making at the metalworking table. Khalid, however, was not taking chances. He nodded to his men who moved forward, weapons primed lest Yinsen be preparing some sort of trick or trap, as unlikely as such a thing might be.

Khalid unbolted the door and tried to push it open. Nothing happened.

Raza got to his feet. Now he was positive that something was wrong. But he wasn't sure if there was anything he could or should do; Khalid was acting in the right and proper manner, clearly ready for anything. Still, he couldn't shake the feeling that there was something he was overlooking, something unexpected . . .

The door.

The door might be jammed because Yinsen and Stark had jammed it. And that might be because they had done something to it, rigged it in some manner that needed an impact rather than the door just being opened. An impact that would do . . . what?

Raza didn't want to know.

Suddenly he knew what Khalid should do: Back up, roll a grenade to the door, and blow it open from a distance. He grabbed his radio, snapped it on, and tried to raise Khalid on it.

Khalid, meantime, had clearly not engaged the same thought process as had Raza. Instead, confronted with a barrier, he selected the most obvious means of dealing with it: He slammed into it with his shoulder. As he did so, the final irony was that the motion was accompanied by Khalid's glancing down at the walkie-talkie he had on his hip. It had just beeped at him to inform him that Raza was trying to get through.

Then Khalid vanished.

Raza saw the result before he heard it: a massive explosion. Seconds after his visual on the monitor filled with smoke and debris that completely wiped out anything he could make out (including whether Khalid and his men had survived the impact), a thunderous detonation roared up the halls of the cave hideaway.

Everyone instantly began shouting at once. Most had

not been looking at the monitor and were convinced that they'd been located by the United States Air Force, which was doubtless proceeding to drop bunker busters on them. It took Raza precious seconds to rein in his lieutenants, and he finally was only able to grab control of the situation by shooting one of his junior officers in the knee, thus guaranteeing their instant attention. Once he'd done that, even more time was eaten up as word had to be spread throughout the compound, both via radio and in person, that they were under attack not from without but from within.

The entire time he kept scanning the monitors, looking for some sign of Stark and Yinsen attempting to flee. There was none. The idiots were still hiding in their lab, pinning themselves down. That was a mistake, and one that Raza would make them pay for immediately and with finality.

The IED 44 cylinder that Tony Stark had filled with propane gas earlier had worked exactly as they had expected it to. The second that Raza's men had ruptured it when they'd attempted to storm the room, it had exploded just as designed. Stark didn't know how much time it was going to buy them, but he had to hope and pray it was going to be enough.

Yinsen wasn't even glancing at the door. His attention was split between the computer activity that he was monitoring and the bulky chest piece that he was in the process of sealing Tony Stark into. His pneumatic wrench shrieked as it joined the front section to the back.

"It's frozen," Yinsen said. He was trying to keep his voice steady, but there was clearly an edge to it. He pointed at the laptop screen. "The systems aren't talking to each other. Reset!"

Stark knew that resetting was not an option. However much time they had before they were under full assault, it certainly wasn't sufficient to accommodate rebooting the whole system. He looked at the screen, studying the program bars. It had taken no time at all to translate the movements of his leg into a single small armature, but this was something very different. This was attempting to download every possible movement his body could make into a program that would enable a massive life-sized mechanism to function. Essentially, he was trying to turn his entire nervous system into a byte torrent of information. It wasn't exactly the type of task an eight-hundred-buck laptop that someone had probably boosted from Radio Shack was designed to accomplish. Hell, those things froze up while reading e-mail; this was the equivalent of downloading the entire United States Postal System.

If Yinsen was correct—if a reboot was required—then they were toast.

Stark was relieved to see, however, that Yinsen was not in fact correct. "No, they're moving. Very slowly."

Yinsen looked again and then nodded, realizing that Stark was right. He didn't appear any happier about it, though.

Seconds dissolved into minutes, ticking by. The bars continued to creep upward with maddening slowness. In the distance Stark heard shouting. That had been pretty much a constant since the door had blown. But before, even though Stark couldn't speak a word of Arabic, he could tell that it was confused shouting. People bellowing at each other, asking questions, terrified, not knowing what was going on. They probably thought, as Stark had anticipated, that they were having bombs dropped on them. It had been that confusion that he'd been counting on to give them the time they needed. Time was running out, though. That much was evident by the fact that the shouts were no longer sounding confused. Instead, there were what sounded like orders being tossed around, and the stampeding of feet. It was hard to tell for sure since loud noises tended to echo, but it certainly sounded as if they were heading in the direction of the lab.

"Get to your cover," said Stark briskly. "Remember the checkpoints—make sure each one is clear before you follow me out."

"That is a good plan," said Yinsen as he watched the bar. Then in a low voice, he added, "But it will not be good enough."

With that comment, and without a look back, Yinsen bolted from the lab.

Yinsen ignored Stark's alarmed shouting of his name. There was no point in responding because he had been watching the speed with which the bars had been loading, had projected how much more time would be required, and had determined that what time remained to them would not be sufficient.

So he would buy the time, utilizing the only currency he had available to him.

He slowed only to pick up a weapon from the dead fingers of one of Raza's men . . . Khalid, he believed this one was called, although it was hard to be sure. There was not much left of him, but the weapon was in superb shape. One had to credit American ingenuity where one could.

He was free. It was the first time he had been free in what seemed an eternity.

He would not waste it.

But he would not stoop to their level. No matter what it took, he would make clear to them that he was not the same as they.

There was a large pair of double doors in front of

him, extra security doors. They were hanging open. Khalid and his men obviously came through them. He stepped through them, slammed them shut, bolted them. He wished that the lock were on the inside; he could seal himself in, ride out the storm. But it was on the outside. Instead, it would seal Stark in and only slow Raza's men for seconds. With every second counting, though, no gesture was too small.

He kept going, rounded a corner and found himself face to face with Raza's men. He opened fire. He did not shoot at them, but rather over them, screaming and shouting. They outnumbered him three to one, but they were cowards, cowards to the core. Because of that simple fact, they turned and ran, startled and caught off-guard by his unexpected assault upon them. He was like a small cat, arching its back in such a way that attackers thought it was far bigger and more formidable than it really was.

He had no idea there was this much anger still in him. He had thought that he was dead inside. He was exhilarated and, at the same time, found it interesting from a clinical perspective. He continued to scream, shout, buying time for Stark, scaring his enemies, assuaging his soul over the indignities he had been forced to endure.

He entered the outer cavern.

A dozen guns were pointing straight at him. Pitiless, merciless eyes, like those of sharks, were glaring at him.

He could have fired at them. There was just enough time to take out at least a couple of them before the onslaught began.

But he did not. Even at the end, even with this last opportunity to lash out, he would be better than they were.

He lowered his gun, closed his eyes. The first of the bullets thudded into him and it did not hurt nearly as much as he would have thought. It is as if someone had just punched him in the heart. But no, no pain at all, because these bastards cut his heart out ages ago.

Then he left his feet, propelled backward by the impact of more rounds striking him.

He never felt himself hit the ground.

Tony Stark wanted to leap off the table and go after Yinsen immediately. But it was impossible: No matter what, he was now literally locked into the current plan. Any attempt to disengage himself from the worktable would end in failure because he was counting on the computer to finish downloading the information. He couldn't move before it was done; the device in which he was now contained was simply too damned heavy.

He heard Yinsen's voice growing fainter and fainter as he sprinted down the corridor, the clang of doors slamming shut, then muffled bursts of gunfire, a single weapon. Those sounds were enough to enable him to picture in his mind's eye exactly what was going on. He marveled at Yinsen's sheer determination and guts.

Suddenly Yinsen wasn't shouting anymore. Everything had become very quiet.

Frantic with fear, Stark's eyes flashed to the computer screen.

The computer bars finished their cycle.

The device went on line.

Stark rose inelegantly from the table like a latter-day Frankenstein's monster. He wasn't thinking about the parallels or about any sense of accomplishment over what he was doing. All he was thinking about was getting to Yinsen in time.

Then he heard the chatter of a large number of guns. The burst was quick, brutal, and final. He even imagined that he could hear a body fall, although it was too far away for him to have been able to detect it.

Within his iron chest, his heart broke.

And then it went cold. Cold as steel.

Omar and Ahmed charged down a corridor toward the lab. They were backed up by two of Raza's men, and they were confident that no matter what tricks the foolish American had cooked up, they weren't going to do him a damned bit of good. Certainly they hadn't done a thing to protect the old man, Yinsen.

They approached the security door that guarded the main entranceway down to the lab. It was closed. The old man must have shut it behind him as he had made his short-lived, ill-advised escape attempt. Ahmed wondered what Stark could possibly have said to the old man to convince him that such a precipitous action could possibly do him any good. Unfortunately, the old man would never be able to provide any answers.

Ahmed strode forward confidently, reaching for the lock. But when his hand was inches away from the door, something slammed into the portal from the other side.

Something big. Something heavy. Something capable of leaving a massive dent in an armored door.

Startled, Ahmed stumbled backward and would have fallen if Omar hadn't caught him. "What the hell—?" muttered one of Raza's men.

The door bucked again as the same mysterious object on the other side slammed into it. There was another outward bulge, this one even bigger than the first. The sound of the impact echoed around them, and now all four men were backing up. They had their guns leveled. Ahmed's pulse was pounding against his head. He had no idea what was going on. It was as if an elephant or some other great beast was on the other side, trying to smash its way through. But where would Stark have gotten an elephant? It made no sense, none of it.

A third smash, and a fourth, and the two armored doors began to buckle off their hinges.

Ahmed's radio crackled. *"What's going on down there?"* came Raza's confused voice.

"I don't know!" Ahmed shouted. *"I don't—"*

Accompanied by one final crashing noise that rent the air, the doors practically exploded off their hinges.

Something glowing drifted through the air at them. In the dimness of the cave, it seemed like a floating disk, a miniature sun coming at them. Then Ahmed realized that it wasn't merely flying along on its own. It was instead part of something larger.

Much larger.

It stepped forward out of the darkness, and Ahmed and the others were able to see it clearly for the first time. Initially, just for an instant, Ahmed thought it was some kind of tank. It was dull gray, metal glinting in the limited light that the small fixtures mounted in the wall provided.

But then he realized it had arms and legs.

It was a man covered head to foot in armor.

A man made of iron.

Tony Stark had been living in fear for so long that he had almost forgotten what it was like to feel empowered.

Not anymore.

Now every slight, every second that he had felt as if his life was going to be snatched from him at any time, was going to be repaid in spades.

And standing right there in front of him was the man he most wanted to see: Ahmed, who was still wearing Jimmy's Mets watch on his wrist.

Secure inside his armor, Stark strode forward. He went straight for Ahmed. Ahmed backed up, shooting. Inwardly, Stark braced himself. He knew that the armor should be able to withstand just about anything they were going to throw at him—certainly bullets shouldn't present any difficulty—but knowing it was very different from staring down the barrel of a machine gun that was firing at you point-blank.

He needn't have worried. Bullets ricocheted off him as if he were being pelted with water droplets. It was loud, God, was it loud. It was like being inside a gigantic swinging church bell. But if he came out of this with nothing more than a ringing in his ears, then he would certainly have gotten off lightly.

He advanced on Ahmed, grabbed the machine gun from his hands, and broke it in half. Even in the dimness of the hallway, he saw all the blood drain from Ahmed's face. He reached for Ahmed and, had he managed to grab his skull, would have closed his fist and crushed it between his fingers.

His armor allowed him to do many things, but moving quickly was not among them. Ahmed darted back, out of range. Then the others closed in, firing as fast as they could, as hard as they could. Stark reeled under the collective impact. The armor was handling the bullets, yes, but the sustained fire was beginning to take its toll. Stark perceived small dents beginning to appear, and he started to worry that the seams might not be able to withstand the stress.

He kept moving forward, backing them up. Omar was just a hair slow, allowing himself to get within reach. Stark grabbed him and swung him around, sending him crashing into the other two. They went down, dropping their weapons, and Stark methodically stepped on the guns, crushing them beneath his armored boot. He looked around, trying to spot Ahmed. There was no sign of him. He'd run. Coward.

Stark stomped down the corridor, the ground crunching beneath him. With quiet having settled around him since the shooting had stopped, he was able to hear his own steady breathing within his helmet, like a diver underwater.

Suddenly, from just ahead of him, tracer bullets whizzed through the air. It was as if a swarm of fireflies had invaded the corridor. They pinged off his armor and Stark kept moving. He caught glimpses of the stunned insurgents ahead of him as they backed up in the face of this iron monstrosity.

He passed a cross corridor and something thudded against his head. A single bullet, and then he heard something hit the ground. His peripheral vision was for crap, so he had to turn his entire torso in order to see that, lying dead on the ground next to him, was Ahmed. There was a bullet hole squarely in the middle of his head. For an instant Stark thought that Ahmed had committed suicide, but then he realized what had happened: The idiot had tried to ambush him by coming in from the side and firing at point-blank range. The bullet had instead ricocheted off the helmet and drilled its way right through Ahmed's skull.

Stark wanted to reach down and remove the wrist-watch from Ahmed's wrist. But he couldn't bend over, and even if he could, he wouldn't have been able to accomplish something as delicate as removing a watch while wearing his gauntlets. So he settled for stepping on Ahmed's wrist, crushing the watch beyond repair so no one else could use it. As justice went, it was woefully inadequate, but Stark would have to settle for it.

The insurgents, having had their first glimpse of the iron man, were clearly trying to screw their courage to the sticking place and mount a concerted assault. Stark didn't slow down. In fact, he picked up speed, gaining confidence in his construct with every step. He tossed aside attackers like poker chips, sending them crashing into walls, ceilings, and one another.

He should have felt a flicker of concern because he could see that the suit was beginning to shred. The pockmarks were becoming deeper, the damage more profound. Curiously, it didn't bother him. The adrenaline was pumping now, the sheer energy carrying him through battle. Tony Stark, who had built weapons his entire life, had never once, not once, been in an actual fight of any kind, much less utilized his own weaponry for both offense and defense. Despite the wear and tear the suit was enduring, he felt . . .

—he felt . . .

—*invincible. Yes, that's it. That's the word. I am . . . invincible.*

He rounded a corner and stopped dead in his tracks.

Yinsen was lying on the ground, which had turned red beneath him. He was face up and, until Stark was standing right over him, Stark was convinced that Yinsen was already dead. It seemed impossible that anyone could sustain that much damage and still be hanging on.

His murderers were nowhere to be seen. Either they had engaged in the futile assault on Stark, or else they had fled outright upon hearing what was coming their way.

Stark began to stride toward Yinsen, and then—to his utter shock—Yinsen spoke.

"Stop! Stop!" the dying man shouted in alarm.

Stark didn't understand how Yinsen could still be alive or why he should stop, but nevertheless he did as he was bidden. Then he was rocked back on his heels as an RPG streaked from a cross corridor and rocketed through the air directly in front of him. It exploded against the wall, causing not only a section of the wall to collapse but a chunk of the ceiling to crumble as well. Had the missile impacted with Stark's armor, it might well have been more than the already battered suit could endure.

He turned and glared down the corridor. Raza was there, wearing a flak jacket and reloading the rocket launcher as quickly as he could. Other insurgents were pouring into the tunnel behind Raza, shouting encouragement.

Stark brought his arms up and tried to engage his flamethrowers. He heard the misfire, the clicking that failed to ignite, and for a moment he felt a surge of panic like bile in his mouth. Raza brought the launcher to bear and Stark quickly shook out his arms, hoping that all he was dealing with was a clog in the fuel line. He turned out to be correct. As much to Stark's surprise as the insurgents', twin plumes of flame ripped out from his arms.

Seeing the flames coming his way, Raza acted entirely on instinct: He dropped the launcher, grabbed the nearest of his men, and thrust him directly between himself and the oncoming flame. The man screamed, transformed from a living being to an instant funeral pyre. He staggered, waving his arms like a burning piñata, and collapsed. As he did so, Raza and the rest of his men beat a hasty retreat while Stark continued to purge the tunnel with flame, an armored exterminator cleaning out a rat infestation.

Stark turned away from the smoldering remains of Raza's man and realized that he felt his gorge rising. He fought the impulse to get sick; the last thing he needed was to vomit inside his helmet.

He went back to Yinsen and stood over him. For the first time since he had donned the armor, he spoke. His voice vibrated, sounding distorted courtesy of all the electrical equipment within. That was fine by him. Should he wind up saying something to Raza, it would make him sound even more inhuman.

"We could've made it. Both of us. You could've seen your family again."

Yinsen looked as if he thought he was focusing on Stark, even though he was actually looking two feet to his left. "I am going to see them again," said Yinsen weakly. There was a bubbling in his throat. "They're waiting for me."

That was when Stark understood. Yinsen had always spoken about his family in such a way that Stark thought they were still alive. Except, they were not. They had died at the hands of the insurgents, and as Yinsen stared into nothingness, it wasn't that he couldn't see where Stark was standing. Instead, he was looking at someone else—someone whom only he could see, beckoning to him, welcoming him with open arms and a smiling face.

With tremendous effort, expending the last energy in his body, Yinsen lifted his hand and placed it atop Stark's gauntlet. "This was always the plan. My life ends here . . . and your life begins here. It begins . . . by finishing what we started. Finish it . . ."

"I will. I swear to you, I will."

Yinsen smiled and then, just like that, he was gone.

Stark stood there for a moment. No one outside could have known that, inside, within his suit, he was trembling with fury.

He closed his eyes, blind with pain. When he opened them again, his voice was roaring within his helmet, and he strode forward no longer Tony Stark, but an iron avenger.

Raza and his men had fallen back outside the caves. He'd lost the rocket launcher, but his men were still well armed and determined to stop the armored man who was mowing through them.

There was no question in Raza's mind that it was Stark inside the suit. There was no one else it could possibly be. His fury over having underestimated the American was escalating, though he took pains to place most of the blame on Abu, who had clearly mismanaged this entire debacle every step of the way.

There was just as equally no question in his mind that Stark wasn't going to leave. Let him come stomping out in his armored suit. They would fire and keep firing, and sooner or later he'd run out of flame. Plus, they were in the desert, miles away from any sort of civilization. Stark could tromp across the plains to his heart's content, with Raza and his men harrying his every step. Stark wasn't going to get away. Time and location were on Raza's side.

"He's coming! The iron man is coming!" screamed one of Raza's men who clearly had not made the obvious association to realize who their attacker was.

Sure enough, the iron man emerged from the cave. In the naked light of day, Raza saw the damage that the armor had sustained and his hopes were buoyed. The iron man might not even make it out of the encampment.

"Fire! Fire!" shouted Raza, and they unleashed a massive hail of bullets upon the iron man. He continued to move forward, the gray armor scarred and sizzling.

Then Raza realized that he wasn't simply wandering aimlessly; Stark was heading straight for the ammo dump, and he was raising his arms in the same manner he had before when he'd unleashed the flamethrowers.

"Cut him off!" Raza said, as he ran and continued to fire, hoping to drive Stark away from the ammo dump. But Stark was relentless, and within seconds he had turned his flames loose upon the boxes and boxes of ammunition. The fire began to eat into the crates, and the Stark logos on all of them crisped and burned away.

"Concentrate your fire! Knock him over!"

"B-b-but," one of his men stammered, "he is a thing of iron!"

"He is a man and can die as readily as any man!" To underscore his point, he shot down the man who had been bordering on panic, and then pointed at the armored American. "Now take him down!"

Stark saw the world through a haze of red, and that was even before he was igniting everything around him. The crates had been thrown together in such a way that they were almost a maze, but it didn't deter him. He just pushed his way further in and continued to unleash his flamethrowers.

A withering barrage of gunfire, concentrated all in the small of Stark's back, knocked him to his knees. He tried to shake it off. *I am invincible . . . I am invincible . . . I am . . .*

—on fire?

He was.

Instantly he realized what had happened. A stray bullet had caught the hose leading to his flamethrower. Fuel had spilled and he had inadvertently ignited it himself, with the result being that his left arm was now aflame. He batted at it frantically with his right gauntlet, trying to smother it, and suddenly his right shoulder was burning. But it wasn't from flame. He'd been right to be concerned about the seams: All the stress that his armor had endured had resulted in a small fissure, and a bullet had been lucky enough to pierce it and lodge in Stark's upper arm.

This is nothing, this is a setback, nothing more. I'm invincible, dammit!

He struggled to his feet, pushing away any thoughts of fear or panic or anything that didn't relate to the simple mantra that he could not be stopped. The suit made terrible grinding noises around him, like a car stripping its gears. He ignored it, focusing instead on the fire on his left arm. He finished smothering it, leaving scorch marks on his metal that otherwise was unharmed.

He didn't dare reignite his flamethrowers lest he wind up setting his armor ablaze again. But he didn't need to. The conflagration had taken on its own life, leaping from one box to the next. Mirthlessly he watched his name on the sides of the boxes going up in smoke. There was something almost symbolic about it, because he sensed on some level that the man who had built all these weapons was being burned away along with them. It remained to be seen what was going to be left behind, presuming he survived.

More bullets assailed him, and pieces of the armor were starting to shake loose. And now he saw several insurgents sprinting forward, not with guns, but fire extinguishers. They were going to try and put out the fire, and there was an outside chance they might accomplish it.

Like hell.

Stark opened a metal flap on his left arm and flipped a red switch within. A whine began to build within the armor, soft at first but rapidly escalating in volume. The oncoming insurgents heard it and fell back, no doubt thinking that some sort of on-board bomb had just been activated and was spiraling toward detonation.

This had been the trickiest, most problematic aspect of the armor. The bottom line was that he had no idea if this was really going to work or not, and if it didn't, then he was done for.

Raza was screaming at them, trying to get them to move forward, but everyone was hanging back while shouting to one another. So either Raza's voice was being drowned out, or they were just pretending that they didn't hear him, which would in turn serve as their excuse later should there be recriminations.

Stark backed up toward a pile of the boxes that hadn't caught on fire yet. He felt vibrations in his soles, as if he were standing atop a fissure that was about to unleash an earthquake. His heel boosters were firing up, glowing white-hot. He checked the onboard stabilizers, the monitors, and watched the temperature nervously. It was a race to see whether the boots would function as they were supposed to or if the entire apparatus would overheat. If that happened, Stark's armor would be transformed from a protective device into a full-body oven and he would be cooked alive.

Raza shoved two of his men aside, advanced and started firing. Stark had nothing with which to strike back. It was the boots or nothing. The energy continued to build, build, and Stark monitored the levels, trying to ignore the bullets that were hammering him and threatening to shred the armor beyond the point of no return.

Get me to full thrust level, come on, come on, hurry up, hurry up . . .

The boots reached eighty percent of capacity, ninety, and then the small monitor device built into the inner face piece of his helmet informed him that they had *ignition* as a minuscule light shifted from red to green.

The whine had escalated to a full roar, and the boot jets went fully active. They blasted downward, kicking up swirling plumes of dust and dirt so fiercely that even Raza was forced to drop back, throwing his arm across the lower half of his face and trying to figure out where to aim.

In a grimly humorous moment, Stark hummed two bars of "Off We Go Into the Wild Blue Yonder," and suddenly the armor jerked him upward. For some reason he had a quick flash to *Doctor Strangelove,* with the howling cowboy deliriously whooping and hollering while he sat astride a plummeting missile. Stark had done him one better: He'd strapped himself inside the missile. But in both instances they had exactly the same option, which was to hang on and enjoy the ride. Stark could only hope that things ended better for him than the yelling cowboy.

And then he was airborne.

He'd been expecting it, planning it, counting on it. But nothing had fully prepared him for the moment when the armor actually lifted off. It did so slowly at first, and the blast from the jets sliced into the remaining boxes of explosives. It was the final impetus required as the crates of Stark munitions erupted.

Stark wasn't there to see it. The combination of the boot jets and the shock waves from the explosions propelled him skyward, and then the jets really kicked loose. Suddenly he was moving as if fired from a cannon. The terrorist camp was instantly left behind, with the roar of the boot jets eliminating any last audible traces of the insurgents. Their yelling and howling, and the detonation of the munitions, were gone. Stark was enveloped in a deafening roar, as if he were in the funnel of a tornado. He had a brief glimpse of the munitions containers going up, one after the other, a series of incendiary dominos, each one propelling the next over the edge and into oblivion. Then even that was gone, and the ground was hurtling away from him.

He was going straight up. To his horror he realized that if he didn't correct it, he might conceivably wind up in orbit.

Translating thought into action, he adjusted the gyros, which in turn altered the armor's course. Now he was angling away at more of a parabolic arc, which at least eliminated the possibility that the residents of the international space station were going to receive a surprise visitor. With the roar of the jets pounding beneath him, he tried to get a fix on his position as he hurtled across a speeding landscape. He looked down and saw nothing but a flat vista of nothingness.

Then he glanced ahead.

A mountain range was directly in front of him.

As fanciful as it seemed, for half a heartbeat he remembered obliterating a section of a mountain range with the Jericho missile, and he considered the possibility that the obstruction facing him was a distant relative seeking terminal payback. If he struck the mountainside at his current speed, he would go from iron man to iron can.

He struggled with the gyros. They resisted both his silent pleading and his very audible string of profanities. The mountain was coming up horrifically fast and then, when it seemed there was no time left, he coaxed a downward thrust of his boosters, which promptly angled him upward another degree. It was incremental, barely anything, but it was just enough for him to clear the peak, although he did manage to bang his armored knee on it as he passed.

But that final jolt of energy was the swan song of the boosters. They sputtered, tapered off, and then died. His trajectory carried him over the mountain range but then he was in freefall and there was nothing he could do except ride it down.

Ohhhhh yeah, this is going to hurt . . .

Like a crippled armored bird he fell. He wanted to give in to panic, to let out a long, terrified scream. Instead, he engaged his mind in running rapid-fire calculations as to just how fast he was falling and at what angle, and what degree of stress the armor would be able to endure. In short, he was running the numbers in order to determine to a mathematical certainty whether he would live or die. It seemed a better way to pass the horrifically short time he had left than haplessly shrieking.

Three seconds before impact, he finished making his calculations. He wasn't wild about the results.

Then he hit.

An array of sand dunes was spread out before him. They provided some very minimal cushion, but not much, and certainly not enough for his preferences. He slammed into one dune after the next, each one seeming to propel him forward. The moment he struck the first one, pieces of the armor spun away and he continued to shed chunks of metal with each impact. They bounded away across the sand in one direction while he ricocheted in the other like an out-of-control squash ball. A large metal out-of-control squash ball.

When he finally stopped moving, he didn't realize it. His head was spinning so much, the blood pounding in his ears, that at first he assumed he was still going. It was the absence of clanking that was his first clue. He remained where he was, allowing his inner ear to regain its equilibrium. Once that had been accomplished, he made a mental checklist of his body, experimentally flexing his fingers and toes to make certain that they were still responding. That would give him at least some indication whether he'd broken his spine or something equally vital.

No. Everything appeared to be functioning, as unlikely as that seemed. Everything except the armor. That was shot to hell. But it had served its purpose. He was lying on his back, unable to move, as formidable in his armor as a flipped tortoise was in its. Fortunately he had more resources available to him than did the average tortoise.

He realized the ironic debt he owed Raza and his men. Yinsen had sealed him into the armor; if it had remained intact, getting out of it would have presented more of a problem than it did. As it was, the component pieces were barely holding themselves together. So it required only minimal effort for Stark to shove the pieces apart and climb out. He felt bruised and banged up, and there was a sharp, stabbing pain in his side that made him think he might well have busted a rib. He flexed his arm and instantly the pain from the rib became a distant second in priorities. It was replaced by the agony in his shoulder. He reached around, put his hand on it, and came away with blood on his fingers.

He worked up the nerve to look at his shoulder and see if it was still pumping blood. It would really stink if, after everything he had endured, he wound up bleeding to death because of a severed artery. It seemed to his admittedly untrained eye (when it came to medicine) that the wound wasn't bleeding freely. But he was reasonably sure there was still a bullet in there. Between that and the shrapnel that had encircled his heart like Indians around a beleaguered wagon train, he was starting to feel like a walking metal scrap yard.

Walking. That was the ticket. That was what he had to do.

Kicking loose the final armored components from his legs, he staggered to his feet. His shoulder ached and reflexively he clutched it. There was no point in dwelling on it; he needed to focus on where he was going rather than where he'd been. He staggered to his feet, took two steps and fell forward. He landed face down, lay there for a second to try and implore the world to stop spinning, and then got to his feet once more. He started taking it one step at a time, like a toddler essaying the whole "walking" thing for the very first time.

Far, far in the distance, he could hear the explosions continuing. He afforded a glance over his shoulder and smiled grimly as he saw blackened smoke rising lazily above the mountain. It sounded like a war zone, except in this case both armies were in full retreat and one of the armies consisted of exactly one man.

Except that's really not true, he thought. *Mine was an army of two, and one of us didn't make it.*

He stopped and stared for a long minute at the collapsed armor. He thought about Yinsen prodding him for so long, asking what he was working on, and how Stark had been so slow to trust him. His reluctance was understandable; there had been no telling for sure if Yinsen might not be a spy working on Raza's behalf. Now, though, he felt ashamed for ever having doubted him. When he looked at the shattered armor, he saw the handiwork and effort of Yinsen in every bolt, every shard. What appeared to the naked eye to be a shattered hulk of metal was instead a final testimonial to a great man.

A man far greater than I. I, with my corporate jets and fancy house and hundreds of employees, as if all that means anything in the grand scheme of things. I have everything, he had nothing, but he was ten times the man I'll ever be. Yet I'm still alive and he's gone. That has to mean something. There has to be a way to memorialize everything he was and everything he represented. A memorial that's far more than a pile of metal in the middle of nowhere. And I'll find a way to do it. That is, assuming I live long enough.

That last aspect did not appear to be, at first, a safe assumption.

Stark had never had any sort of survival training, but he seemed to recall that in a desert environment, one was better served to find shelter during the day and travel only at night. That was not an option at this point. Sand and nothingness stretched around him in all directions, with not a shred of shelter to be had. Plus, for all he knew, on the other side of the mountain, Raza and his men would be getting their forces together with the intention of hunting him down. Should that happen, there was no question as to whether he would die. The only thing at issue was whether it would be immediate or prolonged. He suspected the latter. Either way, he certainly wasn't simply going to hang around and wait for it to happen. Survival manuals weren't written for men who had killer insurgents on their trails.

Stark started moving.

It was slow going.

The sand kept shifting beneath his feet so that, in very short order, the muscles in his legs were screaming at him for rest. He didn't dare to accommodate them. Instead he had to keep moving, if for no other reason than that—should he be captured and killed—Yinsen's valiant sacrifice would mean nothing.

His lips were parched. He tried to lick them but he had no spit or any moisture in his tongue. In short order his tongue acknowledged this absence, swelling so that it felt as if it were taking up the entirety of his mouth. Automatically he reached up to wipe sweat from his brow, but there was no moisture there either. Several times he had to stop and take slow, measured deep breaths to force air down his throat because he was having problems swallowing.

Sand managed to work its way into just about every orifice he had. He was blinking sand from his eyes, scooping it from his ears. It was in his teeth and under his swollen tongue. At one point he tried to cough and nearly choked himself again.

As he staggered through the desert, his thoughts flew back to a story his father had once told him. There once had been a king who felt as if he didn't have enough hours in a day to accomplish what he needed. He sought the counsel of the court wizard, asking the wizard to find some means of providing more hours in a day. The wizard told him that it was impossible to do so, and the king threatened the wizard's life. This was, after all, a miracle worker, and what else were miracle workers paid for if not to provide miracles?

But the wizard was not deterred. He informed the king that there was indeed a way to stretch time, although it would not be particularly dignified. The king said that such concerns were of no relevance to him; he wanted longer days, period. So the wizard told the king to go out the next morning to the fields where the workers labored to provide food for the kingdom. The king was to pick up harvesting tools and work alongside the other laborers. The king, not understanding, nevertheless followed the wizard's instructions to the letter, and showed up in the field the next day, ready to do as he'd been advised.

Swinging a scythe, he set to work. Many, many hours passed as he swung and cut and stacked, or so it seemed. But after all that time went by and—with muscles aching and sweat pouring down his bare chest and back—he looked up at the sun, he was astounded to see that the great orb was nowhere near its noonday position. Only a few hours had passed.

It was the longest day of the king's life. And when he staggered back to his palace, footsore and bone weary, he informed the wizard that the mage had indeed found a means of extending a day many hours. But the cost was more than the king was willing to pay on a regular basis.

Howard Stark had told that story to Tony to remind him that he should be thankful for the life he led, and never lose sight of the difficulties and hardships that others had to endure, including their own workers.

Except now all Tony Stark could think about was the literal and immediate nature of the tale, because this felt like the longest damned day in his life. The sun was beating down upon him endlessly, and it seemed that night would never come.

Eventually, however, it did.

Stark was unaware of it when it happened, because he was unconscious at the time.

He wasn't sure of exactly when or how it had happened. All he knew was that he was stumbling across the dunes, that he'd fallen yet again, and suddenly he was lying there in the dark. The fact that he had passed out was incredibly alarming to him. He had no idea how long he'd been lying there exposed and vulnerable. The blood had ceased seeping from the wound, but his arm was soaked in red. Considering how much sand had worked its way in, there was no telling what sort of infections might be swimming around in his system by now.

Right. Sure. Like the biggest danger is that you're going to die of an infection, idiot. You're going to die of thirst long before infection becomes an issue.

He tried to stand up. His body ignored him. It tried to convince him that he should just go back to sleep, just rest there and let everything sort itself out. "Like hell," he muttered and this time, when his brain ordered his muscles to function, they were unable to ignore him. He fought his way to standing and stood there like a wavering flag, symbolizing . . . he wasn't sure what. Maybe he just symbolized being too stupid to know when to quit.

He started walking again, but now his imagination was starting to run wild. He became convinced that Raza's men were closing in. The big problem was that it was impossible to say whether he was imagining it or not. They could, indeed, be right behind him, closing in, about to . . .

He fell once more, and this time—even as he tumbled headfirst down a dune—he knew he wasn't getting up again. He flopped at the bottom, spent as a dishrag, too tired even to think about standing.

And then he heard it, and he knew that it was not his

imagination at all, not remotely. Something was bearing down upon him, something large and mechanical. Raza's men had caught up with him. This was it.

He sent out a silent prayer to any deity who might be listening to just take him, please, take him, right now.

A dark, massive shape rose from behind the dune. A light pierced the night and he squinted against it, morbidly amused that he had strength to maneuver his eyebrows.

It kept rising and that was when Stark realized it was hovering. It was a helicopter, although in the darkness he was unable to discern what sort it was. He didn't recall Raza having any choppers at his command, but that alone didn't necessarily mean anything.

Then the chopper descended. He tried to move his head to follow its path but couldn't manage it. So he remained where he was, staring up at the night sky.

A face appeared above him, looking down at him. There was astonishment in its eyes, and then a slow smile spread across it.

"Saving your ass is getting to be a full time job," said James Rhodes.

Then Rhodes's eyes widened, and his body stiffened. "What the hell—?" He dropped down next to Stark and pulled at his shirt. His face literally was lit up as he looked down at the radiant circle on Stark's chest.

"Those bastards," whispered Rhodey. "How much time—?"

Stark shook his head, uncomprehending.

"How much time until the bomb goes off, Tony!" His voice was rising with urgency. "Is there a cut-off switch?" Quickly he was uncorking his canteen and was trying to ease water down Stark's throat. "I'm not abandoning you now, buddy! Not after all this! But we gotta disarm that thing, and if—"

Stark coughed up water, but it wasn't because he was

choking. It was because he finally realized what Rhodey was reacting to, and it was damned funny. He tried to speak and his voice was barely a croak as he said, "Not . . . a bomb, not a bomb."

Rhodey stared in confusion at the miniature Arc reactor implanted in Stark's chest. "Then what the hell is it?"

It glowed softly in the darkness. A beacon of light.

"A reminder," said Tony Stark.

xi.

Pepper Potts stood on the runway at Edwards Air Force Base. The heat shimmered around her, coming in waves off the tarmac. Happy Hogan was standing nearby her, leaning against the Rolls-Royce Phantom Silver. He looked nonchalant, but he couldn't fool her. He was as relieved as she was.

Okay, probably not as relieved, but still significantly so.

She scoured the horizon, waiting for some sign of the plane. She knew it was on its way; she knew that he was safe. But she still refused to believe it until he was there in front of her.

Finally she saw the plane, a C-17, in the distance. The little girl within her wanted to clap her hands in joy, but she knew that Hogan was watching. Besides, she was a professional and needed to project that professionalism whenever humanly possible. That was what she had kept telling herself when she'd been crying uncontrollably in the limo on the ride over. Hogan, bless his heart, had said nothing. He hadn't offered conciliatory words or meaningless assurances of "There, there, no need to cry, he's okay." He had instead merely kept the supply of tissues coming until she had cried herself out. She supposed that, on some level, she shouldn't have been shocked at her breakdown. She had held herself together for months. It was only now, when Stark was safe and they had been en route to Edwards to pick him up, that she had the luxury of letting her long-repressed fear manifest.

After what seemed an endless amount of waiting, the C-17 finally landed and taxied toward them. The engines shut down and a ramp descended from the rear of the airplane. She held her breath and then saw Rhodey and Tony.

"Oh my God," she whispered.

Tony Stark looked like a fragile ghost of himself. She had no idea how much weight he had lost. His skin was pale, and there was fatigue in his eyes that she could discern even from this distance as he squinted furiously against the sun's blinding light. He was seated in a wheelchair, adding to the general look of frailty. Rhodey was holding the wheelchair firmly from the back and now he carefully wheeled Stark down the ramp.

"You just like pushing me around, don't you," Stark said.

"Yeah," said Rhodey, "you got me pegged."

It sounded on the surface like light banter, but there was an undercurrent of frustration in Stark's voice. Clearly he felt helpless, and it was not a sensation that he was either accustomed to or willingly accepting of.

His impatience with the situation was quickly evident the moment they got to the bottom of the ramp. "Help me out of this thing," he said to Rhodey, unwilling to endure what he saw as an indignity an instant longer than he needed to.

Then, without waiting to be helped, he tried to pull himself out of the chair. His anxiousness to prove his independence turned out to be a mistake because, as he struggled to his feet, he nearly fell. The only thing that prevented him from doing so was Rhodey, who caught him and steadied him. "I got you, pal," he said in a tone that was clearly meant to be reassuring. But Pepper saw the look in Stark's face and could almost read the thoughts going through his mind: *I'm weak. I'm weak and everybody here knows it.*

Nevertheless, he did nothing to pull away from Rhodey, leaning his weight, or what was left of his weight, on Rhodey as they walked forward. Stark seemed to be focusing his efforts on keeping his feet moving.

Pepper's eyes locked with Rhodey's as they drew near. He nodded to her.

"Thank you," said Pepper softly.

"Don't mention it," said Rhodey.

She rested a hand gratefully on his forearm for a moment and then squeezed it. He nodded again and then she turned to face her boss. She had allowed herself her initial stunned reaction when she'd first seen him emerge into the daylight of Edwards. Now she maintained her composure and smiled as if she were simply picking him up at the end of a gala event.

He looked at her closely. "Your eyes are red," he said finally. "A few tears for your long-lost boss?"

"Tears of joy," she said. "I hate job hunting."

Stark nodded as if this explanation were remotely acceptable. Hogan, meantime, was holding open the limo door for Stark. "Good to see you again, sir."

Tony Stark scrutinized Hogan. "You do something new with your hair?"

"Wouldn't dream of it, sir."

Stark nodded approvingly and patted Hogan on the shoulder as Rhodes eased him into the limo. Hogan then looked at Rhodey the same way, Pepper thought, as she just had. Then he saluted. Rhodey promptly straightened his shoulders and snapped off a responsive salute. Message sent, message received.

Pepper climbed into the back of the limo with Stark as Hogan slammed the door.

"So," said Pepper the moment she was settled in. She

was studying her electronic organizer with the intention of rattling off various obligations that Stark had. She felt it was best to try and jump right back into things in order to give him something to think about, and the rest of his ordeal could be dealt with later. But the next words died in her throat, because Stark wasn't looking at her. Instead, he was gazing out the window. He looked like his thoughts were thousands of miles away, which they probably were.

Pepper's eyes met Hogan's in the mirror. She gave a small shrug. Briskly, Hogan said, "Where to, Mr. Stark?"

"We're due at the hospital," she reminded them.

"No," said Stark. He spoke more forcefully than she would have expected, given his wan appearance and general air of fatigue. "I was just held captive for three months. There are two things that I want. I want an American cheeseburger and I want—"

"A hot blonde?" said Pepper. When he looked at her with a smile, she continued, "You thinking about how well I know you?"

"Actually, I was thinking about how well you knew me. Past tense. The second thing I want is a press conference."

"*Really.*"

"Yes. And no, the press conference isn't about my not being in the mood for a hot blonde . . . although I suppose some would consider that lapse to be news-worthy."

Moments later the limo was gliding away from Edwards. As an uncomfortable silence hung in the car, Hogan filled it with, "Did they get them?"

"Them?"

"The guys who, you know . . . did this to you."

"Oh. Right." Stark grunted. "By the time I directed the Air Force to where they'd been, they were already gone. Nothing left of the camp but some smoldering ashes."

"They'll find them. They'll pay, one way or the other," said Hogan.

"Yes," said Tony, but left it there.

There was very little discussion the rest of the way to Tony Stark's corporate headquarters. Pepper was, for the most part, busy making phone calls to arrange for the press conference that Stark had wanted. Hogan was watching the road. Every so often as she attended to her boss's request, she would cast a glance in Stark's direction to see what his condition was. He said nothing, gave no sign of what was going through his mind.

As requested, they stopped for a cheeseburger. Displaying the slightest flash of his famed puckish humor, Stark insisted the limo pull into the drive-through of a Burger King. Pepper had to admit to herself that it was worth it just to see the face on the girl at the take-out window when the gleaming silver Rolls glided up. Stark had handed her the money himself, giving her a fifty and telling her to keep the change. It raised Pepper's hopes that perhaps her boss's resilience far surpassed anything she would have considered possible.

Stark had finished eating the cheeseburger, although he had yet to touch either the french fries or the Coke he'd ordered. He was just in the process of picking off bits of melted cheese from the wrapper when the vehicle pulled into the center of the Stark Industries complex. The centerpiece was naturally the towering main building, a glass skyscraper that looked like a beacon of pure light when the sun was at the right angle. Howard Stark, upon its opening, had proudly proclaimed that it was intended as a source of illumination to light the way to greatness—high-flown words, and maybe even somewhat overblown, but one had to admire the rhetoric. Smaller buildings of various sizes radiated out from the main building. The entire area was on a vast, elevated plaza that was ringed by several main traffic arteries. The highways frequently suffered from traffic backups simply because people would slow down while passing Stark headquarters in order to get a better look.

Naturally everyone at SI knew that the man whose name adorned the upper reaches of the building was arriving. There had been no details released of just how Stark had managed to escape and survive. Pepper was intensely curious, but she didn't feel it her place to ask and Stark didn't seem inclined to volunteer the information. She reasoned that, when he was ready to talk about it—presuming he ever was—then he would. That, as far as she was concerned, was the end of it.

Still, the lack of information didn't translate to lack of support or interest. The result was that there was a massive group of employees waiting for Stark when the limo rolled up. Obadiah Stane was at the forefront.

Pepper felt concern building. Stark was still frail. How was it going to look if he stepped out of the limousine and five hundred or so people saw their boss sprawl on his face onto the sidewalk?

Clearly Hogan was having the same worry. "Boss," Hogan was saying, "maybe you should just, you know, wave out the window so they know you're okay, and then head straight home."

"So they'll know I'm not really okay," said Stark. He folded the paper from the burger. Pepper took it from him and then passed it on to Hogan, who dumped it in a small garbage bag in the front. "I don't think so. Pull us over, Happy. Let's do this."

Pepper was not thrilled about the "this" involved, even as Hogan—having parked the limo—came around and opened the door for Stark. She held her breath and watched as Stark put his feet down, first one and then the other, on the sidewalk. Hogan extended a hand to help him out, but Stark waved it off. Then, with a slight grunt, he hauled himself out of the limo and stood. He even gave a slight bow. Pepper exhaled in relief.

The employees were applauding thunderously. Stane approached with arms outstretched. "See this? Huh? Huh?" he called. Pepper was unsure whether the "this" Stane was referring to was the crowd of well-wishers, or the sight of Tony Stark having survived an ordeal that most of them could never imagine.

He threw his arms around Stark, hugging him fiercely. For an instance Pepper's breath caught in her throat, because she thought that Tony's knees were buckling. But then he caught himself and pulled himself up to standing.

Without even a backward glance at Pepper, Stane turned Stark around and guided him toward headquarters.

Pepper felt her eyes beginning to sting. As if he were psychic, Hogan handed her a tissue. She dabbed at her eyes quickly, pulling herself together, and then she was out of the car and following the receding crowd as quickly as she could.

She had despised the notion of calling a press conference, but Stark had insisted and he was the boss. So she had done as she had been instructed. Now she followed the mob as they headed in the direction of the Howard Stark Memorial Speaker's Center. It was the room in the main building where various high-capacity functions were held, and certainly a press conference of this magnitude qualified.

The place was already packed by the time she arrived. Reporters were crowded in at the front, and the back areas were rapidly filling up with employees who were curious to see what was going on and what Stark wanted to talk about.

Pepper shook her head at the barely controlled insanity of it all. Stark was nowhere to be seen. She reasoned that Stane had wisely taken him around back so that—rather than force his way up the packed aisle, through the herd of jackals who represented the free press—he'd be able to step directly out onto the podium from the backstage door.

Then some man she'd never seen intruded into Pepper's sightline, blocking out her view of the podium. He was a tall man, with a high forehead and thinning hair brushed in a not-especially-flattering manner across his head. He had an air of smug superciliousness about him, as if he belonged here and she was merely someone who was occupying space that might otherwise have provided air for him to breathe. She took one look at him and was already annoyed.

"You'll have to take a seat, sir," she said, and tried to sidle past him.

"Oh, I'm not a reporter. I'm Agent Phil Coulson with the Strategic Homeland Intervention, Enforcement, and Logistic Division."

She blinked. She'd just figured he was another pencil jockey. "That's a mouthful," she said, not knowing how else to reply.

"I know. Here."

He handed her a card. The font on it was minuscule in order to accommodate the agency's name; she was having a hell of a time reading it. Giving up, she said, "Look, Mr. Coulson, we've already spoken with the DOD, the FBI, the CIA—"

That was a bit of an exaggeration. It wasn't "we," it was Tony. He'd have been home days sooner if it weren't for the endless need of various agencies to subject him to one questioning session after another abroad.

"We're a separate division with a more . . . specific

focus," said Coulson. "We need to debrief Tony about the circumstances of his escape. More important—"

"Well, great, I'll let him know," she said, cutting him off. What she really wanted to tell him was to go read any of the half-dozen reports that the other agencies had surely generated. Problem was, since they were into secrecy, they probably couldn't be bothered to share the information with one another. So poor Tony had to go through yet another session reiterating everything he'd already said? Forget that.

She tried to step past him but Coulson blocked her path without seeming bullying about it. "We're here to help. We're here to listen. I assure you Mr. Stark will want to talk to us."

"I'm sure he will," said Pepper, who was in fact sure of quite the opposite. "Now if you could just take your seat," and she pointed firmly.

Coulson looked prepared to argue some more, but something in Pepper's expression must have prompted him to rethink it. He bobbed his head instead and, providing an insincere smile, found a seat while Pepper walked away, shaking her head. *God save me from agents,* she thought as she found herself a seat and waited to see what in the world Tony Stark had to say that simply couldn't wait.

There was a tap on her shoulder. She looked up. Rhodey was standing there, looking as bewildered as she'd ever seen him. She wondered how he had found out about the detour and then reminded herself that she shouldn't have been surprised. Rhodey had the governmental equivalent of an all-access pass to Tony Stark's life. If there was anything unusual going on with her boss, then he was going to know about it.

"Uhhh, weren't we taking him to the hospital?" Rhodey said.

She shrugged.

"Where is he? Pepper, what's going through his mind?"

"I wish I knew," she said.

Stark moves through the narrow hallway that will put him directly onto the podium. The only one there with him is Stane, following right behind as if he's guarding Stark's back even though no one else is around. "You know, there's a lot of reporters in there," Stane says, and he sounds a bit uncomfortable for the first time. "What's going on?"

"You'll see," Stark says. He speaks with an assurance that he does not feel.

He has no idea what he feels.

His mind, his emotions, everything remains scrambled, tumbling about within his brain. He is someone who has spent his life exhibiting a laserlike focus. That focus is now gone. Knowing that he cannot be what he was, he has no idea what he is to become. This press assemblage has been a deliberate ploy on his part, a sort of shock treatment. He is afraid that he may well withdraw into himself, or worse, into a bottle, if he does not find some fast way to face directly what has happened to him. As the cliché goes, he has clambered out onto a limb and is now about to saw it off behind him.

The ruckus from the other side of the entrance door is a solid wall of noise. Stark finds himself wishing that he was wearing armor again. Except, something better looking. Something constructed with the finest materials to which he has access. An image takes hold in his mind and will not let go. He does what he typically does at such times: creates a mental file folder, inserts it, and tucks it away, knowing that he can and will revisit it at his leisure.

He throws open the door and moves quickly across the stage to the podium. There is an immediate swell of noise—people cheering him, reporters hurling questions. Then the noise subsides. It's Stane's doing: He's putting out his hands, gesturing for silence, and the crowd is attending to him. Credit the man for having considerable charisma, that he can command an assemblage like this with some simple hand movements.

It takes perhaps another ten seconds before everyone is quiet and waiting, and Stark had been hoping that during that interval something would pop into his mind. Nothing is coming. His hands are resting lightly on the podium and now his fingers curl underneath it, gripping it firmly and then relaxing. Long seconds pass. He feels vulnerable, scattered. Stane has been standing a few feet away but now—like an actor stepping in to help a cast mate paralyzed with stage fright—he is moving toward Stark with the obvious intention of guiding him away.

"I . . ." Stark says. It's a word. All right, a pronoun. But it is a start. He takes a deep breath, lets it out and the words come with it: ". . . can't do this anymore."

Dead silence. They're waiting for a follow up, a smart remark, a punchline—something.

He has nothing.

But he has anticipated this. Unwilling to trust himself to convey his thoughts, he is counting on the reporters to do their job. They will draw him out of his shell.

One finally does what Stark has been expecting.

"You mean you're retiring?"

"No, I don't want to retire. I want to do something else." He doesn't know what else. But something else. He simply needs someone to help him articulate it.

Another uncomfortable silence. Then another reporter prompts, "Something besides weapons?"

"Yes, that's right."

Suddenly the room is a hive, with questions hurtling around him like berserk drones. It is all he can do not to slap them away. And then one question, bellowed by

*one reporter who Stark swears must have had opera
training because his voice carries above all the others.*

"The official report was sketchy. What happened to
you over there, Mr. Stark?"

*Tony Stark points directly at the reporter with such
intensity that the reporter takes a step back, as if concerned that Stark's finger is loaded. And now it all comes
out in a rush, the force and intensity and confidence
building with each word.*

"What happened over there? I had my eyes opened,
that's what happened. I saw my weapons, with my name
on them, in the hands of thugs. I thought we were doing
good here . . . I can't say that anymore."

*He notices Pepper seated toward the back. She ap-
pears transfixed. Rhodey is next to her, and he looks
stunned.*

"What do you intend to do about it, Mr. Stark?" *says
the same reporter.*

*Stark feels as if he's standing two inches taller than he
had been moments ago. Not to get messianic, but this is
his Sermon on the Mount . . . a mountain built upon
human suffering that is his fault, and he will descend
from that mountain now.* "The system is broken—
there's no accountability whatsoever. Effective immediately, I am shutting down the weapons manufacturing
division of Stark Industries, until a time when I can re-
assess the future of this company."

*The room is now in chaos. Everyone is shouting at
once, arms are waving frantically to get his attention.
Employees look stunned, glancing at each other because
apparently they cannot believe what they have just
heard and are wondering what the future of this company can possibly be. Surprisingly, some are nodding in
approval. Apparently he has come around to some
epiphany that they had already had. Good for them.*

They're ahead of him on the curve; he's going to have to do some sprinting to catch up, apparently.

Stane has now stepped in very close to Stark and he is trying to restore order. It's not working this time. Stark has thrown open the floodgates and the tidal wave will not be turned back. Fortunately Stark has a microphone, and his voice can carry above the cacophony easily enough. "We've lost our way. I need to reevaluate things. And my heart's telling me I have more to offer the planet than things that blow up."

"So you're saying . . . what are you saying?" come the overlapping voices of other reporters.

Stark senses that Stane is about to cut him off. He won't allow for that. He drapes an arm around Stane's shoulders and says, "In the coming months, Mr. Stane here and I will set a new course for Stark Industries. 'Tomorrow Today' has always been our slogan. It's time we try to live up to it."

The questions are now coming fast and furious, but Stane has permitted all he is going to. He shoves his face into the microphone on the podium in front of Stark and says firmly, "Okay, I think we're going to be selling a lot of newspapers here. What we should take away from this is that Tony's back, he's healthier than ever, and as soon as he heals up and takes some time off, we're going to have a little internal discussion and get back to you. Thank you for coming by."

Tony Stark didn't depart the podium the way he came in. Instead, he went forward, moving through the crowd. Pepper watched in utter astonishment as the crowd actually parted for him. The reporters were still hurling questions, but it was from a respectful distance.

Respectful.

It occurred to her abruptly that that had never been the case before. The press, the public, had been fascinated by Tony Stark, intrigued by him, appalled, amused, and a dozen other things. But pure respect for what he had to say—that was new.

This was new.

He was new.

Or was he? Was he on the level with this? Or had he simply created some sort of persona that he was trying on experimentally like a new suit? It was hard to be sure; one never quite knew what one was getting with him.

He walked right up to her and stopped. Then he glanced from her to Rhodey and back to her. He appeared to be waiting for them to say something. No one else in the room mattered to him.

"You mean that?" she said, accommodating him. Then, with a raised eyebrow, she added, "Or is this some clever stock maneuver?"

"Wait and see," Tony said challengingly, and then walked past her. She watched him go and felt as if she were seeing him for the first time.

And maybe she was.

She started to head out after him, but Rhodey stopped her from going. "Pepper, there's something I've got to talk to you about."

"Rhodey, can it—"

"No. It can't wait," he interrupted her.

She caught a glimpse of that annoying Coulson person trying to get to her, but he was swept away by the crush of bodies of people trying to follow Tony Stark, ask him questions, thank him, criticize him, whatever. She turned back to Rhodey, blew air between her lips in an annoyed fashion, and said, "Okay, thirty seconds."

He leaned in close to her and spoke quickly and firmly.

"He sustained some sort of massive damage to his heart. I'm a little fuzzy on the specifics, but the only thing keeping him going is a portable reactor implanted in his chest that he managed to cobble together from God-knows-what. It's like an amputee having to attach his own claw prosthetics. The entire experience may have seriously traumatized him, and there may well be nothing more dangerous on this planet than Tony Stark not being in his right mind. So keep an eye on him before he blows up himself or you or the West Coast." He glanced at his watch. "Twenty-three seconds. Any questions for the remaining seven seconds?"

Stunned, Pepper shook her head, and decided right then that she would never ask her boss for a raise. Money could never become an issue because no salary in the world was commensurate with the sort of thing she had to deal with.

The famed Stark Industries Arc reactor was housed inside a simple, eight-story-tall building that didn't look like much of anything from the outside. That was fine with Tony; what he had always loved about the Arc reactor was its simplicity of design.

The reactor itself looked more or less like a doughnut. A ten-foot-tall, thirty-foot-diameter doughnut that was an astounding construction of blue metal tubes wrapped around a pulsing purple plasma core. That constituted the first floor of the building; the remaining seven floors were basically an elaborate coolant system. The entire thing rested on a network of pipes and circuitry inlaid into the floor. It bore a striking resemblance to the device that was currently inset into Tony's chest. Unconsciously his hand drifted toward the implant. He touched it tentatively, then lowered his hand as he gazed at the readouts from the reactor. The plasma density was at three, the tesla field was at seven, and the auxiliary heating was at fifty megawatts. In other words, as always, it was on standby, providing the minimal output that the Arc required in order to be prepared to function at a higher capacity.

He had not gone straight from the hall to the Arc reactor building. Instead, he had swung by the car and picked up his fries and soda. Now he sat on the floor, crosslegged, like a Buddha, slowly savoring the taste of each fried potato. Then he lifted the cup of soda and took a long, lingering sip through the straw. He closed his eyes and sighed.

He heard a familiar footfall behind him and didn't have to bother to turn around to know that Stane was right behind him. "You know," he said thoughtfully, gazing lovingly at the french fry, "if we just carpet bomb everyone who hates us with fries, they'd grow to love us."

Stane didn't respond to that. Instead, tossing a rueful glance in the general direction of the building they'd left, he said blandly, "That went well."

Tony sighed. "Did I just paint a target on the back of my head?"

"*Your* head?" said Stane, clearly disbelieving. "What about *my* head? What do you think the over-under on the stock drop is going to be tomorrow?"

"Forty points." If Tony had ever tossed around such an overnight forecast in his father's presence, that would have been sufficient to kill Howard Stark if he were not already dead. But he felt detached, even bored, as if the number meant nothing.

It obviously meant a great deal to Stane. "Minimum." He sighed, hung his head, and then crouched next to Tony and put a hand on his shoulder. "Tony, Tony. We're iron mongers. We make weapons. That's what we do. We're a weapons manufacturer."

"I don't want a body count to be our only legacy."

"What we do here," and Stane gestured around them, obviously intending to encompass the entirety of

Stark headquarters, "keeps the world from falling into chaos."

Tony leaned back and looked straight at Stane. He felt pity welling within him. How could he possibly explain this? Stane had a lot on the ball, but ultimately he was just a businessman. Conveying to Stane what he had experienced was simply impossible; Stane didn't have the tools to comprehend. It was like trying to explain flight to a gopher. "Well, judging from what I just saw, we are not doing a very good job," said Tony, unable to keep the bitterness from his voice. "There are other things we can do."

"Like what?" said Stane challengingly. He looked as if he was genuinely interested in what Tony could possibly come up with. His question was laced with sarcasm, but curiosity was still evident in his tone. "What do you want us to do? Make baby bottles?"

In response, Tony gestured toward the reactor. Stane looked at it and slowly started shaking his head. "Oh, come on—!"

"A new kind of power generation, Obadiah," Tony said insistently. "Remember? Clean. Safe. Won't hasten global warming. One Arc reactor, built upon Repulsor technology, could serve the power needs of the entire state."

"In theory," Stane emphasized, "in theory, Tony. Remember that part?"

"Theory only becomes fact if we work on it—"

"But it didn't work! Tony, you remember! At the end of the day, the Arc reactor was a publicity stunt. We built it to shut the hippies up."

"It works."

"Yeah, as a science project. It was never cost effective. We knew that before we built it. I mean, don't get me wrong," he said in a conciliatory manner. "If it hadn't been for the Arc reactor, we never would have realized the weapons possibilities that Repulsor technology represented. Thanks to the reactor, we have the Jericho missiles and other weapons applications."

"Yeah, that's us all over," Tony said bitterly. "Try to find ways to save the world and we wind up finding ways to blow it up. Iron mongers, just like you said."

"I didn't mean to rain on your parade, kid. All I'm saying is that, when it comes to being utilized as a means of generating energy, Repulsor technology is a dead end, right?"

Tony's response was guarded. "Maybe."

"There haven't been any breakthroughs in thirty years, right?"

Now Tony looked straight at Stane since what Stane wasn't saying became far more significant than what he was saying. Stane tried to keep his face neutral and failed utterly. Tony laughed. "You're a lousy poker player. Who told you?"

"Come on," said Stane, impatient, obviously knowing there was no point in pretending anymore. He pointed at Tony's chest. "Let me see the damn thing."

"Was it Rhodey?"

"Just show it to me."

With a frustrated sigh, feeling like a high school science project, Tony pulled open his shirt and yanked up his undershirt. The glow of the miniature Arc reactor suffused the room.

Stane shook his head, astounded. Then he shrugged as if this was at least the third Arc reactor he'd seen implanted in someone's chest that week. "Well, everyone needs a hobby."

"Yeah, it was either craft a scientific breakthrough out of stray missile parts or take up stamp collecting. But I hate getting the sticky part of the stamps on my fingers."

Tony started to pull his shirt down over his implant.

Stane helped him, aiding him in buttoning the shirt. "Listen, we're a team," he said, gently but firmly. "There's nothing we can't do if we stick together. No more of this ready, fire, aim business. No more press. Can you promise me that?"

In the exact same tone of caution that he'd used when Stane had first been asking about advancements in Repulsor Tech, Tony said, "Maybe."

Stane would not be put off. "Let me handle this. I did it for your father, I'll do it for you, but please, you just got to lie low."

Tony held his gaze for a long time, and then smiled and nodded.

"I'll see what I can do."

xii.

Tony Stark's house came to life.

As night fell, the windows and lights began to shift, with the windows no longer opaque and the lights coming on to their fail-safe level: romantic. The television came on automatically to CNN.

Some of the shifts were backward. Normally the television came on first thing in the morning, not in the evening. But Tony had been home less than forty-eight hours, and he had not acclimated himself to the correct time zone yet. He had been sleeping for hours on end, and not remotely conforming to his customary day/night sleep cycle.

This presented no challenge for the computer entity known as Jarvis. Jarvis had simply waited for Tony to stir. When Tony awoke as if it were morning instead of night, Jarvis adjusted the household patterns accordingly.

Tony trotted down the main steps into the living room, rubbing his eyes as he went.

"Hello, Mr. Stark," said Jarvis in clipped British tones.

"Hello, Jarvis.."

"What can I do for you?"

"I need to build a better heart."

The voice paused. Obviously it was processing the statement. Tony had written every bit of the coding and could practically see Jarvis endeavoring to approach the remark from multiple directions and make sense of it.

Failing to accomplish that, Jarvis said—with the slightest hint of regret—"I'm not sure I follow, sir."

"Give me a scan and you'll see," said Tony as he headed for his workshop.

A few minutes later, in his workshop, Tony was sitting naked from the waist up in front of a 3-D laser scanner. He was wearing goggles to protect his eyes as a series of beams played across his body, mapping every molecule of his structure. On assorted monitors throughout the workshop, terabytes of data raced past, every scrap of information going directly into Jarvis's data banks.

"What were your intentions for this device?" Jarvis said.

"It powers an electromagnet that keeps the shrapnel from entering my heart. Can you recommend any upgrades?"

On the main monitor, Tony's chest device became magnified. Jarvis effortlessly dissected the image, breaking it down into its component parts. They flashed, one after the next after the next. Tony knew that he could have explained to Jarvis step by step how he had constructed the device, but it wasn't necessary. Jarvis was essentially reverse engineering the mini-reactor's creation. It would take Jarvis far less time to figure it out than it would require Tony to tell.

"It is difficult to offer counsel," said Jarvis, "in light of the fact that your stated intentions are inconsistent with your actions."

Tony was bewildered by the response. "What are you talking about? That is ridiculous. That is exactly the purpose of this invention."

He glanced at the monitors and was struck by the design of the device. Granted, he had put the entire thing together himself, crafted every circuit. Still, seeing it here on the monitors, as Jarvis dug deeper and deeper through the strata of the device.

God, it looks like a small city.

The disembodied computer voice continued, "The energy yield of this device outperforms your stated intention by eleven orders of magnitude. You could accomplish your stated goal with the power output of a car battery."

Tony felt a twinge of annoyance. Jarvis was acting as if he—it—he knew better what was going through Tony's mind than Tony did. As calculations continued to flash with astounding speed upon the monitors, Tony stepped out from the booth. "Upgrade recommendations. List," he said as flatly as he could.

The shift in tone was not lost upon Jarvis. "Why are you talking to me like a computer?" Jarvis didn't sound hurt; merely curious.

"Because you're acting like one."

Jarvis contemplated that for a long time—which, by Jarvis's standards, was three seconds—and then asked politely, "Shall I disable random pattern conversation?"

"No. It's okay." Tony smiled, but the smile was tinged with regret. He thought about the family that he had told Yinsen he didn't have, and the family that Yinsen had but would never see again. The world seemed lonelier to him. "You're the only one who understands me."

"I *don't* understand you, sir."

Tony looked up as if Jarvis were standing directly in front of him. "Were you always this dry? I remember you having more personality than this."

"Should I activate sarcasm harmonics?" said Jarvis, always designed to please.

"Fine. Could you please make your recommendations now?"

Jarvis's accent changed, going from polished East End to a resident of Liverpool. "It would thrill me to no end."

"And that's more like it."

Tony continued to watch as the designs on the monitors changed, developed, evolved before his eyes. He felt a flash of regret: Imagine if Yinsen had been able to see this in action. Yinsen had been such a brilliant man; imagine what he could have accomplished with the right tools, the right environment.

How many more Yinsens are out there? How many people who could have bright, incredible futures filled with achievement, but are trapped by their personal circumstances? How many people would be able to flourish if they had even a fraction of the opportunities that had been handed to Anthony Stark . . . who had, in turn, been too stupid, too smug, too filled with notions of entitlement to appreciate them all?

"Should I begin machining the parts?"

The question shook Tony from his reverie. The flashing images on the screen had ceased. There was a new model of the reactor on the screen. Paradoxically it was both more complex and more simple . . . or perhaps more streamlined might be the better way to put it.

Tony nodded slowly. Then he took an armload of raw metal stock and lay it down onto a lathe. "Machine away," he said.

He stood and watched as robot arms descended from overhead. They were long, angular, with efficient claws mounted on the end. Briskly they began organizing the sheets of metal and, once everything was properly stacked, selected a sheet and lay it upon the lathe. Pinpoint laser beams, adjusted for the proper cutting width, sliced through. What would have taken Tony hours to do, the computer-guided lasers and robot arms sorted through in minutes. As each piece was cut to its exact size down to a margin of error of one thousandth of an inch, robot arms would descend, pick them up, and sort them into individual piles.

As Tony worked with his various tools milling parts,

the new generation of the reactor in his chest began to come to life. He smiled grimly.

Jarvis had been right. He knew it and Jarvis knew it. He had plans for something far more than a heart reactor. And he hoped and prayed that, sooner or later, he would have the opportunity to implement those plans against his former captors.

He realized that he was almost wolfishly looking forward to a reunion. He couldn't wait to see the look on Raza's face.

There was not much left of Raza's face.

As he crouched on a sand dune in the Afghan desert, he brushed away flies that seemed especially interested in the horrific wounds that adorned his forehead, cheeks, and what was left of his scalp. All of the damage was courtesy of the jet boosters that Tony Stark had employed in his escape.

Even the slightest passing thought of Tony Stark was enough to send Raza flying into a rage. Thanks to Stark, they had had to pull out of their hideout, to find new caves, new locations where they could feel safe. Thanks to Stark, they were on the run. Thanks to Stark.

Oh yes, he wanted to thank Stark, all right. He wanted to thank him with a bullet between the eyes.

As it so happened, however, Raza had something else to occupy his mind besides impotent fury aimed at Tony Stark. His focus instead was upon what appeared to be metal fingers protruding from the sand. Raza began digging into the dune, clearing sand away until he had managed to remove the entirety of a right-handed gauntlet. He stared at it in wonderment, turned it around and around. He shook his head. Then carefully he set it down on the ground next to him. Alongside him was another discovery that he had already managed to unearth: A battered iron helmet.

His men were scattered around, scavenging the immediate area, while their horses waited patiently and the engines of their pickup trucks idled. They had to be ready to flee the scene at any time should armed forces be detected in the area.

Raza gathered up the helmet and glove and headed toward his vehicle, a large Toyota pickup with a machine gun mounted in the back. A stiff desert wind was coming in from the east, enabling the banner to fly that was attached to a pole on the right bumper. It bore the proud interlocking symbol of ten rings.

Several other pieces were already in the back of the pickup—a boot, a large panel that appeared to have come off the torso section, a few miscellaneous shards that might well have been useless or, perhaps, incredibly vital. It was impossible for Raza to say.

Staring at the helmet, he envisioned having Tony Stark's head inside it. No body; just the head. That thought gave him such pleasure that he actually smiled. That turned out to be a mistake because the burns all over his face caused the smile to hurt something fierce. He resolved never to make that mistake again as he called out to his men, "Keep looking! I want all of it!"

His men heard, acknowledged, and continued the search. Raza picked up the helmet once more and glared balefully into the eyeholes.

He wasn't sure how it would happen yet, but he knew beyond question that, sooner or later, Tony Stark was going down.

xiii.

"Down, baby! Tony Stark is going down! Think of it as the Middle East Trifecta. Since he came back from Afghanistan, Iran as far as I could, and the stock is going to drop like Iraq! Booyah!"

Pepper Potts sat in her work alcove off Tony Stark's living room and moaned softly as he watched Jim Cramer's antics during this latest segment of *Mad Money* on CNBC. Cramer was being his usual manic self, which typically didn't bother Pepper. But this time Tony Stark was the target of his rants about what stocks to buy and what to avoid, and she couldn't say she was enamored of it. Tony was just going through a difficult period of adjustment, having endured an ordeal that would have broken most other men. And instead of backing off, cutting him some slack, they had to pile on him? It wasn't as if it was limited to television. The newspapers had been just as merciless: "Stark Raving Mad?" "Stark Lunacy?" Those had been some of the more mild headlines. None of it seemed fair.

It was easy to chalk it up to *schadenfreude*, that charming German concept involving taking pleasure in someone else's misfortune. Pepper began to think, though, that it was even more fundamental than that. Maybe people were just, by and large, cruel and cowardly, and that was all there was to it.

On the flatscreen television, Cramer continued his rant. "Stark Industries: I've got one recommendation.

Ready? *Selllll!* Abandon ship! Does the *Hindenburg* ring any bells?"

Cramer slammed a large red button on his desk and the sounds of panicked "aoooogah" shrieking resounded. Pepper buried her face in her hands. Tony didn't need this. She didn't need this. Did anyone?

Unable to focus on her work, she muttered, "Please, God, give me something to distract me."

The phone rang. She glanced heavenward, mouthed, *Thank you,* and aimed the remote control at the flatscreen. The TV promptly went off, the screen receded into the wall, and an abstract painting slid into place to obscure it. Then she picked up the phone and answered it.

"Hello. This is Agent Coulson with the Strategic Homeland Inter—"

"Yes, I remember," Pepper said. "What can I do for you?"

"I've left a number of messages trying to get something on the books with Mr. Stark."

"I know this is a priority for him," said Pepper, rubbing the bridge of her nose and suddenly becoming nostalgic for Jim Cramer. At least she could dispose of him with a click of a mute button. This was, in fact, not remotely a priority for Tony, if for no other reason than that it wasn't a priority for Pepper. Here she was busy fretting about whether or not Tony Stark had truly gone around the bend, and yet another government stooge was not something she felt like dealing with at this point or even in the near future. "The next few weeks are a bit up in the air and I can't set appointments without speaking with him first."

"Do you know when you will be speaking with him again?"

"Not sure."

The intercom on her desk suddenly beeped at her. Before she could cover the speaker of the phone, Tony's voice came through: "Pepper? How big are your hands?"

"What was that?" It was Coulson, who had obviously heard Tony.

"Agent Coulson, I really have to go. Let me get back to you later." She hung up, cutting off Coulson's beginning of a protest, and then tapped the intercom response button. "What?"

"How big are your hands?"

She stared at her hands. "I don't under—"

"Just get down here."

Shaking her head, she left the living room and ran down to the workshop. It took a moment for her eyes to adjust once she got there, because the room was so dimly lit. She remembered having likened the workshop to a physical reflection of Tony Stark's mind. Since his return, the workshop had become dark and foreboding. The symbolic parallels were not lost on her.

Tony was seated in a chair in the middle of the room. He was shirtless and his chest was glowing.

Pepper desperately wanted to look away, but was unable to do so. Instead, the sight of it transfixed her. Tony had not spoken of the device in his chest since he had returned home. All the information she had on it was from what Rhodey had told her hurriedly after the press conference the other day. Since then Rhodey had been calling in regularly to check on both of them. By the third time he'd called, Pepper had assured him that calling wasn't necessary. Rhodey would be able to tell if things had gone awry by the large mushroom cloud that would doubtless be rising from the cliffside crater where Tony Stark's house used to be.

If Tony found her gawking at him to be annoying, he gave no indication of it. He said, in a flat and even voice, "Show me your hands."

"What?"

"Just show me your hands."

She held them out. He took them by the wrists and turned them around and over, inspecting them from all angles. "Perfect. They're small. I need you to help me."

Pepper nodded in order to acknowledge that he had spoken, but she was still staring at his chest. "So . . . so that's the thing that's keeping you alive?"

"That's the thing that *was* keeping me alive. It is now an antique. *This* is what *will* be keeping me alive for the foreseeable future."

He pointed a short distance away and she turned and looked. Tony gestured for her to go over and pick it up and she did so. She turned it over in wonder, inspecting it from all sides. She wasn't remotely in Tony's category of technical expertise, but even she could see that she was studying a newly fabricated, higher tech replacement for the chest piece.

"Amazing."

"I'm going to swap them out and switch all functions to the new unit."

That made her a little uneasy. She supposed on some level it wasn't any different than switching out spark-plugs in a car. The problem, naturally, was that she wasn't dealing with a car but with a human life. "Is it safe?" she said, unable to keep the queasiness out of her voice.

"Completely. First, I need you to reach in and—"

She took a reflexive step back. "Reach into where?" she said, having an uncomfortable feeling that she already knew.

"The socket."

"What socket?"

"The chest socket. Listen carefully, because we have to do this in a matter of minutes."

"Or else what?"

"I could go into cardiac arrest."

He sounded so matter-of-fact about it that at first she laughed because she was certain that he was making one of his patented deadpan jokes. Then she saw it in his eyes: He was dead serious, emphasis quite possibly on "dead." She couldn't speak at first, and when she found her voice, she said, "I thought you said it was safe."

"It is for you. You'll be fine, except of course you'll be unemployed if this goes wrong, what with you being my personal assistant and me being dead. But don't think of it as something daunting. Simply think of it as you holding the fates of me, all my employees, and possibly the free world in your hands. Bottom line, I don't want you to panic."

"Oh my God—" Panic was starting to sound like the best option available to her.

He put his hand atop hers to steady her. "Stay with me," he said gently but firmly. "I need you to relieve the pressure on my myocardial nerve."

"I don't know how to do that."

"I'm telling you."

"Sorry—"

"*Listen,*" he said, trying to shake her out of the fugue state she was in danger of entering. "I'm going to lift off the old chest piece—"

"Won't that make you die?"

"Not immediately. When I lift it off, I need you to reach into the socket as far as your hand can fit and gently move the housing away from my heart. Do you know which direction that is?"

"To the right."

"To my right. Your left."

"To the left."

"Right."

She stared at him, trying to get focused once more and not succeeding. "Wait, left?"

"Left."

"Right," she nodded, certain that she had it now. "Left."

Tony frowned and said, "Maybe in the future we should consider the advantages of saying 'correct' when we're replying in the affirmative and save 'right' purely for directions."

"Right. I mean, correct. Good idea."

In a sure, firm manner that Pepper would have thought impossible under the circumstances, Tony carefully pulled the device from its receptacle in his chest. Then he nodded to her to indicate that she should do as he had requested. Taking a deep breath to steel herself, Pepper began to reach in.

"How deep does this go?" It seemed insane to her. She was reaching into her boss's chest, for God's sake. What the hell kind of life was she leading?

"Keep going," Tony said.

She inserted her hand more deeply. It felt vaguely perverse for some reason, and even oddly sexual, although she couldn't quite fathom why.

"That's it," said Tony. "Deeper. Now press."

She felt it then. It was some sort of latch release. Her fingers were poised right atop it. She pressed down upon it and Tony Stark's head flopped lifelessly back, a puppet severed of its strings. Pepper, her hand frozen in place by her wide-eyed panic, gasped out, "Tony!"

Promptly his head snapped back up and he grinned lopsidedly. "Just kidding. I'm fine."

"Oh, for—!" She resisted the urge to belt him and instead, with her hand still in his chest, said, "Is it . . . ?"

"Yes. It's releasing."

He indicated that she could extract her hand. She did so and felt ill when she saw that it was covered in a nasty pink slime.

"*Eww!* Pus!"

"It is not pus," he said, and sounded annoyed. Not

that she gave a damn at that moment, considering the goop covering her hand. "It's an inorganic plasmic discharge. It's from the device, not my body."

"Well, it smells," she said, her nose wrinkling. "Am I done?"

"Yes. Thank you."

"Can I wash my hands now?"

He nodded. She walked to the sink as Tony cleaned out the discharge from the opening. "The new unit is much more efficient. This shouldn't happen again."

"Good," she said, soaping up her hands. She had a feeling she was going to be compulsively washing her hands for the rest of the day, perhaps even the rest of the week. " 'Cause it's not in my job description."

"It is now."

She moaned, not welcoming that bit of information at all. She turned back, drying her hands, and was about to ask if he needed help getting the thing installed in his chest. But it turned out to be unnecessary. A robot arm was coming down from overhead and inserting the brand-new device into Tony's chest.

Hoping desperately that she might be able to inject a shred of normalcy into the proceedings, Pepper said, "I don't suppose you want to go over things. Business-related things, I mean. I can just grab them off my desk and—"

His voice laced with irony, he said, "Can it at least wait until I install my new untested groundbreaking self-contained power source and lifesaving device prototype?"

Pepper had no idea how to respond to that. She had thought that the matters she needed to discuss with him were pressing, but somehow now . . . much less so. "I suppose," she said and backed up.

As she did so, she spotted the previous chest piece perched on a table. She hadn't seen it wind up there and assumed that one of the ubiquitous robot arms Tony had created must have placed it there. She glanced over toward Tony. He was busy supervising the installation of the new unit. The sight of it chilled her. Rather than dwell on it, she chose to pick up the old chest piece and examine it.

"Throw that thing out," said Tony.

"Don't you want to save it?"

"Why?" The notion seemed to surprise him. "It's antiquated."

Pepper actually had to laugh at that. The thought that he could take something that was such a monumental achievement and dismiss it in the same manner that he would the previous year's computer model—it just stunned her. "You made it out of spare parts in a dungeon. It saved your life. Doesn't it at least have some nostalgic value?"

"Pepper," he said as the robot arms finished fitting the new piece into his chest, "I have been called many things. Nostalgic is not one of them."

The robot arms moved off and there was a long, nervous moment—nervous for Pepper, at least, although Tony seemed sanguine enough about it—when the chest plate sat there, doing nothing. She imagined the metal shards slowly advancing on his heart. *Hurry up, hurry up.*

Then the new reactor bloomed to life like a lighthouse. Pepper let out a long, relieved sigh. Tony simply nodded in approval. For all the emotion over this astounding accomplishment that he displayed, he might have just finished changing a spare tire. "There. Good as new. Thank you."

"You're welcome. Can I ask you a favor?"

"Shoot."

"I don't do well under that kind of pressure," she admitted. "If you need someone to do something like that again, get somebody else."

"I don't have anyone else."

He said it so matter-of-factly that it took a moment for it to sink in. He seemed—it was hard for her to say— regretful? Resigned to it? Indifferent? Sometimes it was so difficult to get any sort of read off Tony Stark. He kept his innermost thoughts and feelings, his very soul, walled off.

It was Voltaire who said that God was a comedian playing to an audience too afraid to laugh. There was some truth in that. Life was typically filled with horrific ironies, and this struck Pepper as one of those instances. Tony Stark, a man of science who kept his heart very much to himself, now had a heart that was under perpetual attack and needed science in order to survive. In so doing, he had created a device that actually shielded his heart from penetration. Science was preventing his heart from being broken.

It made her want to slowly applaud God for what was perhaps His most ambitious and on-point jest yet.

Instead, she simply asked, "Will that be all, Mr. Stark?"

"That will be all, Miss Potts," he said with a slight incline of his head.

She walked out and Tony Stark, after a moment's thought, got back to work.

As diligently as Tony labored over the next few days, his thoughts kept returning to Pepper as she held up the first model of the chest plate.

There was no way to explain to her what was really going through his head. That every time he looked at it, it brought back memories of Yinsen that were becoming increasingly painful. He couldn't look back. He had to focus entirely on moving forward because the past was too difficult for him to cope with.

Since when is that anything new? Tony asked himself with morbid amusement as he finished the soldering work on two sculpted metal boots. Sketches and diagrams were splayed out all over the worktable. No one else would have been able to figure out any of it. In Tony's case, it didn't matter what order they were in; they were just sitting out so that he wouldn't have to go dig them up. In point of fact, by this time he was carrying all the specifics around in his head.

"Still having trouble walking, sir?" Jarvis said.

"These aren't for walking."

Once he had finished the work on the boots and allowed them to cool, he lay down a test circle on the floor with pieces of tape. *Yeah, real high tech* he thought. He had wired the boots to a chest bandolier that was lined with sensor equipment to monitor and modulate the energy flow. He was holding hand-controlled joysticks in either hand.

"Ready to record the big moment, Jarvis?"

"All sensors ready, sir."

"We'll start off easy. Ten percent."

Tony activated the boots using the joysticks.

He had anticipated that he would get the same reaction off the boots as he had from the previous model: A slow buildup followed by rapid acceleration, all of which he was certain he could handle, especially since he was only operating it at ten percent of capacity.

Unfortunately Tony had badly miscalculated. All he knew was that one moment he was on the ground and the next he was hitting the ceiling. The instant he did so he lost his grip on the joysticks. That was actually a good thing. He had intended the joysticks to function as a dead man's switch. They operated as intended and the jet boots promptly shut off. As a result, he simply ricocheted off the ceiling rather than plowing through it. He wound up crash landing in a corner, knocking over a table and sending diagrams, schematics, and spare parts tumbling all over the workshop. He lay there for a moment, gasping for breath. As he did so, Jarvis calmly informed him: "That flight yielded excellent data, sir."

"Great," said Tony, experimentally flexing his lower body to make sure he wasn't paralyzed. "I, uhh, think I know what this needs."

As Tony approached the hangar at Edwards Air Force Base, he heard Rhodey's voice delivering a lecture. "Manned or unmanned: Which is the future of air combat?" Tony stopped at the doorway and watched quietly as Rhodey paced in front of a Global Hawk drone. Student pilots were assembled before him, watching him with rapt attention, all of them taking notes on pads and scribbling as quickly as they could.

"For my money, no drone, no computer, will ever trump a pilot's instincts," Rhodey said. "His reflexes, his judgment—"

Tony couldn't resist any longer. "Why not take it a step further? Why not—a pilot without the plane?"

He stepped forward and a grin split Rhodey's face. "That I'd like to see." He made a sweeping gesture toward Tony and announced to the class, "Look who fell out of the sky."

They turned as one and looked. A couple of them had blank expressions on their faces, but most of them reacted with astonishment and awe. Tony felt a twinge of pain: They reminded him of Jimmy and the other young soldiers who had lost their lives.

What the hell is wrong with me? It's bad enough that the previous chest reactor is tied up with memories of Yinsen. Is everything going to start reminding me of that hellhole?

Doing his damnedest to shake it off, Tony clapped his hands together briskly and said, inclining his head toward the drones, "Who wants to take these apart and put them back together?"

Several hands immediately shot up, but Rhodey said to the pilots, "All right, let's wrap it up."

The pilots got to their feet and trickled out of the hanger. A number of them stopped to shake Tony's hand, say "Good going," or otherwise congratulate him on his return to civilization when the popular opinion had been that he was done for. Tony nodded and smiled and accepted the accolades and agreed to sign a couple of autographs, even though Rhodey's glare at the autograph seekers indicated that there would be some payback for that.

Finally, when the last of the pilots had left, Rhodey shook Tony's hand and said, "I didn't think I'd be seeing you for a while."

"Why not?"

"Figured you'd need a little time."

Tony glanced heavenward as if seeking an answer from on high. "Why does everybody think I need time?"

"You've been through a lot," said Rhodey with a shrug. "Thought you should get your head straight."

"I've got it straight," Tony said insistently. "And I'm back to work."

Rhodey looked surprised. "Really?"

Tony dropped his voice and said softly, "I'm onto something big. I want you to be a part of it."

"I knew it," said Rhodey, thumping his fist into his open palm. "I knew when you said you were done with weapons systems, that it was just crazy talk."

"Rhodey . . ."

"Man, a lot of people around here will be happy to hear that. To hear that you're getting back in the old saddle. What you said at that press conference really threw everyone."

"I meant what I said."

That brought Rhodey up short. He spoke slowly, as if dealing with a raging drunkard who was insisting that he was stone-cold sober. "No, you didn't. You didn't mean that at all. You took a bad hit. It spun you around."

Tony stared at him for a long moment.

His heart grew cold.

What did you expect? He comes across like he's your friend. Maybe he even thinks he is. But what he sees you as, what he really sees you as, is a resource. A military resource. A means of providing new and exciting ways to kill people by the hundreds.

How do you explain it to him? How do you explain that what you've created until now has been the technological equivalent of broadswords, hacking through and annihilating guilty and innocent alike? That you're transforming yourself from a butcher into a surgeon, preparing the equivalent of a scalpel that will excise the brutes and bullies and monsters like Raza while leaving innocents untouched. The world is simply too complicated, and bigger and better boom-boom toys don't come close to providing answers. What you're doing, on the other hand, can make things better for everyone. You owe it to Yinsen, to his family, to all the people who have died whom you didn't give a damn about until now. How do you say all that to a man who's waiting for you to shake it off and hop right back into making bigger and better killing machines?

"Maybe I do need a little time," Tony said, giving no outward indication of everything that had been running through his mind.

Rhodey studied him for a moment and then nodded.

"All right, then." He patted Stark on the shoulder. "Good seeing you."

"Likewise."

Tony walked from the hangar, and he had already left Rhodey far behind in his thoughts. Instead he was dwelling on those old 1950s B movies that his father had always laughed at. Movies in which scientists would develop new and dangerous inventions and then would recklessly test them on themselves.

Tony Stark hadn't intended to be one of those. Upon realizing the power and potential of what he was developing, he reasoned that the best person to test it would be James Rhodes. After all, why in God's name should Tony—an amateur at best when it came to actual field-testing—be thrusting himself headlong into such conditions as these when Rhodey was an experienced hand? He'd figured he would bring Rhodey into the loop, show him everything that he had in mind, and James Rhodes, top test pilot, would get the honor and glory of being the first to operate Tony Stark's newest and greatest brainchild.

But by that point Tony had realized he had, once again, miscalculated. Rhodey's priorities lay with tapping Tony Stark's mind for one purpose and one purpose only: waging war. Rhodey was nothing but a cog in the vast war machine, and that wasn't what Tony needed. It wasn't what the suit needed.

Like a B movie scientist, Tony Stark realized that if anyone was going to be the subject of his experiments, it was going to have to be him. As he had said to Pepper: He had no one else.

xiv.

Tony was perfectly aware that Pepper had entered his workshop. He did not, however, say anything to her, although he did acknowledge her presence with a quick wave of his hand.

A week had passed since Tony's abortive visit to Edwards, and it had galvanized his efforts. Everything in the way Rhodey looked at him, the way he had reacted, convinced Tony that he was on the right track.

He didn't hold any hard feelings toward Rhodey. He was what he was: a military man. And a military man, well, he had a certain mindset that looked at the world one way and only one way, allowing nothing for variations. The irony was that Tony owed his life to that kind of thinking. It was Rhodey's one-track mind that had kept him looking for Tony Stark when so many others were convinced it was a dead end. Tony knew that he was indebted to the very sort of thinking he now considered limiting. *Classic double-edged sword,* he thought.

Night had fallen and Tony was working as aggressively on his new designs as he had been since he'd rolled out of bed that morning. He was "in the zone," as he was fond of saying. He was in the process of testing the prototype gauntlet that he'd devised. Clipping the gauntlet wires to the bandolier, he extended his arm and aimed it at the first thing that caught his eye: a toolbox.

The Repulsor technology had proven astoundingly versatile, and now he was endeavoring to expand its horizons yet again. A small raised circle set into the palm of the gauntlet glowed, and then emitted a controlled burst of Repulsor rays. The gauntlet absorbed the kickback of the rays, for even Tony Stark couldn't overcome the laws of action and reaction. But he wouldn't have cared in this instance if it had knocked him ass-over-teakettle, because the results were exactly what he'd hoped for: The toolbox tipped over, scattering wrenches all over the floor.

"Thought you were done with weapons."

Pepper's voice startled him. Playing it up, Tony grabbed at his chest, miming a heart attack. Pepper was standing in the shadows and now moved forward, and her mouth became a very thin line. She was not amused. Tony promptly stopped trying to mess around and instead said, "It's a flight stabilizer."

"Well, watch where you're pointing your flight stabilizer, would you?" She chucked a thumb over her shoulder. "Obadiah's upstairs. Should I tell him you're in?"

"Be right up."

She'd been holding a small package under her arm and she now laid it down upon the workbench. Tony looked at it curiously as he removed his gauntlets and then shifted his gaze to her, but she had already turned her back and walked out. Intrigued, he went over to it, hefted it, and then tore open the wrapping.

"I'll be damned," he murmured.

Pepper had taken the miniature reactor, dubbed it "Mark I," and mounted it on a Lucite stand. It was glowing faintly, as it was typically going to do: Left to its own devices, the glow would last years. There was an inscription on the Lucite. It read:

"Proof That Tony Stark Has A Heart."

He smiled and then chuckled softly. Trust Pepper to make a point in the most imaginative way possible.

He sat it down proudly on his worktable and headed upstairs.

* * *

Stane had "gotten" it.

Tony had been concerned. He had admitted it not only to himself, but had gone so far as to admit it to Stane as well. The fact that Rhodey had kneecapped him before he'd even managed to get the fundamental concepts across to him still rankled, and he'd been understandably cautious when he'd begun broaching the concept to Stane.

But Stane had warmed to it immediately. The moment Tony began talking, Stane was nodding. Moreover, Stane had gone out of his way to make Tony feel as comfortable discussing the project as possible. He'd done something as mundane as order in pizza. Tony had been talking nonstop from the moment Stane had placed the order until the guy had delivered it twenty minutes later (normally forty minutes, but it was amazing what a promise of a fifty-dollar tip could accomplish).

As Stane set the pizza down on the living room table, flipping open the lid, Tony continued to pace, propelled by such manic energy that he would probably have needed the gauntlets' kickback to slow him. "This, this is the big-big idea," he said. "It can pull the company in a whole new direction."

"That's great," said Stane. He'd been saying that, or variations on that, the entire time. *That's great, that's amazing, that's fantastic.* He was offering nothing but constant support of Tony's vision. Tony couldn't have asked for a better partner in his endeavors. "Get me the design as soon as you can. We've got a hungry production line that can knock out a prototype in days."

Tony looked at Stane and it was all he could do to choke back the emotion he was feeling. "You know, I had a moment there where I was . . . reluctant."

"Why? Because of what you told me about Rhodey's reaction?" When Tony nodded, Stane made a dismissive gesture. "Look, it's just like you told me. He wouldn't understand it. He's part of the war machine. He's not a man of vision."

"No. Not like us," said Tony. "But I know now I made the best decision. I feel like I'm doing something right. Finally. Thank you for supporting me in this." He grabbed Stane's right hand and shook it eagerly, so much so that he almost caused Stane to drop the slice of pizza he was holding in his left hand.

Stane squeezed Tony's hand in response, obviously moved by Tony's gratitude. Then something in his face changed. He looked apprehensive, as if he had to discuss something that Tony wasn't going to like. Sensing a shift in the mood, Tony released Stane's hand and waited. "Listen," said Stane. "I have something to talk to you about. I really wish you'd attended the last board meeting like I asked you to."

"I know, I'm sorry. What did I miss?"

"The board's filed an injunction against you."

It took a moment for Stane's words to process through Tony's stunned mind. When they finally did, Tony gasped, "What?"

Stane shrugged, as if he was bringing up something that was so ridiculous it barely warranted discussion, but nevertheless had to be hashed out. "They claim you're unfit to run the company and want to lock you out."

The world seemed to be swirling around Tony. He had been riding such a euphoric high, and now to be faced with this? With mutiny in the company that bore his name? Yes, what about that little fact? "How the hell can they do that? It's my name on the building. My ideas drive that company!"

"They're going to try," said Stane. His tone was calm. He could just as easily have been discussing the construction of an additional speed bump in the main driveway of Stark Industries. "We'll fight them, of course."

Tony was still having trouble comprehending how something like this could be happening. "With the amount of stocks we own, I thought we controlled the company?"

"I don't know. Somehow they pulled enough votes together." Stane appeared at a loss over how to explain it, and that alone was enough to jack up Tony's worry quotient. Stane was one of the canniest businessmen, the smoothest operators that Tony Stark had ever encountered. If Stane had been blindsided by this . . .

Stane leaned forward, clearly sympathetic to Tony's growing consternation. "Listen, the world doesn't share your vision, Tony. The more people have to lose, the more frightened they are of new ideas."

He had finished the slice of pizza and was now pouring two drinks from a bottle of aged Scotch. He slid one toward Tony. Tony stared at it. Once upon a time, he would have picked it up and tossed it back without giving it a second thought. Now he waved it off. Stane raised a surprised eyebrow. Then he shrugged and said to Tony, "Now listen, I don't want you to get all in knots. You know how many times I protected your father from the wolves?"

Tony nodded, but he still felt troubled over what Stane was telling him. How could things have gotten so far out of hand? Was Tony that inept a leader, or so incompetent that he'd been unable to convey to anyone the breadth of his vision? What the hell was happening? He felt unable to get a handle on the world.

Stane obviously saw the turmoil in Tony's eyes. He put a hand on Tony's shoulder in a fatherly gesture. "Get back to your lab and work some magic. You let me handle the board. Oh, and Tony? No more press conferences."

Tony nodded. "Okay. Fine. No more press conferences. Are you sure you can handle the board? Do you want me to come in and talk to them?"

"Better to let me be your public face to them. Tony, no offense, but if you square off against them, I'm worried you're going to come across as too vulnerable. That will just make things worse. To deal with these kinds of situations, you have to build up a pretty thick shell."

"That," said Tony Stark, "is exactly what I had in mind."

It was literally starting to come together.

The armor looked like a partially constructed human body, as if someone were building a person and there were sections that were completed, but others were still in process while the entire nervous system was on plain display. The suit consisted of Tony's stabilizer belt, partially chromed propulsion boots, gauntlets, and the entire shebang connected via a crazy quilt of tubing and wires. Tony fired up the boots, this time making sure to keep a firm control on the energy output (he had screwed up the input/output ratio in his first endeavor; that was what had bounced him off the ceiling like a squash ball).

The boots lifted him a few feet off the ground but he began to tilt wildly. He wasn't capable of keeping his body absolutely, unmovingly straight. He wasn't sure if anyone could, and the problem was that the slightest movement of a muscle caused him to tip. But he'd prepared for that, and he fired the Repulsor rays in the gauntlets to stabilize himself. He hung there for a moment in mid-air, weaving, tilting, as if he were surfing on waves of breeze. Slowly he began to get the hang of it, learning to compensate for whatever small movements or twitches his body might make that could impact his flight orientation. Once he had managed to build up his confidence somewhat, he started gliding around the lab, slowly at first but then picking up speed. He discovered that it only required minimal effort to glide himself around equipment and assorted pieces of furniture. He maneuvered his way through his car collection and only had near-hits. But he wound up not so much as chipping the paint job on any of them.

The only hitch was that the propulsive force of the jet boots was still formidable. As a result, the boots were knocking over small objects as he moved, just from the force of their blasts. But having to deal with a little bit of cleanup later was certainly a small price to pay for the power, the sheer joy of flight.

"Nothing to it," said Tony, as if he were doing something as simple as trotting up an escalator. He cut the propulsion, dropped to the floor, and stuck the landing. "Let's get to work."

It was a week later when Tony strode through his workshop, encased in the revised, updated, computer-assisted, Mark II–edition of the armor. It was far more form-fitting than the previous version, although rivets and seams were still visible. Ailerons and air brakes popped as Tony moved his head and arms, stretching, trying to get a feel for his new "body." When he had been in the process of developing it, he had come to think of it as an exoskeleton. It was more accurate, more . . . scientific, somehow. But now that he was wearing it, gazing out at the world through the narrow eyes of the helmet, it was what it was: armor.

The suit began to hum as it powered up. He flexed the arms, stretched the legs. Then, just as an experiment, he bent over and touched his toes. No problem there. The suit was far more flexible than the first model. Certainly it was more comfortable and maneuverable. There was still a degree of awkward clanking involved, but in the first armor—by contrast to this one—he'd felt as if he were twenty feet underwater, trying to wade forward across a spongy ocean floor while manacles were attached to his ankles. Here he could actually walk.

But why walk when one could fly?

"Stand by for calibration," he said to Jarvis.

"Standing by, sir."

Tony fired up the gauntlets and boots and, just as he had a week earlier, rose from the ground. He prepared to steady himself as he did so.

Unfortunately he had not accounted for the accelerated strength that the armor provided him. When he'd simply been wearing the gauntlets and boots, he had been maneuvering with his own muscle power. Wearing the armor, every movement was accentuated and heightened. As a result, when he moved his arms to balance himself as he had a week earlier, he flipped himself over and crashed.

Even more unfortunately, his gleaming silver Saleen S7 was between him and the floor. He slammed down on the hood, crushing it and setting off the car alarm. Tony stumbled off the car, automatically tried to reach into his pocket to get the keys and disengage the alarm, and discovered the obvious flaw in that plan. Annoyed, he raised his gauntlet and fired off a quick blast of his Repulsor ray at what was left of the hood. The blast took out the alarm, along with the carburetor, the ignition, and the fan belt.

"Swell," muttered Tony, and then he said, "We should take this outside."

"I must strongly caution against that," Jarvis's disembodied voice cautioned him. "There are terabytes of calculations still needed."

Considering that Tony's previous venture in road testing armor involved wading through a barrage of machine gun fire and crash landing in a forbidding desert, he wasn't especially daunted by the prospect of tera-bytes of calculations still needed. "We'll do them in-flight."

"Sir, the suit has not even passed a basic wind-tunnel test."

Tony Stark, the living crash-test dummy. "That's why you're coming with me. Load yourself into the HUD."

Within the helmet, readouts were projected against the lenses that covered the eyeholes and they provided Tony with a constant stream of information about both his own body and the performance of the armor. The technical term for it was "Heads-Up Display," or HUD. As Jarvis did as instructed, downloading his monitoring capabilities and observational protocol into the armor, Tony reignited the boots and gauntlets. This time he was careful enough to maintain an even keel, and the armor floated him down the driveway that led out of the work-shop.

"I suggest you allow me to employ Directive Four," said Jarvis.

" 'Never interrupt me while I'm with a beautiful woman?' "

"That's Directive Six. Directive Four: 'Use any and all means to protect your life should you be incapable of doing so.' "

Tony shrugged, although the gesture would not have been visible to someone looking at him. "Whatever floats you, Jarvis."

Moments later, Tony emerged from the workshop. The night sky beckoned to him. He rose slowly, taking his time, but quickly began to gain confidence and move faster. The confidence was short-lived, however, as he discovered yet again that even the smallest movements altered his trajectory in unexpected ways. This was the exact sort of thing that Rhodey would have been perfect for. The far-more-experienced pilot would have had a faster learning curve. But Tony realized there was no point in thinking along those lines. Rhodey was out; Stark was in. It was as simple and straightforward as that.

At least the HUD was helping him. It flashed on a pitch-and-yaw display with crosshairs that enabled him to anticipate when he was starting to go off track. He started developing the ability to course correct before it had a noticeable impact on his trajectory. The HUD also continued to give him a steady stream of altitude, power levels and vital signs monitoring.

But the horizon was still tilting in a disorienting fashion more often than he would have liked. He experimented for a time, trying to find the ideal balance that would provide him the maximum amount of control. Eventually he discovered a combination of jet and gauntlet booster angularity that enabled him to fly straight and true. Just like that, he was in complete control of his trajectory.

He angled down along the ribboning concrete of the Pacific Coast Highway, curious to see whether he could follow it. He found that he was able to do so, matching the twists and curve of the road effortlessly. He could also see that cars were slowing, people far below sticking their heads out their windows or gaping straight up courtesy of the lowered roofs of their convertibles. Doubtless people were yanking out their cell phones to try and snap pictures of the bizarre UFO that was cruising through the skies. He wasn't concerned; he'd be long gone before anyone could even begin to focus anything on them. He would be, at most, a blur, less useful than that grainy picture of Bigfoot.

He stretched out his left hand, which countered his direction, sending him hurtling out toward the Pacific Ocean. He let out a long, delirious whoop, like a kid on a roller coaster. For months he had been staring at death and that pall had hung over him ever since he came back. For the first time in ages—perhaps the first time in his life—he felt truly alive.

The waves flashed by him, fifty feet below. For an instant he considered the prospect of just going and going, perhaps winding up in Hawaii, lying on a beach, sunning himself and sipping frosty cocktails while hula girls gyrated around him. Then the more practical aspects of such a prospect presented themselves: He'd run out of power long before he got to Hawaii, crash into the ocean, and sink like a rock. And even if he made it there, he'd never get any kind of decent tan inside the armor.

So instead he arced high into the air, pulling a loop-de-loop before angling back toward the California coastline. He saw the Santa Monica Pier ahead of him and angled toward it. There was a kid in a Ferris wheel, and his eyes went wide with shock as Tony hurtled past him. Tony wondered whether the kid would tell anyone, or figure that it was smarter to keep his mouth shut lest he be called a liar or an idiot or both.

The moon hung high above him, full and ripe, reaching out to him, summoning him. Tony accepted the invitation, flying straight upward, an armored bird on the wing. Ice crystals began to form on his mask as he continued his ascent. He paid them no mind. The moon was calling to him.

Could I make it that high? Seriously? Would it be possible? How close could I come?

Visions of standing on the moon, facing the American flag that had been planted by men wearing suits that were as primitive compared to his as a caveman's club was to an M-16, filled his thoughts. Beneath his helmet he grinned foolishly, caught up in his visions. A small part of his brain tried to shout at him, gain his attention, and inform him that he wasn't thinking straight. That he was caught up in some sort of flight-related euphoria that could undercut, even ruin the entire experiment. He paid it no mind. His thoughts were elsewhere.

Jarvis's voice came in through his helmet, giving real-world voice to the internal ones that Tony was ignoring. "Power: fifteen percent. Recommend you descend and recharge, sir." When Tony didn't respond, Jarvis said, "Acknowledge, Mr. Stark."

Tony, intoxicated as the moon beckoned, did not acknowledge. His mind was a million miles away, or, more technically, two hundred and thirty-eight thousand miles away. He didn't notice as all the indicators in his HUD began flashing red. His armor was doing everything to warn him short of punching him in the face repeatedly with a spring-loaded boxing glove, and still he didn't notice.

"Power at five percent," Jarvis told him coldly. "Threshold breached."

The armor, the running lights, almost the entire HUD suddenly went dark. That was finally sufficient to snap Tony from his reverie. The only illumination the HUD was displaying was being powered by the emergency backups, and all it said was, "System shut down." Fortunately that was sufficient to regain Tony's complete and undivided attention.

"Uhh, Jarvis? *Jarvis?*"

No answer.

The jet boots fritzed out and died, and the gauntlets had nothing to offer. The suit was a dead hulk; for all the control he had over the situation, he might just as well have sealed himself up inside a barrel and had it thrown over Niagara Falls. Actually, the barrel would have been preferable; he might at least have had an outside chance of surviving that fall.

He plummeted toward the Earth in total freefall, the world pinwheeling around him. He plunged through the clouds and continued down, down. The lights of the downtown Los Angeles grid spread out far below him, so far away that it almost seemed irrelevant to his predicament. But he was falling fast and gaining speed (*thirty-two feet per second,* his mind told him, *which means that you should reach terminal velocity in—yeah, okay, can we think about something else that doesn't involve the word "terminal"?*).

"Status, status!" Tony was shouting. "Reboot!"

There was a series of popping noises, a surge, a sputter. The power cut out again, and then suddenly flared back to life. Energy surged through the suit.

"Temporary power restored," Jarvis said, and there was a faint scolding in his tone. "Descend immediately."

Tony worked the boosters to get the suit back under control, and it was only at that point that he suddenly realized the suit hadn't failed him at all; Jarvis had shut it down. He was unable to comprehend why in God's name Jarvis would do something like that, but then he started running the events of the last few minutes through his head. He recalled, as if it was being related to him secondhand, Jarvis's voice urging him to return to Earth, trying to get his attention while Tony's attention had been elsewhere.

Even so.

"Jarvis, I think we need to chat about, uh, Directive Four."

"May I remind you, sir," Jarvis said stiffly, "the suit feeds off the same power source as your life support. A zero drain of energy will likely kill you."

"You're a downer, Jarvis." Tony sighed. "But I appreciate the heads-up."

The onboard GPS aided Tony in making it back to his estate, which was a bit more of a chore than he would have expected. Then again, he wasn't exactly accustomed to finding his way home while a thousand feet in the air. He angled himself around so that he was standing and descended toward the workshop driveway. Some stiff wind gusts and a few sputters from the armor, however, were making it difficult for him to hold the stance. He started drifting off course.

"Shall I take over?" said Jarvis.

"No, I got it. I got it—"

As it turned out, he didn't have it. He closed the distance between himself and the ground faster than he thought he would, and as a result punched right through the roof of his mansion. He tried to reverse course but failed to do so. Instead he kept going, smashing through the foyer ceiling in his living room, down through the floor, and continued into the workshop where he smashed into the Shelby Cobra that was parked next to the wrecked Saleen.

As all the cars chorused with their howling alarms, Tony unlatched the helmet and yanked it off. He surveyed the damage. Then, unaccountably cheerful, he shouted over the alarms, "Perfect. Let's do some upgrades."

Minutes later he had shucked the armor and was seated at his computer terminal, typing as quickly as he could. The screens were alive with scrolling data graphics and diagnostic tests. He'd turned on the plasma TV primarily so that he could have some low-level noise in the background. Helped him focus.

"That was quite dangerous, sir," said Jarvis. "Might I remind you, if the suit loses power, so does your heart."

"Yeah, and it doesn't have a seat belt either." He scratched his chin thoughtfully. "A few issues: Main transducer felt sluggish at plus-forty altitude. Same goes for hull pressurization. I'm thinking icing might be a factor."

"The suit isn't rated for high altitude. You're expending eight-percent power just heating and pressurizing."

Tony gave that a moment's thought, and then said,

"Reconfigure using the gold titanium alloy from the Seraphim Tactical Satellite. It should ensure fuselage integrity to fifty thousand feet while maintaining power-to-weight ratio."

"Shall I render, utilizing proposed specifications?"

Tony sat back in his chair and interlaced his fingers. "Wow me."

He focused on the center screen as a new design began to appear. The words "Mark III prototype" glowed at the top of the screen. Work that would have taken Tony Stark days, if not weeks, using pencils and paper, required no more than ninety seconds for Jarvis.

The armored figure seemed to be staring at him, a gleaming solid-gold image.

"Hmm. Bit ostentatious, don't you think?"

"Ostentatious?"

"Yeah. All gold. It's a little too C-3PO for me. Either that or movie stars will want to start thanking the Academy every time they see me." He glanced over at his gleaming crimson motorcycle and found inspiration there. "Add a little red, would you?"

Then he became distracted by what he was seeing on the television. It was a local entertainment reporter standing outside Disney Hall. Tony picked up his remote control and kicked up the volume.

"Tonight's red-hot red carpet is here at the Walt Disney Hall, where Tony Stark's third-annual benefit for the Firefighters' Family Fund has become the go-to charity gala on L.A.'s high-society calendar. But this great cause is only part of the story—"

All around Tony the lab sprang to life as Jarvis activated various high-powered pieces of machinery. As the noise level elevated, Tony increased the television volume.

"The man whose name graces the gold-lettered invitations hasn't been seen in public since his highly controversial press conference, and rumors abound," the reporter was saying. "Some say Stark is suffering from post-traumatic stress and hasn't left his bed in weeks."

They're only saying that because they weren't looking up tonight.

Tony returned his attention to the computer monitor. The armor had now been recolored as per his instructions. The leggings, sleeves, and faceplate remained gold, while the boots, torso, gauntlets, and back of the helmet were red. It was a solid color combination.

"The work could take until morning to complete, sir," said Jarvis.

"Good. I should come up for air anyway." He leaned forward and smiled. "People should start having a positive image of Tony Stark for a change. I'm tired of being the black hole of rumors."

There was a black hole in the armor that had housed Tony Stark when he'd been making his escape from his captors. Light had once glowed from it. No longer. It represented the lifelessness of the weapon that had sent Raza's men scattering and annihilated their entire ammo dump.

That glowing light, however, was the only thing that was missing.

Raza watched, mesmerized, as his men pieced together the entire suit. He envisioned himself wearing it. He envisioned all his men wearing identical armored suits, smashing through troops, laughing off bullets.

He envisioned crushing Tony Stark's head beneath an armored boot of Stark's own design.

It was good to be a man of vision.

XV.

The scene outside the Disney Concert Hall was a typical Hollywood affair, crowded with stars, kingmakers, political figures, and army brass. The hilarious thing—at least to Tony Stark, who was gazing out the windshield of his Audi R8 as it approached—was that all of them seemed fascinated with one another. The brass was fascinated by the movie stars, while the movie stars in turn were fawning over the high profile political hotshots. And the kingmakers lorded it over all, equally worshipped by everyone except, of course, other kingmakers, who saw them merely as rivals or opponents to be taken down.

What was to mere mortals a swarm of glitterati and excitement was, to the eyes of Tony Stark, a massive web of competing goals, preening personalities, and a constant attempt to see where strands of power could be snagged and pulled to one's advantage.

God, he'd missed this.

There was a huge banner proclaiming the gathering to be for the purpose of the Firefighters' Family Fund. It had always been a pet project of Howard Stark's, and Tony had proudly taken up the reins when his father had passed. Since that time, the fund's activities—including the gala that Tony had instituted—had swollen beyond anything that Howard could have conceived. Tony would have liked to take credit for it, but the sad truth was that the annihilation of the World Trade Center, and the many valiant firefighters who had perished in the aftermath of that heinous act of terrorism, put the fund on the map in a way that even Tony's most imaginative efforts never could.

He caught sight of Obadiah Stane surrounded by various celebrities and near-celebrities, has-beens, and never-wases, perhaps hoping to have their moment in the sun if they stayed near Stane long enough. There were always going to be those who needed to bask in reflected glory.

Attendants were parking cars as quickly as they could, as each car pulled up to curbside. Tony, however, was growing tired of waiting. He gunned the Audi around the lengthy string of cars waiting to get in and roared to the front of the line. The parking attendant jumped back as the Audi rolled up to curbside. Horns immediately started honking in protest, and even Stane looked in the direction of the Audi. There was stunned disbelief on Stane's face; Tony reasoned that Stane must have spotted the license plate reading "STARK 4."

Tony swung open the car door, stepped out, and tossed off a wave to the line of honking cars behind him. Instantly the honking stopped as drivers yanked out their camera phones and started snapping pictures.

He flipped the keys over to the attendant, winked, and then strode toward the crowd. All eyes, all cameras, everything had turned away from Stane and was now pointed in Stark's direction. Photographers were snapping away as fast as they could while television news reporters deliriously spoke into their cameras lenses as if Elvis had just shown up. To some degree, he had.

Tony spotted a familiar older man wearing a red smoking jacket, surrounded by three equally smoking women. The older man's back was to him, but the style and entourage typical of Hugh Hefner was unmistakable. Tony walked up to the renowned playboy, slapped him on the back, and said, "There he is. My man."

The older man turned around to face him. It wasn't Hefner. It was someone else . . . some guy that Tony didn't recognize, although he thought he recalled the old fella being connected to comic books in some way. "Sorry. Thought you were someone else."

"I certainly am someone else," the older man said. He pumped out a fist and declared loudly, "Excelsior!"

"Pleasure to meet you, Mr. Excelsior," said Tony. He shook his hand and walked away, not noticing the man's bewildered expression, as he headed over to Stane. Stane looked as if he had no idea how to react, a half-dozen expressions warring for dominance. Tony didn't give him time to make up his mind, walking up to him and draping an arm around his shoulders. He waved to the cameras and they obligingly fired away.

"What are you doing here?" Stane said in such a low voice that he obviously hoped to avoid microphones picking them up. "I thought you were going to lie low?"

"It's time to start showing my face again."

"Let's just take it slow, okay? I got the board right where we want them."

"Great."

He could understand why Stane was nervous. With the board on edge, he was terrified that Tony would say something that would push them right over. But Tony knew he'd never promised he'd lie low; he'd just said there wouldn't be any more press conferences. Fair enough.

Television reporters were already shouting questions at him, but Tony blew them off with a casual wave of his hand and a "See ya inside. Lots to talk about." With that he walked right past them, up the red carpet. They continued to hurl questions at him. He imagined himself back in his armor, the questions bouncing off him like bullets and leaving no trace. Now, that was the sort of positive thinking he could get behind.

Entering the main ballroom where the gala was being held was like stepping back into another time, a more elegant time. A formal band, attired in perfectly turned-out tuxedos, was playing "Begin the Beguine" while equally well-dressed people were dancing in the middle of the room. Tony moved through the room, nodding to some people, saying a few words to others, shaking the hands of the startled men and kissing the knuckles of the thoroughly charmed women. Each and every person looked astounded and pleased to see him. He reasoned that he shouldn't be surprised about that. The newspapers and television programs had painted him as being two sleeves away from a straitjacket. They probably all thought that if Tony Stark were to show up in public, he'd be frothing at the mouth or perhaps hauling all his possessions in a large paper bag while wearing an aluminum foil hat to prevent Martians from reading his brainwaves. That he was here, now, clearly sane, with his act together, as charming and rational as any one of them (and more so than a good percentage of them), could only be seen as a sign of good things to come.

Tony made his way toward the bar. Even those people he didn't stop to talk to were whispering his name. He'd always been impressed how easy it was to pick out one's own name when it was spoken, even if it was in the middle of a crowd of people talking about a hundred different things. The ancients believed that names had power, and perhaps they were on to something, for his attention was always going to be drawn whenever someone said—

"Mr. Stark!"

He turned and saw a tall man with thinning hair heading toward him. He wore a tuxedo the way a fish wore tennis shoes. Apparently he thought that sporting a tux would enable him to blend in. That was, to put it mildly, a mistake on his part.

"Agent Coulson," said the man without preamble.

Tony ran the name through his mental Rolodex. Nothing was coming up. If Pepper had mentioned the guy to him, he'd simply expunged it from his mind as not being worth his time. "Was I supposed to meet you here?"

"No, but you haven't been returning my calls. This is serious. We need to get something on the books or I will have to insist through more official means, if I make myself clear."

Coulson no doubt considered that to be a formidable threat. It might indeed have been, were Tony Stark listening to him.

As it happened, he wasn't. Not in the least.

His attention was focused on the graceful, curving stairway that led into the main section of the room, for coming down those stairs was Pepper Potts, who had never looked more elegant in her life. At least not for as long as Tony Stark had known her. She was clad in a stunning white classic gown, her strawberry blond hair hanging loose and cascading around her shoulders. He had to look twice just to make certain he was seeing what he thought he was seeing.

It took him a moment to remember that the irritating government guy was still standing there. "Yes, you're right," said Tony, patting him on the chest. "I'm going to handle this right now. Let me . . . make a date with my assistant and get back to you." Whereupon he walked quickly away, almost sprinting, leaving Coulson with his mouth hanging open and a question framed on his lips that would never be answered or even heard.

Pepper wasn't looking Tony's way as he approached her. No reason she should be. She wasn't expecting him to be there. So she blinked in surprise when she turned and discovered her boss standing less than two feet away. "Miss Potts, can I have five minutes?"

She looked around for some reason, clearly confused. "You're . . . you're here?"

"Well, my name is on the invitations, so I figured I should be checking them at the door. Wouldn't want any of the wrong crowd to sneak in. You look . . ." He tried to maintain the glib air that he so typically favored, but was unable to do so. Instead he dropped the posturing and allowed sincerity to float to the surface. "You look like you should always wear that dress."

"Thanks," she said and smiled, clearly gratified. "It was a birthday present, from you."

"I have great taste," he said with a shrug, as if that were the most obvious statement in the world. "Care to dance?"

He didn't give her time to say "no" or even think about it as he took her hand and whisked her out onto the dance floor. She let out a startled *eep* as he did so and then he swung her around in a flawlessly executed ballroom move. Then he stopped, standing perfectly still, and drew her to him. He held the pose for just the right amount of time, and then gracefully started to move. His feet glided across the floor, and she followed his lead. But she was stiff, tentative, and it concerned him.

"I'm sorry," he said. "Am I making you uncomfortable? You seem very uncomfortable."

"No, I always forget to wear deodorant . . ."

"You smell great."

"—and dance with my boss in front of everyone I've ever worked with in a chiffon dress."

He smiled ingratiatingly. "Would it help if I fired you?"

"You wouldn't last a week without me."

"I'm not so sure."

"What's your social security number?"

He paused. He even stopped dancing as he pondered it. God knew he'd filled it out enough times on various college documents. One would think that would have drilled it into him. Finally he said, "Five."

"I think you're missing about eight digits. It's 527—"

"Point taken, Miss Potts."

He had to smile at the look of triumph that glittered in her eyes, and a moment later she shared that smile. They continued to dance, and from that point on she moved in a more relaxed manner. She even seemed to be enjoying it.

Lord knew he was. It was almost frightening to Tony how much he was enjoying it. On some level he found that absurd, that he was undaunted over the prospect of hurling himself into the upper atmosphere clad in an iron sheathe but was intimidated by just how much of a good time he was having with a simple dance.

Well, maybe that's it, isn't it? Maybe the dance isn't as simple as all that. Maybe there's more going on here than you care to admit. Than either of you care to admit.

Those thoughts continued to occupy his mind as he danced again with Pepper, and then—at her request, anxious "for some air"—they exited the hall and headed out onto the veranda. Tony had stopped to get her a glass of wine and she was holding it now. The stars glittered above them, and there was, of course, the moon as well. Tony felt a brief tug, the siren call, but then Pepper's arm interlocked through his at the elbow and brought him forcefully, and gratefully, back down to Earth.

"I'm sorry I was so uncomfortable," she said. "I hate being the center of attention like that and that's why this one time in high school when I was supposed to be in a play . . ."

Tony tilted his head, amused. Pepper was always the

picture of total efficiency and poise, so it was delightful to him that she found herself disarmed by the situation. She was clearly aware of both her feeling of social disorientation and his enjoying it, as she continued, "No, never mind." The words and thoughts were pouring out of her now. She seemed as if she wanted to stop talking, but couldn't find a way to do so, and so she kept babbling. "But you know that's why I never wanted to have a big wedding, you know, because I thought everyone would be looking at me wearing a dress." Her eyes widened as she suddenly thought that she came across as if she were expecting Tony Stark to pop the question. "Oh, no, no—I'm not saying, like, 'wedding.' No, not like that. I'm just saying, you know . . ."

He decided to stop the outpouring of emotion and thoughts through the most reasonable, and preferable, means possible. He drew her to him to kiss her. He expected her to pull away. She didn't. Instead she practically melted into it.

But at the last possible instant, they stopped. They gazed into each other's eyes, their lips millimeters apart, and then the moment passed. Tony pulled back, clearing his throat, and tried to figure out what to say next. He noticed that the glass she was holding was nearly empty and opted for something fairly safe to say to her until he could regroup. "Can I get you another glass of wine?"

"A vodka martini, extra dry, with extra olives as soon as possible."

He blinked. "Okay."

He took the glass from her and started to head off the veranda. He was stopped, however, when she said, "And, Tony—" He turned, paused, waited for her to complete the thought. "I'm not a cheeseburger," she said.

Tony hadn't been sure what she was going to say, but

that certainly hadn't been it. Still, he could see why she would. "No," he agreed. "You're not a cheeseburger."

With that settled, or at least as settled as it was going to be, he went back out to the bar. The party had built slowly, but now it was definitely in full swing. Getting to the bar took Tony far longer than he'd thought as well-wishers and fans stopped him every couple of feet to congratulate him on his still being alive. None of them identified themselves as being irate stockholders. Certainly none of them were rude enough to ask him if he'd lost his mind. He was relieved at that, considering how many other people seemed obsessed with the state of his sanity.

Having finally managed to acquire two more drinks, Tony turned to head back to Pepper and came to a dead halt. Standing directly in his path was Christine Everhart. Attired in a red cocktail dress and wielding her tape recorder, she looked rather fetching—in a mercilessly, predatory sort of way.

"Mr. Stark! I was hoping I could get a reaction from you."

Tony forced a smile. "How's 'panic'?" he suggested.

She smiled thinly. "I was referring to your company's involvement in this latest atrocity."

The glib "panic" comment from an instant before was becoming more than just a joke. Obviously in the way she was talking and looking at him, something was going on to which he wasn't privy. He knew he was about to get broadsided, and wasn't the least bit happy about the fact that he had absolutely no clue as to what it might be about. But he certainly wasn't about to admit to any of that. Opting to stick with glib, he shrugged as if he had totally misunderstood her intent and, indicating the party around them, said, "Hey, they just put my name on the invitations."

He knew she was going to lower whatever boom she

had to lower upon hearing that, and he was not wrong. She thrust a dossier of photos out to him. "Is this what you call accountability?"

He looked at the photos, trying to brace himself. He barely managed to succeed. He went stone-faced; if he'd been wearing his helmet, the faceplate would have displayed more emotion.

It was photos of Raza's insurgents. He recognized more than a few of them. The insignia of those damned ten rings were plastered across their vehicles if there had been any shred of doubt left. And the vehicles were shown plowing through a town that was a disaster area of flame and destruction. The insurgents were wielding machine guns that were clearly marked with the Stark logo, and they had Stark RPGs as well.

More photos. He felt as if nightmare images—all the things he'd imagined when Yinsen had described the destruction that Stark weaponry had inflicted on helpless villagers—had been plucked from his mind and brought to 8×10 glossy life. Civilians were being marched in rows toward walls that were already pockmarked with bullet holes and bloodstains. These were peasants being prepared for execution, and Stark weapons were being jabbed into their backs, forcing them to their miserable fates.

He barely recognized his own voice as he spoke. It sounded mechanical, robotic. "When were these taken?" he said, praying that they were from last year, from even six months ago. God, let them be old news, made moot by his change in direction for his company.

"Yesterday. In a village called Gulmira. I'm sure that it's too small for someone like you to have heard of."

Yinsen, he thought bleakly. *Yinsen's home . . . oh God . . .*

"Good P.R. move," said Christine, jabbing forward mercilessly. She could just have easily been one of the pieces of shrapnel that was trying to shred his heart, and there was no magnetic generator in the world that could pull her away. "You tell the world you're a changed man. Even I believed you." She sounded disgusted with herself that she had been taken in. *Join the club, sweetheart. What I did to you months ago with your consent, someone just did to me and I still had my pants on.*

"I didn't approve this shipment."

"Well, your company did."

"Come with me" was all he said.

Whatever it was that she was expecting him to say, it certainly hadn't been that. Without waiting for her to say anything further, Tony turned away from her and made a beeline for the red carpet up front.

Stane's words of caution about not causing a scene, keeping a low profile, and for God's sake no press conference, all echoed in his thoughts. But they were also drowned out by a furious pounding in his head.

No. It wasn't just a pounding. It was a screaming, and it wasn't his own voice. It was his imagining the cries of those people suffering, dying, thanks to the weapons that he had manufactured.

We're iron mongers was what Stane had said to him. *No, Obadiah. We're bloody bastards, and someone's going to have to stop the hemorrhaging.*

Tony strode straight down the red carpet as if he owned it—which he did—and headed toward the paparazzi who had their cameras ready. Christine was desperately trying to keep up with him, but she had fallen significantly behind, high heels not being conducive to footraces. In a loud voice, Tony said briskly, knowing that in speaking to the press his words were going to be carried to the entirety of the world, "I made some promises I'm not going to be able to keep. I suggest you pull all your money out of Stark Industries immediately."

Stane was suddenly there. Tony had no idea where he'd come from or how he'd gotten there so fast. Was Stane present the entire time or—even more chilling a prospect—had he been keeping an eye on Tony and made a point of sprinting after him the moment Tony looked like he was about to make a scene? Before Tony could even ask, Stane was steering him away from the assembled press and back up toward the entrance steps. "Is this like a tic for you?" said Stane. "Some sort of nervous tic? Whenever you have a feeling, you start going to all the people who don't trust you, who don't protect you." He pointed at the press who were fruitlessly shouting questions at Tony's retreating figure. "They're going to put a spin on everything you say!"

Tony was so furious that he found that anger transmuting into, of all things, giddiness. He couldn't say what he wanted to Stane because if he did so—if he started tapping into the roiling emotions associated with the death and destruction that he'd caused, the blood that was on his hands—he sensed that he was simply going to lose it. That was all. Just lose it. Have a complete and total meltdown right there on the steps of Disney Hall, and it was going to wind up on YouTube with a half a million hits inside of twenty-four hours.

But somehow he had to deal with what he was feeling. He had to. Operating in what only could be termed self-defense, his brain cross-wired itself and jumped straight to non sequitur. "Wait a minute. I got to ask you something. I'm dead serious about this," said Tony, and his voice dropped to an *entrez-nous* level. "I'm not kidding. Am I losing my mind, or is Pepper really cute? Do you think she's attractive and interesting, or is it just that her hair is down? I've been out of the game for a while."

Stane wouldn't be distracted. "Are you out of your mind?" he said. His voice rose, clearly more than he would have liked, and he fought to bring it down to a manageable level, obviously keenly aware that the microphones had considerable range. "You're messing with the 'guys in the rooms'! We're talking about billion-dollar interests, the world order—"

"I'm not worried about that right now."

"You should be. You'll disappear. I can't protect you against people like that."

Suddenly there were flashes in their faces. The photographers had literally crossed the line, sneaking in close to snap more photographs. Stane rounded on them, tossing aside any semblance of self-control, and bellowed, "Do you mind!" They fell back, although not far, as Stane grabbed Tony by the elbow and pulled him further up the stairs.

"Tony, don't be so naive."

"Naive?" Tony knew he was on the verge of losing it. He couldn't hold on to the glibness, to the carefree manner that he was desperately affecting to cover the turmoil in his soul. The pulsing anger crept into his voice and he was making no effort to hide it, although, interestingly, the angrier he got, the softer his voice became. "I was naive before, when I was growing up, and they told me, Don't ever cross this line, this is how we do business. In the meantime we're double-dealing under the table. We don't even deserve to represent the United States—"

"Tony, you're a child!" said Stane, sounding like the disappointed father figure Tony knew he was.

Such words coming from Stane would have stung Tony deeply once upon a time. But it was a funny thing—when one spends months where every day could bring violent demise, and one has witnessed carnage and death and even caused some of it, harsh words somehow didn't have the impact they once might have. "You don't believe I can turn this company around, do you?" said

Tony, sounding no less disappointed in Stane than Stane was in him.

"You've got about as much control over things as a child riding in the backseat of your father's car with a red plastic steering wheel in your hand."

Tony was seeing Stane's words no longer as opinion, but merely a tactic to try and make him feel small, puny, and helpless. It wasn't going to work. Tony Stark had known true helplessness, and when it came to inflicting that sensation, Obadiah Stane was a rank amateur compared to Raza and his crew. Instead he said easily, unperturbed, "Maybe I'll just get out of the car."

"You're not even allowed in the car." Stane paused and abruptly played the one card that Tony was not prepared for: "I'm the one who's filing the injunction against you."

Tony was paralyzed with shock. The capper was what Stane said next, as if he and Tony were remotely on the same side or shared the same priorities anymore: "It's the only way I could protect you."

Stane had clearly had enough of providing fodder for the press. His men gathered in a circle around him, bundling him toward his car. Staying behind on the steps, Tony pointed at him and shouted, "This is going to stop!" But the words sound empty, even to his own ear, a hollow threat from a helpless child.

His mind filled with turmoil, he barely remembered the next few minutes. Functioning entirely on autopilot, he had his car brought around and tore out of there so fast that he left tire marks.

The moment he got home he went straight to his workshop, throwing himself into it for solace. No, not just for solace: for protection. It was like a return to the womb for him, the only place in the world where he felt totally safe. The newly minted armor pieces were waiting for him, and he promptly started putting them through their paces. He had wired up the Mark III gauntlet to his chest piece and was studying the power levels. Not satisfied with what he saw, he made minute adjustments with a screwdriver and finally nodded in approval. The flatscreen TV on the wall behind him was carrying the latest news feed. It was describing the ongoing tragedy unfolding in the small, war-torn postage stamp of a village called Gulmira.

"The ten-mile drive to the outskirts of Gulmira can only be described as a descent into Hell," intoned the voice of the on-air reporter. "Into a modern-day *Heart of Darkness*. Simple farmers and herders, from peaceful villages, driven from their homes at the butt of Western rifles and the turrets of modern tanks. Displaced from their lands by warlords and insurgent groups emboldened by their newfound power—a power fueled by high-tech weapons easily purchased with poppy money, further destabilizing a fragile region that for decades has been a tinderbox of tribal feuding and ethnic hatred."

Each word cut into Tony as he wondered how many of those Western rifles and modern tanks had come through his factory. He aimed the gauntlet at an overhead light fixture and unleashed a blast. The fixtures sparked, shattered, and fell from the ceiling.

"The villagers have taken shelter in whatever crude dwellings they can find—in the ruins of other razed villages, in the cold barren scrublands, or in the remnants of an old Soviet smelting plant. Our translator relayed to us one human tragedy after another. A seven-year-old boy, thin as a scarecrow, clutching yellowed photographs and holding them out to anyone who would stop, with a child's simple question: 'Where are my mother and father?' A woman, begging for news of her husband, who'd been kidnapped by insurgents—either forced to join their militia, or shot without reason."

He wondered if any accompanying images were appearing on the screen and couldn't bring himself to look. Instead, he adjusted the gauntlet again, jacking up the power level. He aimed at a window in the lab and fired. The impact blew the window to fragments and knocked a painting from the wall. It was pure, mindless destruction, and it was a mirror of the self-loathing that he was feeling. He was taking out his pain on himself.

"With no political will or international pressure, there is little hope for these new refugees. Refugees who can only wonder two things: Is the world watching, and who, if anyone, will help?"

Tony swept the gauntlet around and fired straight at the plasma television. The screen blew apart. He didn't flinch as pieces of it tumbled all around him. He just stood there for a long time and watched it smoking.

He disconnected the gauntlet, removed it, and then started gathering the armor pieces. He had designed them to be flexible, even collapsible. He pulled out a specially designed storage container, about the size of a large suitcase, and loaded in the armor. His mind was racing with everything that needed to be done, and he had just finished stowing the armor when he heard a soft clearing of a throat from the door.

He turned and saw Pepper standing there, and it was only at that moment that he realized he'd completely forgotten about her. The last thing she'd known, he'd gone off to get her a drink after a dance that was borderline romantic, and she hadn't seen him again. Whereas she had been shining in the environment of the gala, here, in her beautiful chiffon gown, she looked woefully out of place.

She looked around the shambles of a workshop, trying to keep her face impassive. She regarded the shattered lights, the destroyed TV screen. Then she glanced

up and saw the gaping holes in the ceiling. Her only reaction was a carefully arched eyebrow. Whatever was
going through her mind, whatever anger she was no
doubt feeling toward Tony Stark at that moment, she
was far too professional to put it on display. Instead she
spoke in a flat voice that only suggested mild curiosity,
as if she were asking which necktie he was planning to
wear next time he went out. "Are you going to tell me
what's going on?"

For all that she was containing her emotions, it was
nothing compared to Tony. He was positively stoic, his
voice hollow. He offered no apologies for running out
on her, no explanations for the disaster area that his
workshop had transformed into. All he said was: "Get
my house in Dubai ready. I want to throw a party."

Pepper's veneer cracked every so slightly. She looked
flustered for a moment, but then recovered enough to
say, "Yes, Mr. Stark."

He heard her heels clicking on the parquet floor as she
walked away to attend to his wishes. Then he stopped
listening to her, because the screams of terrified children
and adults and the roar of Stark-generated weaponry
had taken over in his mind.

Is the world watching? the newscaster had breath-
lessly wondered.

*Let's hope they're watching. Let them watch Tony
Stark in Dubai, so a hundred people can swear I was
there, just in case someone tries to connect me with Gulmira. Because I'm going to give them one hell of a show.*

xvi.

He moves through his villa at dusk, where festivities are in full swing, with expensive cars pulling up and discharging passengers while valets scurry as quickly as they can. Beautiful people are everywhere.

He used to be one of them. Now they disgust him with their shallowness and self-obsession.

They are a cover for him now. A shield. Something to hide behind and protect him from scrutiny while matters of greater import call to him. They call, and he will answer.

Tony moved through the sea of glitzy guests, pumping hands, smiling, clapping people on the back and laughing in all the right places at all the right jokes. There was no second-guessing here among the guests, no questions about stock options or what Tony's long-range plans for Stark Industries were. This was Dubai, another world entirely, and all anyone was interested in was a good time. The closest any of the beautiful people came to questioning their good fortune was one guest who inquired, "Tony, you never said—what is the big occasion?"

"Ever known me to need one?"

The guest, a major oil tycoon, laughed in response, which was exactly what Tony expected.

The party amped up in direct proportion to the setting of the sun. The festivities in full tilt now, guests were dancing everywhere, splashing about the pool, grabbing all the free food and drink they could. Tony moved through it all like the king of the castle that he was, an exotic girl on either arm. He had absolutely no idea what their names were, nor did he care.

Pepper approached him. She was back to business as usual. Tony thought he saw a hint of disapproval in her eyes. As far as he was concerned, that was for the best.

"Well, you seem back in old form," she said.

He shrugged. "Life of the party. Isn't that what everyone wanted? Cue the fireworks in five, would you?"

The girl on the left, so tipsy that she could barely stand up, giggled at what she perceived as a double entendre. "Kinky," she said. The girl on the right looked confused a moment, and then she got it as well. She started laughing uncontrollably, which only made the one on the left giggle all the harder. Tony maneuvered the two of them toward the house, making sure to sway a little himself so that he would look hammered.

"Sure. Don't hurt yourself," Pepper called after him. He heard the edge in her voice. It should have cut like a razor.

Instead he felt nothing. He wouldn't allow himself to.

He hauled the tipsy beauties up to the master bedroom, keeping a lascivious smile plastered on his face as guests he passed snickered or gave him a thumbs-up. Once he was there, he closed the door behind himself and allowed the girls to tumble, still giggling, onto the huge bed.

"I'll be right back. Why don't you two get started without me?" he said.

They laughed in response (what a shock). Tony glanced at his watch, then slipped out a side door of the bedroom that led to a private study . . . and from there down to a workshop that couldn't quite compare to the one he had back home, but it was sufficient for his purposes.

The moment he stepped out of the bedroom, his entire manner and demeanor changed. Gone was any hint of inebriation—the bubbly he'd been imbibing that everyone assumed was champagne was, in fact, ginger ale. Granted, he had more tolerance for alcohol than most mere mortals, but he couldn't take any chance of being less than 100 percent on his game. The stakes were too high.

For just an instant, he regretted not being completely honest with Pepper. Indeed, it was the only thing he regretted. She'd had her hands in his chest, for God's sake. Certainly that entitled her to a full measure of candor on his part. But he hadn't been able to bring himself to do it for one simple reason: He knew perfectly well that the moment she heard what he had in mind, she'd try to talk him out of it. And he didn't know which would be worse: if she failed to do so, or if she succeeded. So he had sidestepped the entire issue, knowing that seeing him falling back into his old ways would hurt her. He forced himself not to care.

Funny—he'd never cared about her disapproval before. He wondered exactly when it had come to matter so much.

Pepper mingled with the crowd watching the massive fireworks detonating high above. The night sky was alive with the hiss and boom of the rockets, and people oohed and aahhhed and clapped enthusiastically.

Even though she was in the midst of the throng, Pepper felt alone. She was trying to figure out what had happened to Tony Stark, and she wasn't coming up with any easy answers.

That wasn't entirely true. The easy answer was that he was a selfish jackass. The more complicated answer was that he'd simply reverted to the behavior she'd come to know so well. The attitudes he had expressed, the way he'd acted at the gala—those were all the direct result of post-traumatic stress disorder. But now he was turning back into good old Tony Stark, executive playboy . . .

Except that didn't make sense to her. She'd learned that Tony had had some sort of dustup with Stane, although she still hadn't managed to ascertain exactly what that was all about. The personality change, the reversion, had occurred after that. What had Stane said? What had Stark said in response? Had Tony Stark really reverted to type, or was this all some sort of grand scheme that he'd concocted in order to . . . to . . .

She shook her head. She knew that she was reaching. Occam's razor: The simplest explanation tended to be the correct one. Tony had drilled that into her. And in this case, which was the simplest explanation? That Tony had arranged all this in order to accomplish some convoluted goal that he hadn't shared with her? Or that Stane had simply told him that it was time to return to the man he'd been before he sank his entire company, and Tony—after some initial resistance—had heeded the advice?

Not much of a contest, really.

As she faced away from the display that so fascinated everyone else, she noticed that one of the rockets appeared to have gone astray. It shot off at a different angle from the others and, unlike them, didn't explode. Instead it became smaller, smaller . . . and eventually vanished from view into the darkness.

She hoped that it didn't cause any damage when it eventually came down.

The boy's name was Ezil. His father had been dragged away by the invaders who had overrun their town while Ezil, his mother, and his younger brother—clutched to his mother's bosom—watched from hiding. There were plenty of places to hide these days, with so many buildings reduced to shells of themselves thanks to the constant bombing. Ezil's father had been out foraging for food for his desperate family, and invaders had captured him a mere ten feet from his family's latest hiding place. Ezil had wanted to run to his father's rescue, but his mother held him back, whispering frantically in his ear that his father would be fine, just fine, and until they were reunited that Ezil would be the man of the house. Ezil did not bother to point out that they no longer had a house for him to be the man of, and that at all of nine years old, he was too young to be a man anyway. But he had tried to live up to his mother's expectations.

So he had spent the next few days laboring to keep his family safe until he, too, had been captured while trying to find food for them. He had been several blocks away from their hiding place, which meant his mother would never know for sure what had happened to him. It saddened him, but perhaps it was better that way. He would never have to face her disappointment in him and in his utter failure to do what needed to be done.

Along with a mix of children and adults, Ezil was shoved toward the town square. The little carts and stores that used to populate the square were gone or shuttered. Instead armed insurgents were overseeing the unloading of large wooden crates from waiting trucks. Ezil knew what was in them: weapons. Weapons that the insurgents would no doubt be using against his own people and the people of other villages. There was a sadistic irony to the fact that the villagers were being compelled to aid in the unpacking of weapons that spelled their own destruction. It was like forcing a condemned man to dig his own grave before shooting him and tossing him into it.

Then Ezil's eyes widened as he saw a drawn, haggard-looking man struggling under the weight of one of the crates. *"Father!"* he screamed, and ran toward him.

His father nearly dropped the crate when he saw his son. Then an insurgent stepped in between them. The insurgent looked like someone who had been in a fight. His nose was broken and there was still severe bruising under his eyes. He had a gun in one hand but didn't need to use it as he swung his open hand. It struck Ezil in the side of the head and knocked him off his feet.

Ezil went down, his face slamming into the ground. He tasted his own blood swelling from his lip and he spit it out.

Then he heard something. It sounded like something streaking through the air.

The insurgent who had struck him had likewise heard it. He looked up, squinting against the sun, shielding his eyes to try and get a clearer view. There appeared to be nothing there.

Ezil's father had put down the crate, clearly looking ready to try to get to his son. The insurgent faced him, looking angry. The tableau terrified Ezil, who was certain he was about to see his father gunned down. How many times did one child have to lose his father, anyway?

Ezil prayed to the Prophet, high and unseen in heaven. He didn't just pray for the Prophet to save his father. He prayed for the Prophet to come down and get his hands dirty on behalf of his people. *Let enough be enough.*

And then, before the insurgent could squeeze the trigger and take Ezil's father from him, something dropped down from on high like a meteor.

It was a man. A man made of metal, or covered in metal. He said nothing, but his eyes were glowing.

"The Prophet," whispered Ezil, and then he sobbed with joy.

* * *

Within his helmet, Tony smiles grimly. He enjoys seeing the startled looks on the faces of the insurgents. He recognizes several of his former captors, including Abu, who had been aiming a gun at a helpless villager.

He glances around at the crates. They contain weaponry manufactured by Stark Industries. The knowledge fills him with cold fury. He realizes that he cannot let it overwhelm him. He must remain focused.

Surgeons typically play recorded music to help focus them and even calm them when they're in the midst of a difficult operation.

Tony Stark is a surgeon as well, excising the cancer that has embedded itself into the body of this village. So if it's good enough for doctors, it's good enough for him.

He brings his sound system on line. What else could possibly suit not only the mood, but the thematic consistency of his endeavors, than heavy metal? He cranks up Metallica. The first strains of ". . . And Justice for All . . ." pound through his helmet as he launches into battle.

"Hammer of Justice crushes you," he hums. "Overpower."

Nothing can save you.

This is turning into a damned good day.

Abu had no idea how the day had gone completely to hell.

Everything had been proceeding according to routine thus far. They had a job to do and they did it. They derived no enjoyment from it. It was nothing personal. There were simply plans for this particular piece of geography, and the current residents were not a part of those plans. The ones who were young and healthy enough to help them with the grunt work were kept alive long enough to make themselves useful. The ones who weren't were disposed of immediately. On the plus side, at least the residents weren't putting up much of a fight. And since this was simply an impoverished land with no oil or any other natural resources to provide an incentive, Abu's men could operate with confidence that the United States and other countries would take no interest in what was transpiring.

Then this boy had shown up, yelling about his father, and Abu had been about to make an example of the father, or possibly the boy—and possibly both.

That was when the missile that walked like a man had slammed to the ground. The missile or robot or whatever it was remained in a crouch for a moment and then straightened up.

As Abu stood there and watched the terrifyingly powerful figure take in his surroundings for a moment and suddenly attack his soldiers, three words emerged from his lips:

"It can't be . . ."

Tony is caught up in a rush of pure, pounding adrenaline as a soldier charges him, gun in hand. Without hesitation, muscles powered by his servos, Tony swings a roundhouse punch that sends the insurgent flying. He arcs through the air at least twenty feet and crumbles in a heap.

He turns and sees a soldier about to fire an RPG. Tony doesn't flinch. Instead he advances and thrusts his palm forward. His would-be attacker looks straight into the Repulsor port, which starts to crackle with energy.

"Geneva convention?" he says hopefully.

Tony isn't in the mood. Like a gunfighter, he fires off a shot with his Repulsor ray that blasts aside the soldier with the RPG, and yet another who is wielding a machine gun. The weapons go flying.

He spins, looking to see who else is foolish enough to challenge him.

No one. Instead they are trying another tack.

The desperate insurgents have grabbed some villagers and are hiding behind them, holding guns to their heads. They are screaming in Arabic which, naturally, Tony doesn't understand. But their meaning is clear: Lower his hands or the villagers die.

The moment calls for a change of tactics and music.

He lowers his hands even as he switches to Black Sabbath. Ozzy Osbourne's voice pumps through Tony's veins as his HUD quietly and precisely targets the insurgents, delineating between the captors and captives. Suddenly flaps in his shoulders rise, unleashing finely honed projectile blasts at the insurgents. They go down one by one, ducks at a shooting gallery. As they do, Ozzy snarls in Tony's ears . . .

> *"Heavy boots of lead*
> *Fill his victims full of dread"*

Ezil embraced his father, drinking in his presence. The other villagers, freed from the oppression of their captors through the miraculous appearance of either the Prophet or the living sword of the Prophet, ran to one another. Families and lovers were reunited, hope presented them for the first time in what seemed an eternity.

Their savior stood in the middle of the square, looking around, clearly trying to make certain that no other insurgents posed a threat. Then Ezil spotted someone whom he thought might be of interest.

He went straight to the man of iron and rapped on his leg. The clanging, if not the feeling of it, attracted his attention. He looked down with those glowing eyes and Ezil pointed to his right.

* * *

Abu quavered in his hiding place under the truck. The sounds of battle had ceased. Now the only option left to him was to wait for some sign that the armored figure had departed the area. Then he could, perhaps, gather his men and—

Suddenly the car flipped off him. He looked up in terror, knowing what he was going to see.

The armored figure reached down and grabbed him by the scruff of the neck, shaking him like a cat with a mouse.

"Where did you get these weapons?" Tony demands, having momentarily shut off the music.

Abu, terrified, mumbles something in Arabic. To make clear his intentions, Tony brings his palm up so that it is within inches of Abu's bruised and battered face. The Repulsor glows so brightly that it nearly blinds him, and Tony allows the charge to start building up audibly.

"Where," he says again, "did you get these weapons?" He nods in the direction of the crates.

Despite his supposedly nonexistent command of English, Abu suddenly becomes a quick study. "From Tony Stark! Tony Stark! Stark Industries!"

It is everything Tony can do not to break him in half. He throws Abu down in disgust and launches himself skyward, determined to find more of his weapons. The others—perhaps foolishly, perhaps not—he leaves to the people of Gulmira so they can arm themselves against oppressors. Now all he needs to do is find whatever heavy armament might still be out there that no one should possess.

Abu watched his attacker fly off and breathed a sigh of relief. His sense of reprieve lasted exactly as long as it took for the villagers to descend upon him. He barely had enough time to see the satisfied look of a young boy snarling, "The Prophet showed you!" and then blackness enveloped him.

Tony soars over the village and then his HUDs lock on to exactly what he has been afraid he would find: a stockpile of Jericho missiles, set off from the village, under a tarp.

Before he can angle down toward them, Jarvis, in a masterful example of understatement, informs him, "Incoming ordinance, sir."

The missile slams into him before he can either course correct or muster any defensive maneuver. It knocks him from the sky, sending him plummeting down, down into a dirt road and crashing with such force and velocity that it leaves a sizable crater. A moment passes, and nothing stirs save dirt floating lazily in the air. Then Tony slowly pulls himself out of the crater, running diagnostics to make certain that everything is online and functioning properly.

He turns and sees a tank rolling forward, its turret swinging around to target him. It rolls over makeshift hovels to close the distance.

The fact that it is a Stark-designed tank is more than mere irony. It means that he has all the schematics already online and prepped to go. They run across his HUD. The tank was designed to withstand anything that existing technology had to throw at it, but his suit didn't exist when Tony developed the tank. In other words, the old technology can't stand up to the latest thing.

His schematic overlay identifies a weak spot on the tank, one that no other weapon could possibly exploit. His armor, however, enables him to do so. He raises his arm and a miniature missile pops out of the forearm. Under ordinary circumstances it would require a one-in-

a-million shot from an attacker who was reckless enough to get within fifteen feet of the tank to take advantage of the tank's vulnerable spot. But with the armor's onboard tracking capability, the odds skew from one in a million to ten out of ten.

He fires the missile and it blasts into the underside of the tank, rupturing the fuel lines and disrupting the electronics. Sparks fly, igniting the spilled fuel, and the tank immediately goes up like a volcano. Seconds later it explodes. No one gets out alive. Tony doesn't care. "Spread the fear," he mutters.

He turns then, targets the cache of Jericho missiles, and fires. Had the missiles been active, the combined firepower would have been sufficient to reduce the entire area for miles around into a great blackened pit. But they weren't, and thus Tony's blasts instead merely transform the missiles to useless scrap.

Pleased with the day's work, he rockets skyward, unaware that smoldering eyes set within a scarred and ruined face—Raza's face—are watching him go.

Stark. It had to be Stark.

Raza knew it beyond question. The armor may have been different, but it could have been no one else.

The plan had been so perfect. Storing the weapons in the houses of the Gulmiran villagers, using the people as shields against Western intervention, presuming that the military industrial complex of the Great Satan would shake off its apathy and decide to get involved.

And in less than an hour, Tony Damned Stark had marched in and annihilated everything.

This was not going to go over well with the man to whom Raza answered. Not well at all.

xvii.

Major Julius Allen walked briskly into the Combined
Air Operations Center at Edwards Air Force Base in response to a late-night summons. Late night for him, that
was; in Gulmira, which was being monitored via huge
screens offering grainy satellite views of what was happening on the ground, it was mid-morning.

Allen was tall and wasp-thin and brought a sense of
urgency with him as he entered the CAOC. He was still
rubbing the sleep from his eyes with one hand while ad-
justing his necktie with the other. Never once did it
occur to him that he might have been summoned without good reason. If Allen, the foremost expert that Edwards had when it came to weapons systems, was told
that his presence was required, then it was required and
that was all there was to it.

Allen went straight to the central screen and looked in
astonishment at a very different scene than he'd expected. He knew that the murdering insurgents had been
moving through the helpless country, and had expected
to see soldiers using some new sort of weaponry on fleeing citizens. Instead, to his astonishment, it was the soldiers who were clearly in full retreat. But what were they
running from?

He leaned forward and muttered, "What *is* that?"

A vague figure was moving through the haze and
smoke of battle. He couldn't make out any details.

"Are *we* in there?" he said.

"Negative, it's a local skirmish, green on green," said

Lieutenant Dowling from the main monitoring console. He was trying to adjust the feed so more details would be available.

Allen, the weapons expert, was feeling distinctly behind the curve. It galled him to admit it, but he was clueless. "Anyone want to tell me what the hell I'm looking at?"

"A drone? An advanced robotic? We don't know what it is, sir."

Shaking his head, Allen realized that this was out of his depth. He was conversant in every weapons system there was, but this was something that didn't already exist. If it was something in the hopper, he sure as hell hadn't gotten the memo. "Get someone down here from Weapons Development—now."

Tony reflects on all that he has accomplished thus far. Yet he keeps thinking about Yinsen's words, and cannot shake the feeling that this is still merely the beginning. There is so much more to do.

He turns off Black Sabbath. He will fly back in peace.

Less than ten minutes of flight and one phone call later, the peace is irrevocably shattered.

"So what do we have here, Rhodes?"

James Rhodes paced the CAOC at Edwards as he stared at the SAT-images of the assault on Gulmira. Finally he shook his head. "I don't think it's Russian or Chinese."

"Then where did it come from?"

He considered the question as Major Allen waited for an answer. Unfortunately nothing occurred to him. "Let me make a call," he said finally.

He punched a phone number into a console. He hated phoning Tony up about this, especially considering everything the guy had been through lately. It seemed poor Tony's entire world was flying apart. The stress he was under must have been monumental. Rhodey's mind kept returning to that incident days ago when Tony had approached him about something. He had thought at the time that what Tony needed was a good, old-fashioned, no-nonsense reminder of what his priorities should be. The more Rhodey considered it, though, the more he was starting to think that what Tony had really needed at that point was a supportive friend. Tony had been enthused about something and Rhodey had essentially shut him down. He'd been trying since then to figure out some way to make things right between them, but nothing had come to mind. Or maybe it was just Rhodey's pride that was making it difficult for him to come up with anything.

So he hated the idea that, with things still unsettled between him and Tony, he was going to him with questions about some bizarre new robotic weapon that was stampeding across Gulmira. But Major Allen was staring at him expectantly while pixilated images of this new whatever-it-was shimmered around them. Rhodey didn't see much choice, especially since this weapon wasn't merely ground-based. Eight minutes earlier it had actually lifted off like a rocket and was heading due west with astounding speed.

"Yeah?" came Tony's voice over the console.

"Tony, it's Rhodey." He frowned. He could barely hear Tony over what sounded like a blast of rushing air. "What the hell's that noise?"

"I'm in the convertible. Not the best time."

In the convertible? What was he doing, driving through a cyclone? Rhodey moved on: "I need a quick ID. What do you know about unmanned combat robotics with air-ground capabilities?"

"Never heard of anything like that. Why?"

"Unmanned Aerial Vehicle has entered the no-fly

zone," said Dowling. "Repeat, UAV has entered the no-fly zone." A topographic map that was tracking the flying form showed the dot representing the armored bogie had crossed into territory it should most definitely have avoided.

"Because," said Rhodey, "I think I'm staring at one right now, and it's about to get blown to kingdom come."

Alarms promptly went off in the CAOC. Allen shouted, "Rhodes! You got something for me?"

"Uhhh . . . kingdom come?" Suddenly Tony said hurriedly, "This is my exit. Gotta go."

The connection went dead.

Rhodey rolled his eyes. Friend or no, guilt feelings or not, there were times when he had to feel that Tony Stark simply had no sense of priorities.

Proximity alarms scream as two USAF F-22 Raptors flash out of the clouds like sharks. "This is my exit. Gotta go," Tony says hastily to Rhodey, and cuts off the connection. Then he goes turbo, accelerating and rolling away in a treacherous banking descent.

"A no-fly zone, Jarvis," he growls through clenched teeth. "You charted me a course back through a damned no-fly zone?"

"It wasn't a no-fly zone earlier. Hold on. Let me check . . . ah. Apparently it was declared such at oh-six hundred hours in response to the Gulmira situation. Some concern over neighboring countries airlifting weaponry to the insurgents. Request processed four days ago."

"And just implemented now?"

"The military data base only just recently updated, sir."

"So I'm being chased by our own planes because you didn't get the memo."

"One is often struck by life's little ironies, sir."

Tony snarls something else that Jarvis doesn't quite catch, or at least later claims not to have caught, even as Tony banks hard in a desperate attempt to put as much distance between himself and the planes as possible.

At Edwards Air Force Base, Rhodey was watching the entire confrontation via the electronic readouts. In the meantime, the two planes, designated Viper One and Two, were attempting to close so that they could make visual contact and have some imagery that was clearer than grainy satellite shots.

"Ballroom Control, this is Viper One and Two checking in. UAV is in sight."

"Viper, target at 330 for ten miles," said Major Allen.

The Vipers drew within range, and suddenly the CAOC screens filled with images of the bogey being tracked. Rhodey's jaw dropped when he saw it, and a room that was populated by seen-it-all, hard-core Air Force men was filled with gasps and startled exclamations of *"What the hell is that?"*

It looked like something out of a science fiction writer's imagination or perhaps off the shelves of a local toy store that stocked Japanese robot stuff. It was a red-and-gold streak hurtling ahead of the F-22s, which in turn looked like they were having a hell of a time keeping up.

"Ballroom, contact appears to be an unmanned aerial vehicle—"

"Ballroom copies, you are cleared to engage."

They were able to hear the voice of the Raptor's on-board system, or "Bitching Betty," as it was called. "Locked on. Locked on," Betty informed them.

Rhodey watched, fascinated, as Viper One fired a Sidewinder missile.

"This should take care of it," said Major Allen.

For no reason that he could readily determine, Rhodey had a strange feeling that Allen was dead wrong.

The HUD informs him that a Sidewinder missile is closing in.

This is not how Tony had expected the day to go. Jarvis informs him coolly, "Incoming Sidewinder in five . . . four . . . three . . . two . . ."

Tony is so paralyzed by his predicament that, for four seconds, his brain locks up. Then he suddenly, almost too late, remembers the countermeasures he built into the suit. He had never expected to have to utilize them, but his dad had always said, "Expect nothing, anticipate everything."

A hatch opens in his belt section and countermeasures are triggered. Chaff unspools from the armor and, as Tony angles away, the missile strikes the chaff and erupts in a ball of fire.

Tony keeps going. He doesn't have to glance behind him to know the two Raptors remain on his tail; his HUD is doing a fine job of keeping him apprised of that disastrous little fact. The F-22s remain glued to him, despite an array of dizzying evasive maneuvers.

He angles downward, accelerating. Not being an experienced pilot, he is unaware of the risk that he is taking as the g-forces pile upon him. He becomes all too aware of it, however, as he begins to feel incredible pressure, as if a vise clamp is closing upon every muscle in his body. The world is beginning to swim around him and an emergency indicator kicks the g-force meter into the red zone.

"Sir," says Jarvis, and if a machine can possibly feel concern, then it is being reflected in Jarvis's voice. "May I remind you that the suit can handle these maneuvers. You cannot."

Message received, but before Tony can make an adjustment, there is cannon fire being sprayed in his path. The F-22s aren't cutting him the slightest slack. Tracer rounds streak past Tony, exploding around him, hitting him, ricocheting off the armor but jarring him violently nevertheless. The suit can withstand a considerable pounding, but the man inside is starting to feel it.

"Jarvis! Air brakes!"

The reverse thrusters slam into action and Tony instantly drops down a quarter of the speed he was moving. The jets blow right past him, eagles outpacing a sparrow.

He makes his move.

"That was not a drone!"

Viper One's startled voice came over the squawk at Edwards. "Checking scope!" it continued. "Nothing. Repeat, I've got nothing on my scope."

"Where the hell is it?" came Viper Two's voice.

That was what everyone else in the large control room wanted to know. Rhodey kept his vision focused on the camera images provided by the planes. They were frozen images from the initial encounter—the bogey was currently MIA. The longer he stared at it, the more convinced he was that it should mean something to him. That there was something in all this that he was missing.

Meanwhile, in the real-time feed, there was nothing but blue skies and clouds ahead of the Raptors. No sign of the bogey.

Dowling turned to him and called out, "Lieutenant Colonel Rhodes, I have Tony Stark calling."

"Put him through."

The call fed directly into Rhodey's headset. He could still hear that wind tunnel–like roaring coming through. Tony really needed either to put the top up in his car or roll the windows up or get the muffler checked—something. This was ridiculous. "Tony? You there—?"

"Rhodey, I had Jarvis run a check," Tony's voice came back, shouting over the noise around him. "I might have some info on that UAV. A piece of gear like that might exist. Might definitely exist."

"Wouldn't happen to be red and gold, would it?"

"Viper Two! He's on your belly! Shake him!"

It had been the voice of Viper One and naturally it pulled Rhodey's attention back to the screen. He was astounded at what he saw: The bogey had indeed attached itself to the underside of Viper Two. Viper One had noticed it at almost exactly the same time that it came into view on the big control screens.

"What?" said Viper Two.

"You got a hitchhiker! I said shake him! Ballroom, that is definitely not a UAV!"

"What is it, then?" said Major Allen.

"I think it's . . ." Viper One hesitated, hating to say something so completely insane, but he continued, "I think it's a man, sir."

And when the pilot's voice said that, everything came flying together for Rhodey. The look in Stark's eyes, the determination. His fierce certainty at the press conference that the time for weapons creation was over and he had to embark on a different direction. He was on to something new, something big. That day at the hangar . . .

Why not take it a step further? Why not a pilot without a plane?

Rhodey shouted into the headset, uttering a four-word phrase that both encapsulated his own realization and also described perfectly the man he was addressing.

"*Son of a bitch!*" he shouted, getting no more than glances from the others in the command center, who just assumed he was reacting to the same stunning information the rest of them were receiving. Dropping his voice, he snarled in a harsh whisper over the headset, *"Tony!"*

He thought he heard the beginning of a response, but then Viper One was heard saying, "Still there, Viper Two! Roll! Roll!"

Viper Two did as he was bidden and the plane spun like a berserk pinwheel in an attempt to send its unwanted passenger hurtling away.

At that moment the line to Tony Stark went dead. And for all Rhodey knew, Tony Stark was about to go dead along with it.

The world has become a centrifugal blur around Tony. He is cursing himself. This hitchhiking trick worked fine when Han Solo pulled it on the Galactic Empire. It is just Tony's luck that apparently the pilots has seen the same movie.

Warning buzzers are screaming in Tony's ear, just in case he didn't happen to notice the flashing lights and the readouts that inform him power is at twenty-eight percent. All he needs to really drive home his jeopardy is a toy bunny banging cymbals together.

"Sir, two minutes and there won't be sufficient power to get home," Jarvis tells him. Jarvis sounds calm. Jarvis can afford to sound calm. Jarvis is a damned computer, safe and snug at home in the mainframe. Tony's the one with his iron ass sprouting grass and two F-22s serving as lawn mowers.

Before Tony can decide what to do, it's decided for him. The magnetic couplings he's utilizing to cling to the plane are jarred loose as, this time anyway, centrifugal force trumps magnetism. He tumbles away from the F-22 and collides with the other Raptor that had been pacing him. He reaches out reflexively for something to halt his trajectory and only succeeds in tearing loose the

Raptor's tail fin. Crap. Bet they bill me for that, *he thinks, and then tumbles away.*

"I'm hit!"

Rhodey and the others watched helplessly as Viper One spiraled out of control. Seconds later the canopy blasted loose and the pilot of the doomed Raptor ejected from his ship.

"Viper Two, do you see a chute?" said Major Allen, wanting to ascertain the safety of the pilot.

The response that came back was a chilling one: "Negative! No chute, no chute! There's—the UAV! The UAV is going after him! It's attacking!"

Tony manages to gain control of his plunge and right himself. Jarvis's voice continues to remain flat, but there is a distinct urgency that will not be ignored. "Power critical. Set course for home immediately."

He is about to do so when he sees the tumbling pilot. He hovers a moment, just to make sure that the parachute releases.

Nothing.

"Come on, come on," he mutters.

Still nothing.

Tony does not hesitate. He hurtles through the sky, bearing down on the plummeting pilot.

It takes him only seconds to catch up. For a split second, the pilot and Tony are face-to-face. The pilot is gaping at him, his shocked eyes visible through the visor. God only knows what he thinks Tony is. Alien. Robot. Alien robot. Anything's possible. He probably thinks Tony is about to kill him.

What a life.

Tony instantly sees the problem: The chute mechanism is jammed. He knows this make and model: Fujikawa International, one of his competitors, manu-

factured it. FI delights in undercutting Stark bids. This is a design flaw that Tony spotted when the parachute was first manufactured. He'd dropped the Air Force a note warning them and it had been round-filed somewhere. Perhaps he should have begun it in some manner other than: Memo to the Air Force: You get what you pay for.

He yanks the mechanism free with a simple application of muscle power that would not be available to the typical plummeting pilot. Instantly the chute deploys, yanking the pilot up and out of view.

Tony tosses off a salute.

Then he realizes that his trajectory is taking him dangerously close to the ground. He banks sharply, thinking that with this display of good intent, the entire misbegotten encounter is ended.

He keeps on thinking that right up until the other Raptor closes and goes weapons hot.

The voice of Viper Two was jubilant. "Good chute! Good chute! You're not gonna believe this, Ballroom . . . but that thing just saved his ass."

Rhodey let out a sigh of relief, but the sigh caught in his throat as Major Allen said, "Viper Two, re-engage."

"Wait!" said Rhodey.

Allen stared at Rhodey as if he'd just lost his mind. Without taking his eyes off him, Allen said, "Take the target out!"

Rhodey quickly crossed the room to him and said with mounting urgency, "Major, call off that Raptor. You don't know what you're shooting at."

"We'll find out when we recover the pieces."

The voice of Viper Two's Bitching Betty came across the speaker: "Locked on! Locked on!"

Viper Two continued after the bogey, engaging in a barrel roll, but the pilot sounded confused. "Ballroom, understand, you want me to engage the UAV?"

"Copy," said Allen.

Rhodey cut in quickly. "Negative, Viper Two, disengage."

"It's not your call," said Allen, and there was unmistakable threat in his voice that Rhodey couldn't possibly miss. "That thing just took out an F-22 inside a legal no-fly zone. Viper Two," he raised his voice, "you get a clean shot, you take it."

Rhodey knew by then that arguing was pointless. But what the hell was he going to say? That Tony Stark was flying around up there? He didn't have a shred of proof. Major Allen would think that Rhodey had completely lost his mind to even suggest it. And then he would just try to blow Tony out of the sky anyway.

Rhodey's eyes were locked on the screen as Viper Two fired its missile.

He can't believe it. He cannot believe it. Has the world gone completely insane? He goes to a suffering country and provides relief. He saves a pilot who would be dead right now if it weren't for him. And they're still trying to kill him?

I've heard that no good deed goes unpunished, but this is ridiculous.

His HUD informs him a missile is closing on him. As every reading tells him that he may not have enough energy to get home, he dives into evasive maneuvers and releases more countermeasures to thwart the missile. It strikes the chaff and detonates, but it's close, much too close, and Tony is knocked out of control by the erupting fireball and the concussive force of the blast.

"Viper Two, can you confirm the kill?"

Viper Two's voice came back, "I got him good. He went down, he was smokin'. But I cannot confirm."

Rhodey felt as if the world was tilting around him. He reached back, found a chair behind him, and sank into it. When he looked up, Major Allen was staring down at him. His voice flat, Allen said, "Is there something you'd care to tell me?"

"Not a thing, Major," said Rhodey. "Not a single thing."

Pepper Potts couldn't bring herself to go upstairs and tend to Tony Stark's latest conquests.

The party in Dubai was long over. The rising sun had caused the glitterati to scatter like cockroaches when a kitchen light came on. Pepper had supervised the cleanup of the party. Now, well into mid-morning, everything had been put away. The only thing remaining was to put on a happy, peppy face and deal with whatever requirements "the girls" might have.

The problem was that she just didn't have the stomach for it. She knew she was supposed to be professional and turn a blind eye to the fact that Tony Stark clearly had the morality of a hummingbird, but—

There was the sound of feet tromping down the main stairway. She looked up and saw the girls. They look disheveled and not a little hung over.

"Where is he?" asked one of them.

Pepper blinked in confusion. She knew Tony hadn't emerged from the bedroom. "I . . . thought he was with you."

The girls looked at each other as if she had just spoken in a foreign language, and then back to her. They shook their heads in unison. Pepper tried to force a smile but it didn't seem interested in coming willingly. "Well, I guess he had something early he had to attend to. I certainly hope you all had a good time. I can arrange for transporta—"

"I didn't have a good time. Did you have a good time?" one girl said to the other.

The second one shrugged. "After Tony left last night, there didn't seem to be much—"

"Left? He left?" Pepper couldn't quite believe she'd heard properly.

"Yes. Just after he brought us upstairs, right?" She needed affirmation from her friend, who nodded.

Pepper was dumbfounded. "Where did he go?"

"We don't know. We asked you, remember?"

Ten minutes later, Pepper had packed the girls off in a cab and looked in every room in the house. Nothing. No sign of him.

At first she started to come up with worst-case scenarios, such as that he'd been kidnapped. But that made no sense because there would have been ransom demands by now. Or perhaps he'd simply found some girl at the party even more intriguing than the other girls. That didn't work for her either, though, because Pepper had seen everyone off.

Finally, Pepper went to poolside and sat on a bench. Her thoughts were racing; she was uncertain what to do, whom to call. Every instinct told her that wherever Tony was, he had gone there willingly. But where was that? When would he come back?

She didn't give any thought to the fact that she hadn't slept in thirty-six hours. But that reality finally caught up with her as she eventually slumped over on the bench and started to doze.

It was the noise of shattering glass that woke her.

It was so abrupt that she was on her feet before she was actually fully awake, and as a result nearly fell over. The only thing that saved her was the back of the bench, which she clutched like a life preserver. She looked around in confusion and then saw that a window in the side of the mansion had been broken. She thought it was the one that opened onto Tony's upstairs den.

She ran into the mansion and sprinted up the stairs to the second level. Upon reaching it, she went straight to the den without the slightest idea of what she was going to see.

Pepper threw open the door to the den and stopped dead. Her face went ashen, her strawberry-blond hair standing out in sharp relief against it.

Tony Stark was seated in an oversized chair. He was clad in red-and-gold armor like a modern-day Galahad. But the armor looked like it had gone ten rounds with a wrecking machine. It was scarred, pitted, and smoke was rising from several of the joints. There was a helmet sitting next to him on a small table. There was blood trickling from Tony's nose, which he seemed too tired to stop, and his left eye was starting to swell up. He was holding a drink in his right hand, except the glass was shaking, nearly spilling out the contents.

"Get me home," was all he said right before the drink slipped from his hand and he passed out.

xviii.

Obadiah Stane stepped out of his black Suburban and looked around in the darkness. He could not have said that he was especially impressed by what he saw.

A few yurts had been set up and they dotted the wasteland outskirts of Gulmira. The proud insurgents, the so-called militants, were sitting disconsolately around their tents and licking their wounds—literally, in some cases. Night had fallen and the temperature had cooled off a bit, and Stane was grateful for that. But that was the only thing he was grateful for; everything else he saw filled him with a vague disgust.

Stane's private guards had spread out through the encampment, securing the area before Stane even got out of his car. The militants glanced at them with only the mildest of interest. For his part, Stane simply stood in the middle of the encampment and looked around, making no effort to hide the fact that he was sorely unimpressed by this band of devastated insurgents who were no longer surging.

The flap of one of the yurts fluttered and then Raza emerged from within. He sauntered toward Stane as if they were running into each other at a casual garden party. "Welcome," he said, spreading his arms. He might as well have been welcoming Stane to a grand salon.

Stane assessed the scars on Raza's face. Raza saw where he was looking and, a mirthless smile on his face, ran his fingers across them. "Compliments of Tony Stark."

"If you'd killed him when you were supposed to, you'd still have a face."

"You paid us trinkets to kill a prince," said Raza with a growl. "An insult to me, and the man whose ring I wear."

"I think it's best we don't get *him* involved in this," said Stane. "I've come a long way to see this weapon. Show me."

Raza nodded. "Come." Then he paused and, indicating Stane's private security force, said, "Leave your guards outside."

Stane shrugged and nodded to his people that they should give Raza and him some space. He then followed Raza into the large yurt. It was dimly lit, courtesy of a kerosene lamp, but there was enough illumination for Stane to see the centerpiece of the tent.

What Stane could only describe as a massive suit of gray armor was hanging there, strung together courtesy of assorted wires. Slowly he walked around it, shaking his head, amazed. "His escape bore unexpected fruit," said Raza, displaying a surprising knack for understatement.

"So this is how he did it," Stane said in wonderment.

"This is only a crude first effort. But he's perfected his design."

Raza handed him several photographs. They were grainy, but the subject matter was clear enough. An armored figure was at the center of every one of the shots, and it was wreaking havoc on Raza's men, tossing them around as if they were children, demolishing tanks, sending them running every which way. *Tony, my boy,* thought Stane, *who would have thought you had it in you? Not me, certainly.*

He set the photos aside because something else had

caught his attention. It was a filth-encrusted laptop sitting to the side of the armor. Onionskin covered with schematics lay atop it. Stane picked up the schematics and his brow furrowed. "What's this?"

"The inside of Tony Stark's mind," said Raza. "Everything you will need to build this weapon." He took the schematics from Stane, illuminated a light board, and began to lay them together. Stane had to admit to himself that he might well have underestimated Raza. The scruffy insurgency leader had clearly been spending an inordinate amount of time trying to decipher and understand Stark's work, and he'd come an amazing distance in accomplishing that. Then again, Stark had rearranged his face. Harboring that sort of grudge tended to focus one.

Once he had assembled the drawings, Raza gestured for Stane to inspect both the schematics and the armor. A small pot of tea was brewing on a burner nearby. Raza removed the pot and gestured toward it for Stane's benefit, questioning mutely whether Stane was thirsty. Stane, far too absorbed with studying this latest manifestation of Tony Stark's genius, shook his head. Raza poured out tea for himself.

"Stark has made a masterpiece of death," said Raza as he sipped the tea, seated cross-legged on the floor. Stane continued to study the armor. "A man with a dozen of these could rule from the Pacific to the Ukraine. And you dream of Stark's throne. We have," and he paused for dramatic effect, "a common enemy."

Stane poked at the vacant hole in the chest plate. That had to be where the power source was situated, and Stane knew exactly where that source was now. Or at least whose body it was in.

"If we are back in business," Raza said, "I give you these designs as my gift. In turn, I hope you will repay me with a gift of iron soldiers."

Upon hearing that, Stane walked over to Raza and gestured for the insurgent to stand. Stane had his hands out as if he were prepared to embrace Raza in brotherhood. Raza stood, and Stane—grinning broadly—placed his hands on Raza's shoulders.

"This is the only gift you shall receive," said Stane.

Raza looked strangely confused for a moment. It appeared that something was happening to him and he didn't have the slightest idea what it was. Then his body stiffened. His eyes widened in shock and blood was pouring from his ears. He tried to pull away from Stane, but he had no strength to do so even if Stane's grip hadn't been viselike.

They stood that way, a twisted image of two men bonding in friendship, for long seconds, and then Raza crumbled to the floor. Stane stepped back, removed the sonic taser from his palm, and pocketed it. Then he took out the small but effective earplugs that he had inserted before ever setting foot in Raza's encampment.

"Technology: It's always been your Achilles' heel. Don't worry. It'll wear off in fifteen minutes. But that's the least of your problems."

When Raza had been speaking earlier of the man to whom he owed allegiance, he'd flashed a rather distinctive ring. Stane took the opportunity to remove it. He studied it thoughtfully for a moment. Then, slipping it into his pocket, he turned and exited.

When he emerged from the yurt, he saw exactly what he expected to see: Raza's men on their knees, their hands interlaced behind their heads, dazed and bewildered expressions on their faces. Stane's personal guards were standing behind them, their guns to the soldier's heads.

Stane nodded toward the yurt from which he had just emerged. "Crate up that armor and the rest of it."

"And them?" asked one of his guards, indicating the kneeling men.

"Send them to their virgins."

He didn't so much as flinch as the air filled with the sounds of screaming and machine-gun fire. His mind was already on other, more important things.

I have seen the future, and it is wearing armor. And I'll be damned if, when the future comes, I'm not dressed for the occasion.

xix.

The absolute last person that Pepper was interested in speaking to as she sat in Tony's living room, her mind awhirl with everything that had transpired in the last twenty-four hours, was naturally the first person to call the minute she got settled into her work alcove.

She was still processing the last few hours: the hurried flight home in Tony's private jet, the drive from the airport via a private and very discreet ambulance service. The paramedics had taken care of getting Tony squared away, but they had strongly advised Pepper that he be brought to a hospital. She had been forced to agree. Unfortunately, Tony had not agreed, and in the end that was all that mattered.

She answered the phone with a curt, "Yes?"

"Ms. Potts. It's Agent Coulson from the Strategic Homeland Inter—"

"Yes, I know," said Pepper, rolling her eyes. "Unfortunately, Tony is not going to be available to sit down with you for a while."

"Really." He didn't sound disappointed or angry. Instead he sounded challenged. "And why is that?"

"He's, uh, there's a, Tony won't be—"

"Maybe I can meet with you instead."

Pepper slumped back in her chair. Usually she was faster off the mark than this. She was so brain-fried she couldn't think of anything useful to say, much less come up with something clever to cover for Tony. "Why? I don't know anything."

"About what?"

Instantly she knew she had erred. Coulson was suspicious, and she had no one to blame but herself. "About anything," she said, and winced as she did so. She was just getting herself in deeper with answers like this.

The security monitor abruptly buzzed. She looked at the image on it and moaned.

"Pepper. It's Rhodey," he said unnecessarily.

She considered just refusing to buzz him in. But there was no point to it; he wouldn't leave. She knew him too well. "Come in," she said with a sigh and buzzed him in.

Coulson, meantime, was like a child chewing on car keys. "I'd just like to ask you a few questions."

"I'm really jammed right now," Pepper insisted. "Booked solid for the next few weeks. I have to go."

Rhodey had already walked in and was standing there scowling. It was like having the Grim Reaper for a friend. Pepper's finger hovered over the disconnect, but Coulson just wouldn't let it go. "Let's just put something on the books. How about the twenty-eighth? Seven PM at Stark Industries?"

"Great. Perfect. Bye," said Pepper, barely listening, and she cut the connection.

"How's he doing?" said Rhodey.

"Not so good."

"I want to see him."

"You can't see him right now."

He stepped close toward her. His eyes were dark and foreboding. "I was watching from Edwards, Pepper. On the screen. I was watching him with the airplanes. I know what he was up to."

Pepper gave no indication that she knew what he was talking about. Rhodey, apparently expecting her to stonewall him, looked up at the hole in the ceiling. He shook his head in disbelief. "What the hell is going on here? Let me in there, Pepper," he said, indicating the stairway up to Tony's bedroom.

She considered ordering Jarvis to put the house into lockdown. He could do that; he had the capability. Every wing, every room could be sectioned off and made impervious to intruders. One word from her and Jarvis would see to it that a phalanx of Sherman tanks wouldn't get anywhere near Tony Stark.

But she had so much anger in her, and so much fear for the future, that she wanted to share some of it with Rhodey. No, not share: inflict it upon him. "You want to see him?" she said coldly. "Fine. See what you've done to him."

Rhodey went up the stairs two at a time, with Pepper following. When Rhodey got to Tony's bedroom, he stopped in the doorway. Pepper hung back, gladly. It agonized her even to look in on Tony.

He lay in bed, tethered to assorted medical scanners. An IV drip was attached to his arm. He was doped up on painkillers. Pepper had desperately wanted to call a doctor, but Tony wouldn't hear of it, countermanding both her and the paramedics. He had insisted to her that he was capable of treating himself. As far as Pepper was concerned, she was riding a roller coaster that was descending at full speed into hell. She firmly believed that if she had any brains at all, she would have jumped off long ago. But she hadn't, and she supposed that meant that she had no one to blame but herself for the agony she was feeling on Tony's behalf.

Rhodey had walked to Tony's bedside and adjusted a tube away from his face. "You look like crap."

Tony managed a pained smile. "Thanks. Party in Dubai got a little out of control. Totally worth it, though. You should've been there. Great canapés."

"I know what you were up to, Tony."

"Yeah? What was I up to?"

"About mach one point seven. It was you in the armor, Tony. I saw the whole thing from Edwards."

Tony's voice was little more than a whispered croaking. "I did pretty good, didn't I."

"You got blown out of the sky. You call that 'pretty good'?"

"Next time I won't play so nice with your planes."

He made it sound like a friendly jest, but Pepper had the awful feeling that he was at least somewhat serious. Plus there were those two words that absolutely chilled her: *next time*. My God, was he seriously considering another outing of this nature? She wasn't even sure *she* would survive it, much less her boss.

Rhodey had pulled over a chair and was seated at Tony's bedside. His face deadly serious, he said, "I respect what you did, Tony. You ended a nightmare over there. Showed a real warrior's heart. But the way you did it—you can't go it alone like that. You've got to let someone have your back."

Tony tried to reply but couldn't. There was a pitcher of water and a glass on the table next to him. Tony tried to reach for it, but his hand was still shaking. Pepper took a few steps toward him, but Rhodey had already lifted the pitcher and was pouring some water into the glass. He placed the glass into Tony's hand and wrapped Tony's fingers around it to make certain that he had a secure grip on it. Then he guided it toward Tony's mouth. Tony sipped deeply from it, then lowered it.

"You got my back, right?" said Tony.

"Yeah. We ride together, pal. Even if it's straight to the brig."

Tony nodded, apparently satisfied with that. He closed his eyes and started to drift. Rhodey took the glass of water from him and placed it back on the table.

Then he got up from the chair and headed toward Pepper.

Before he got to her, however, Tony's voice said weakly, "I never said thank you."

"For what?"

"For saving my life."

Rhodey held up two fingers. "It was twice, actually."

Tony smiled. Then his head slumped back and he fell asleep.

Rhodey turned to face Pepper. "Are we okay? You and I, I mean."

She stood there for a long moment, arms folded, and then nodded toward Tony. "When he's okay, you and I are okay. Until then . . ." She shrugged, turned and walked away.

"Fair enough," said Rhodey.

The subbasement under the building that housed the Arc reactor was a maze: windowless, lined with pipes that fed everything from steam to electricity to all other parts of the building. No one ever came down there, not even the maintenance crew, since the entire building was never used.

Obadiah Stane had taken over the pipe room.

He was addressing a group of elite engineers, men whom he had handpicked for their brilliance, for their discretion, and for their lack of family members should something . . . untoward . . . happen to them down the road. Stane wasn't sure that would be necessary, but one couldn't be too careful.

Fragments of the gray armor were hung in various sections of the room. Also there, erected on scaffolding, was the barest beginning of another suit of armor. It would have been impossible to look at it in its very nascent stages and get a clear idea of what it was going to look like.

"We've made progress," Stane said to them. "But we're going to have to dig deeper—redouble our efforts. The stakes couldn't be higher."

The chief engineer, an older man named Layton who had a salt-and-pepper beard and a troubled air about him, said, "Sir, we're still having trouble with the propulsion."

"I know, the power, the power," Stane said dismissively, as if this entire matter were a mere triviality instead of the major stumbling block that his people presented it to be. "There is no problem. The solution"— he spread his arms wide, outstretched—"the source, the answer . . . is right above us."

He walked around them, speaking quickly and confidently, giving them his best pep talk. "Listen, gentlemen. Civilization has been preserved by the right people having the right idea at the right time. Technology like this comes along once in a generation—and it's a gift that's been put in our hands. That's because we have a vision—a vision for the future of this company, of this nation, and of the world order."

The engineers nodded approvingly. They liked being told they had vision. If there was one thing Stane was good at, it was finding anyone's major weakness and exploiting it. In this case, it was the engineers' conviction that they were the best and brightest around. In short, their overwhelming ego. As long as Stane could appeal to that, he would be able to keep them happy, in line, and not asking too many questions. "Make no mistake," he went on. "The tool that you are creating, in the wrong hands, could jeopardize civilization as we know it. That's why it's our responsibility to build it first. Are we all agreed?" When they nodded, he clapped his hands together briskly and said, "Let's get to work."

* * *

Tony Stark awoke with a shudder and could not tell at first where he was.

The fact that he was lying in his bedroom, attached to an assortment of machines monitoring his every breath, had a surreal aspect to it, especially when one considered just how he had come to be in this situation in the first place. He'd climbed into an armor suit of his own design and single-handedly tried to make the world a better place. What the hell had he been thinking?

Yet that was the question that was bouncing around in his skull, for before he had awoken to his new status as patient with a possible taste for suicide, he had been dreaming that he was nowhere near there. Instead, he was standing on a flat plain in Afghanistan, staring at the mountain range in the distance where the insurgents had kept him captive. Yinsen was standing next to him, fastidiously groomed as always, his arms across his chest. For some reason, the dream of standing there with Yinsen seemed more real than the reality of his bedroom.

Am I on the right path?

He had not even had to speak. He had simply thought it. Yinsen looked at him in response and said, "Are you on the right path? I don't know. What does your heart tell you, Stark?"

In the dream, he looked down at his heart. There was nothing but an empty black hole there, and blood was seeping from it. He had reached up to apply pressure, to try to stop the bleeding. The gesture in his dream translated to a parallel movement in reality, and it jolted him awake. His hand was resting upon the reactor that was keeping him alive, glowing softly in the dimly lit room.

"Not *too* symbolic," he muttered.

He looked at his reflection in the mirror across the room. He looked sad, even pathetic, hooked up to IV tubes and machinery that was pinging and hissing.

It was starting to seem to him that being part man, part machine was developing into a natural state of being. Perhaps eventually they could just remove his brain from his skull, place it in a jar, and hook him up.

He felt a deep, powerful impulse to give in to despair. He had risked life and limb, it seemed, to no purpose. The Air Force had pummeled him nearly to oblivion, and that was just with two planes. Next time there could well be more.

As tempting as it was to give in to depression, as much as he wanted to think that enough was enough, he'd learned his lesson, and he was never going to embark on this sort of quixotic adventure again, he was already acknowledging a reality that some part of his brain was prepared to accept.

There was going to be a next time, sooner or later.

"What the hell," he said as he carefully began to disengage himself from the monitoring devices. "Might as well be sooner."

Pepper nearly had a stroke. She was positive she could feel a vein exploding in her temple as she stood at the door of Tony's workshop and gaped at him.

He was seated in an oversized chair, the IV still attached to his arm, the bandages visible on his upper body. It was the only concession he was making to the fact that—as far as Pepper was concerned—he was being held together with three pounds of electrical tape and a gallon of willpower. He had already cannibalized sections of his damaged suit, which was suspended from a chain winch, and had transformed them into something else, the function of which Pepper could not even begin to guess.

She had gone up to his bedroom to check on him and been shocked to discover he wasn't there. Upon finding that, the last place she wanted to look for him was his workshop, because that was the last place he should be. Naturally, she went there first and couldn't believe what she was seeing.

As if everything were entirely normal and they were both exactly where they should be, Tony said, "This device will hack into the Stark Industries mainframe. I need you to go to there and retrieve all shipping manifests."

Pepper approached him slowly, so upset that she was trembling. "What are you doing?" When he didn't answer, she realized he wasn't going to, and it was only at that point that she fully wrapped her mind around what he had just told her. "Absolutely not! You should be in bed."

"They've been dealing weapons under the table and I'm going to stop them."

She took a deep breath and let it out slowly. It was absolutely essential, she knew, that she remain calm. Tony had lost his mind, and she was going to have to help him find it. "Look . . . if you want to mess around in the Stark mainframe, can't you do it from here?"

"Yes. I could. If I put all my resources into it, all my effort, and don't sleep for the next three weeks, at the end of those three weeks I will probably have found a way to crack through the firewalls I built to make the system bulletproof against exactly the type of thing you just suggested. But I don't have that kind of time, so I need your help—"

"I'm not helping you with anything if you're going to start this again."

"*There is nothing else!*" Tony shouted, and he slammed his open palm on the table so hard that it sent tools skittering. Pepper was taken aback, horrified. She had never in her entire life seen him act this way. Even when he'd been making that rambling speech at the press conference, even when it seemed that he wasn't in his right mind, he had been cool, wryly amused, always conveying the sense that life was simply too short to get worked up about things. She'd thought the dustup with Obadiah Stane back at the gala had been an aberration due to stress, nothing more. But Stane wasn't here now, and she'd been trying to minimize stress, so what sort of rationalization for Tony's behavior could she possibly present now, other than that he was coming unraveled before her eyes.

Tony was privy to nothing that was going through her head, of course, but something within him prompted him to rein himself in. He did so only with extreme effort. He was clearly fighting to keep his voice and his manner under control, draping calm over himself like an ill-fitting suit. "There's no art opening," he said. "There's no benefit. There's nothing to sign. There are no decisions to be made. There's the next mission and nothing else. There's nothing except this." He pointed across the room and Pepper saw that Jarvis was machine-shopping replacement parts, or possibly a newly created armored suit.

She could not take it anymore. "I quit."

"Really?"

Pepper started to walk away from him, and then she gasped as Tony darted out of his seat, something she would scarcely have thought possible. He stepped around her, blocking her attempt to leave, and his eyes blazed with fury. "You stood there by my side when all I did was reap the benefits of wholesale irresponsibility and destruction and now that I'm trying to right those wrongs and protect the people I put in harm's way . . . that's when you're going to walk out on me?"

"Don't try to turn this into some sort of abandonment issue," said Pepper, allowing her own anger to rise.

"Don't try to make it sound as if all I cared about was the good times, or that I didn't give a damn that you were profiting from other people's misery. I deserve better than that, Tony, and you damned well know it!"

He looked as if he were about to present an angry or sarcastic comeback, but then he apparently thought better of it. Instead he said, "Okay, then, so why? Why are you going to walk out now?"

"You're going to kill yourself. I can't support that."

Despite the seriousness of the moment, Tony actually smiled at that, which did nothing to improve Pepper's mood. "So far, so good. I don't support me killing myself either."

"Tony—," she began in exasperation.

He cut her off, taking her hands in his firmly. He seemed to be determined to project his resolve directly into her, as if he were mainlining emotion. "Pepper . . . I know what I have to do. I don't know if I can, but I know in my heart that it's right. And you do, too. And . . ." He paused and then added what must have been, to him, the most galling truth of all: "I can't do it without you."

She moaned to herself. At that moment, she still opposed every aspect of Tony's plan. But she also knew that it was now just a matter of time until she acquiesced.

Because he couldn't do it without her.

Oh hell, he had me at "retrieve all shipping manifests."

XX.

In all the years that Pepper had been working for Stark Industries, she'd never thought she would hit a point in her life where it would all seem so alien to her.

She was beginning to think that she would never make a good spy. She sucked at looking nonchalant. James Bond could stroll through enemy headquarters in a tuxedo and look like he belonged there. Pepper, who was exactly where she belonged, walked stiffly and nervously, glancing all around, jumping at every passing, "Hey, Pepper," from a colleague, and looking like exactly what she was: a thief in the night.

She hadn't felt this uncomfortable and ill at ease since she had first arrived at Stark Industries. Having become fed up with the emptiness of a life spent standing around and smiling, Virginia Potts had willingly left her modeling days behind to get a job as a low-level administrative assistant at SI because, well, that was what was available for someone with a BA in accounting. She remembered the day she'd been doing a routine check on some project financial numbers that had passed across her desk. It should have been nothing, a mere rubber stamp, since hers were the fourth set of eyes to look them over. But she'd caught something, and it had niggled at her and bothered her until she'd become convinced that the financial projections for the project were just flat-out wrong. She'd brought it to the attention of her supervisor who had brushed her off, told her she was mistaken.

The thing was, if he'd checked her math and made that pronouncement, she'd have accepted it. But he didn't. He just dismissed her concerns out of hand.

Virginia Potts didn't respond well to being dismissed out of hand.

In a breach of protocol that she was fully aware might cost her her job, she had moved with sharklike determination over her supervisor's head to the general manager. The general manager, Mr. Folan, had sneered at her and said, "These numbers were crunched by Tony Stark, so why don't you just take it up with him?" When she said that she was going to do exactly that, he informed her in a loud voice that she was fired. She had ignored him, propelled by her sense of moral indignation, and steamrolled into Stark's office. He had been sitting behind his desk, feet propped up, a drink in his hand, chatting with some woman on the phone (Pepper had never found out who). He had looked up, stunned, as Virginia Potts burst in, waving a sheaf of numbers and demanding to be heard. Stark's secretary had called security, and two bulky men had walked in, prepared to haul her out. In a voice that had carried all the way down the hall— Tony Stark swore to this day that he still had a ringing in his ears from it—she had bellowed to the guards, *"Don't you touch me! I have pepper spray!"*

Tony Stark had burst out laughing. The laughter did nothing to lighten the besieged Ms. Potts's mood, but Stark—having hung up on the woman he'd been chatting up—came around his desk and waved off the guards. He was still chuckling as he looked over the sheets that she had been clutching. Then he stopped chuckling. His eyebrows knit the longer he stared at the totals in the section that she had circled in an accusing red pencil.

"Wow," he had said softly. "I flipped two numbers.

The whole projection is off. How the hell did I miss this?"

"Maybe you had a little too much to drink," she had said pointedly, considering he was still holding a drink.

"There's not enough liquor in the world for me to have had too much to drink," he had said, which was her first lesson in the fact that it was almost impossible for Tony Stark to take offense at anything. He seemed to thrive on insults. Stark shook his head as he studied the numbers. "What department do you work in again?"

"Technically, none. Mr. Folan just fired me."

"Did he now." He looked her in the eyes and smirked. "*Pepper* spray?"

"Yes, well, I lied about that."

"I know. That's why it was so funny. You're the world's worst liar. I've never seen someone fail so spectacularly."

"Fine," she had said in exasperation. "I'm a terrible liar. Always have been."

"Considering the number of people I'm surrounded by who try to lie to me on a daily basis, that's actually a very useful commodity to me. I could use someone who can't help but be truthful." He had looked at one of the security guards. "Bob . . ."

"My name's Tom, sir."

"Good for you. Escort Miss 'Pepper' Potts here to her new office. The big one, next door to mine."

"That's Mr. Folan's office, sir," said Tom. "What do I tell Mr. Folan?"

Stark smiled. "Tell him he can have Miss Potts's old desk."

"I—I don't understand," she had said.

"You, Miss Pepper Potts, are going to be my personal assistant. I need someone who will cover my back while never lying to me. You want the job?"

"I . . ."

"Beats unemployment. Huge salary that I'll come up with during a drunken haze. Come on, Pepper . . . you know you want it."

"Okay, but . . ." Her voice had gone stern. "You've got to stop calling me Pepper."

He had smiled and instead replied, "You'll get used to it."

And she had.

She had been at home there ever since . . . right up until now. Now she was in enemy territory, even though she was on a mission on behalf of the guy whose name was on the building.

Pepper entered Tony's office and sat down at his computer. She fired it up, brought it online, and then pulled a small device about the size of a jump drive from her purse. Tony had crafted it for her to hack into the system. Even though she was alone in the office, she looked left and right as if someone might spring out of the walls. Her hands trembled as she jacked the hacking device into the port that Tony had instructed her to use.

The screen on Tony's computer flickered. Seconds later, Obadiah Stane's account information came up. It flashed past her as the hacking device sliced through Stane's personal passwords, firewalls, and security nets.

She glanced toward the door, certain that she heard someone coming. It was after hours, so Tony's personal secretary, Mrs. Arbogast, had gone home for the evening. Pepper waited for what seemed like minutes but was, in actuality, only seconds, and then the sounds of footsteps faded away. She let out a long sigh of relief and then got busy.

Pepper had brought a small cardboard box with her and she quickly began loading Tony's personal items into the box. As she did so, she kept glancing at the monitor. Tony's hacking device had struck deep into the heart of the system, like a mosquito, and now it was drawing the lifeblood straight out of Obadiah Stane's hard drive.

Suddenly it slammed to a halt and her heart jumped until a prompt appeared on the screen. It took her a moment to remember that this was exactly what Tony had said would happen.

Using the cursor, she moved the arrow to the "Copy All" command and clicked on it. "Copy everything," she said.

Items began to scroll past. It was moving at incredible speed, but Pepper was still able to discern things in generalities. There were orders for Jericho missiles. Shipping manifests. Manifests for things that had not gone into the hands of the army or any branch of the United States Armed Forces. They were instead private organizations, and Pepper was willing to bet that they were all fronts. Siphoning businesses, dummy corporations, the purpose of which was to keep terrorists stocked with weaponry.

Pepper felt ill. More than that, she began to have the faintest inkling what it must be like for Tony Stark, because after all it was his company responsible for creating the weaponry.

"What are you doing, Obadiah?" she muttered in astonishment.

Then something caught her attention.

The screen in Tony's office was now an exact duplicate of the screen in Stane's, and she noticed a video clip icon with what appeared to be Arabic text underneath. Not wanting to wait for the download to be completed, she moved the arrow and double-clicked on the icon.

When she saw the result, she gasped and was nearly sick to her stomach.

It was a grainy video clip of Tony. He looked half

dead and was tied to a chair. The front of his tattered shirt was covered with a dark stain that was unquestionably his blood. Several insurgents were in view and there was a flag behind them with ten interlocking rings.

Pepper had understood intellectually what Tony had experienced. She knew it had changed him. But this was the first time that she had even a clue of what it had been like for him. All things considered, it was astounding that he had come out of the experience as intact as he had; others would have been driven completely insane from it. In that moment, everything that he had done since then became clear. Naturally, naturally, he had donned armor. How else to make sure that no one would ever hurt him again?

They were talking angrily in their native language, whatever the hell that was. "Translate," she ordered the computer, which contained audio response technology in addition to standard functions.

The clip continued to play, but the translation issued from the monitors. It was a bizarre disconnect between what she was seeing—the man on the screen was ranting like a maniac—and what she was hearing: the computer speaking in a calm, detached electronic voice.

"Obadiah Stane, you have deceived us! The price to kill Tony Stark has just gone up."

Pepper had thought that she couldn't be more shocked about anything that she discovered, but now it turned out she had been wrong. The man on the screen continued to complain about a variety of issues which, even translated into English, didn't make a whole lot of sense to her. The man was clearly a lunatic, and it was in his hands that Tony had been held helpless all that time. *My God, if I'd come back from that, I wouldn't have called a press conference. I'd have curled up into a ball under a bed for a year.*

More items were scrolling past. Schematics for something that looked vaguely like Tony's armor, but it was labeled "Iron Monger." The name meant nothing to her, and she knew that she had at least a passing familiarity with every project currently under development at Stark Industries. Layouts for a room lined with pipes. It looked familiar; she thought it might be the subbasement at the Arc generator—

A voice said from the doorway, "So . . ."

She jumped, banging her knee on the underside of the desk. She desperately tried to keep the pain and panic out of her face and voice as she saw Obadiah Stane standing in the doorway, a drink in hand, smiling with what she would have once seen as benevolence. But she knew that it masked something terrible and terrifying.

"What should we do about this?" he said.

The monitor continued to scroll as Obadiah Stane's most important secrets rolled by in plain view. Since he was on the other side of the monitor, he didn't see it. But she had no idea how long that would last.

"Obadiah . . ."

Stay calm. Stay calm. You're Tony Stark's personal assistant in Tony Stark's office. You're nowhere that you don't have any right to be.

She kept telling herself that, but there was another fact that she also couldn't ignore. Tony Stark had hired her all that time ago partly because she couldn't lie worth a damn. The prospect of trying to dissemble now, to Obadiah Stane, while every nerve ending screamed to her that she should get up and bolt from the place as fast as she could, was a daunting one.

There was a deathly silence between them for a moment, and then Stane entered the office and closed the door. Pepper gripped the armrests of the chair in which she was seated. She wished she had a gun. Her eyes strayed across the desktop, looking for a potential weapon. Letter opener would work. Perhaps she could bounce the paperweight off his head.

Stane, meanwhile, appeared oblivious to Pepper's desperate defensive plans. Instead, he strolled across the room to Tony's wet bar. As Pepper watched and information scrolled, Obadiah Stane—whose virtual fly was being unzipped and he didn't even know it—refilled his glass with Scotch.

"Drink?" he asked solicitously, holding up an empty glass.

"Sure. That would be great," she said, and as she spoke her fingers were flying across the keyboard. By the time Obadiah came around the desk, glass of Scotch for Pepper in his hand, the monitor screen was filled with Google want ads.

He sat on the edge of the desk, sipping the glass. Five inches away the hack drive was downloading, its single tiny LCD pulsing steadily to indicate the job was in progress. Pepper was frozen. She was afraid to make any sort of move, unsure what small gesture of body language might tip Stane to what was going on.

"I know what you're going through, Pepper," said Stane.

Ohhh, I'll lay serious money down that you don't.

"I know how lonely you feel," Stane went on, sighing heavily. "The two of us—we're the only ones who know what this is like. I was so happy when he came home."

Yeah, I'll bet you were.

"It was like we got him back from the dead. Now I realize . . . Tony never really came home, did he? He left part of himself back in that cave. It breaks my heart."

Like you have a heart, you son of a bitch.

The hack drive chose that moment to get loud. It whirred and ground for a few seconds. Perhaps it had overheard what Stane was saying and was having its own little meltdown. Trust Tony Stark to create a piece of computer hardware that came complete with a nausea function in the presence of hypocrisy. Stane glanced around, unsure where the noise had just come from, and Pepper spoke quickly: "I don't know where his head's at. He hasn't opened up to me," she said in what she prayed was a fair approximation of frustration, even sympathy. *World's worst liar. No time like the present to learn how. Use everything you can to distract him.*

She had risen from the chair when she had spoken, and now she walked toward the window. She made sure to accentuate the thrust of her hips to draw Stane's attention away from the computer. "He's going over a rough patch. I think what he needs is time."

The ploy worked. Stane followed her over to the window. She wasn't wild about the way he was leaning toward her; it deprived her of an easy move away from him.

"You are a rare woman," he said. "Tony doesn't know how lucky he is." A drift of hair had fallen across her face and Stane moved it aside. Then he put an arm around her and drew her tightly against him. He did it sideways, so it could have come across either as platonic affection, or something more. It seemed to Pepper that he was tossing an invitation to her, dipping his toe in the water as it were, to see whether or not she would respond.

Her hand trembling, she downed the drink in one shot. Then she forced herself to turn toward him and smile. "Thank you, Obadiah."

She made no move then. She had a sense at that moment what it was like for a gazelle standing in the middle of the savannah, remaining stock still lest a predator in the high weeds suddenly make a move toward it. That's what Obadiah Stane was right then to her: a predator.

Since Stane was being given nothing to react to, he

had no choice but to smile wanly and say, "Come on. I'll walk you out." He released his hold on her and she realized she'd been holding her breath the entire time. She let it out, but then saw that Stane was picking up the box of personal effects she had been putting together. Yes, granted, there were some things in there Tony had wanted, but he didn't really need any of it. That had been merely her cover lest someone wonder why she was wandering around. But now the picking up of the box was bringing him dangerously close to the small but noticeable hack drive.

She moved quickly, praying that it didn't come across as *too* quickly, and palmed the hack drive just as he lifted the box. Pepper had no idea if he'd seen her do it, and she braced herself for a demand of, "What's that in your hand?" Instead, he simply turned away, cradling the box of personal effects. For the second time in less than a minute, she had to remind herself to breathe.

Before Stane could react, Pepper took the box from him. "It's okay. I've got it," said Pepper. "And I can see myself out. Good night, Obadiah."

His confusion was evident on his face as Pepper walked out of the office as quickly as she could.

Obadiah Stane wondered what in the world had just happened.

Feeling a little woozy, having drunk a bit more than he should have, Stane sagged down into the chair behind Tony Stark's desk. There was a warning sensation niggling in the back of his head. It was trying to tell him that something had just happened here that had gone right past him.

As bleary as his mind was, he forced himself to run the events of the past few minutes through his head. He replayed for himself everything that Pepper had said, everything she had done, everywhere she had looked . . .

Slowly his attention swiveled to the computer. Experimentally, he called up the screen with his own account and checked to see the last time he had been on.

According to the time log, he had logged off less than a minute earlier.

No one had ever sobered up quite as quickly as Obadiah Stane did at that moment as he started checking through his account's recent activity. He paled as he saw all the delicate files that had just been opened . . . opened and . . .

—copied?

"*Son of a—*" He snarled and leaped up from behind the desk. "*Pepper!*"

Except he knew it wasn't her, or at least not just her. She was merely the puppet. Tony Stark was the puppeteer.

Still, there was no reason he couldn't cut her strings just the same.

He bolted from the room and headed for the atrium balcony that overlooked the main lobby. He arrived with such speed that he had to grab the railing, lest he take a header over the edge. He got there just in time to see Pepper walking across the lobby, carrying the box, heading for the door.

"*Pepper!*" he bellowed, his voice echoing through the lobby.

Pepper froze as she heard Stane's voice. She looked up and saw him glowering down at her from the balcony. The security guard at the front desk who had just waved to Pepper as she passed now saw Stane scowling down, and then looked at Pepper suspiciously.

For a moment the pleasant mask that Stane had been wearing to cover what he really was slipped. The true

Obadiah Stane looked out at her with eyes cold as the nothingness of an empty heart.

"Ms. Potts," another voice came from behind her. She felt besieged from all around . . . and suddenly she recognized the voice.

"*Agent Coulson!*" she said as if she'd suddenly run into her best friend from high school. "*Federal* Agent Coulson!" She made sure to add particular emphasis to that first word.

Stane froze, his mouth open, an order to the guard left unspoken. Pepper was by Coulson's side, wrapping her arm around his elbow. Coulson looked startled as she started pulling him forcefully toward the door. "Ms. Potts, did you forget our appointment?"

"No, of course not. I've been very much looking forward to it. Let's . . . why don't we do this somewhere else?" she said. She kept him moving, guiding him out the door while continual glancing over her shoulder.

Stane never moved from the spot. He remained there until she was gone.

The moment they were out in the courtyard, Pepper began to tremble so violently that she dropped the box. Coulson caught it. "We have to get back to Tony . . ."

"Ms. Potts, I think you need to tell me what's going on before we get back to anyone." She tried to dart past him, but he caught her by the arm. His laconic manner dissipated and he said sharply and forcefully, "All right, that's it. You're coming with me."

Pepper suddenly started to wonder if perhaps she should have taken her chances with Stane. "I can't go anywhere with you. Mr. Stark is . . ."

"We have our suspicions about Mr. Stark, and frankly, Miss Potts, we're wondering if you're not complicit—" He stopped talking when he saw she was dialing her cell phone. "Are you calling to warn Stark of our interest in—?"

"You're damned right I'm calling to warn him, but not about you. Tony! Pick up, dammit! I need to—"

He pulled the phone away from her and looked her in the eyes. "Ms. Potts, we're concerned that your boss has been flipped."

"*Flipped? You're* the one who's flipped. Obadiah Stane has—"

"This isn't about Obadiah Stane. This is about the man who was captured by enemy operatives, then returned to this country and announced he wasn't making weapons anymore. That indicates to us at least a seventy-three percent chance that he has been brainwashed into having sympathies for the enemy. And if he's refusing to develop weapons for us, who's to say he isn't developing them for—"

"Seventy-three percent—?!?"

"That's the—"

"Here's a stat for you! There's a one hundred percent chance that you're an idiot!" Before a stunned Coulson could respond, she held up the hack drive. "It's Stane. The proof of it is right here."

"Then we'll take it back to headquarters and check it out. If it backs up what you're saying . . ."

"We don't have time—!"

There was the sound of several doors slamming. Pepper looked and saw that two black Crown Victorias had pulled up and five more guys, all of whom were dressed similarly to Coulson, had stepped out of them.

"We're making the time," said Coulson.

Out of time, out of time, thanks to her we're out of time.

The words pounded through Stane's mind as he dashed to the laboratory beneath the Arc reactor building. Pepper Potts had the evidence and she had the ear of a federal agent. The only thing Stane had was a nonfunctional armored suit and a squad of useless scientists that he had to pray had made a breakthrough.

His luck, unfortunately, remained consistent.

Layton stood in front of the armor, looking like a tribal primitive who was endeavoring to figure out a way to fire up a Cray supercomputer. There were dark rings under his eyes; he looked as if he could barely stand up. Obviously he hadn't slept for several days. "There's no technology that can power this thing."

"I told you," Stane said in a flat, angry voice as if addressing a five-year-old who had been told repeatedly to stay out of the cookie jar and was standing there with chocolate chips smeared across his face, "miniaturize the Arc reactor."

"I'm sorry, Mr. Stane, I've tried." The fatigue prompted him to speak far more bluntly than he ordinarily would have. "I've driven my team to insane lengths and beyond. Practically beat myself black and blue mentally. Specs and formulas . . . they're floating in front of my eyeballs like gnats. Look there." He pointed. "There's an equation for revised power couplings that went nowhere, drifting past." He closed his eyes, steadied himself, and then said, "What you're asking for can't be done."

"Tony Stark was able to do it in a cave, with a box of scraps."

"Well," said Layton, "I'm not Tony Stark, sir."

Stane stared at him for a long moment, and then said, "No. You're not. In the end, there's only one Tony Stark." He paused and then added, "You know what, Layton? Don't worry about it. You tried your best. Go home, get some sleep. Get a life."

Layton was visibly astounded at Stane's reaction, perhaps having expected something far more cutting and angry. But there was no point to that.

Because Stane had spoken a truth that he had not wanted to acknowledge. There really was only one Tony Stark.

It was time to make use of the one they had.

xxi.

Tony Stark, hard at work in his workshop, blinked in surprise when the power started to diminish unexpectedly.

"What gives, Jarvis?"

"You have a visitor, sir. Obadiah Stane is here."

Tony moaned. This simply wasn't something that he needed to deal with. And he wouldn't have had to if he'd bothered to update Jarvis as to the current situation with Obadiah Stane—namely that he was a lying scumbag that Tony didn't want to have anything to do with. Then Jarvis could have taken steps to make certain Stane didn't get into the house.

"Fine," said Tony after a few moments of mentally kicking himself. He tossed aside his tools and headed out, not even glancing at the digital readout on the phone indicating that Pepper had tried to get through.

Stane was waiting in the living room for him and, shock of shocks, he had pizza with him. "Peace offering? Or . . . pizza offering, as the case may be."

Tony simply stood there with arms folded. There was nothing that Stane could say to him that could possibly be of interest to him.

Perhaps sensing that the time for conversation had long passed, Stane put down the pizza, walked across the room to Tony, and produced a letter-sized envelope from his jacket pocket. "I'd like you to proofread something for me."

"Would you like me to spell check it, sir?" said Jarvis.

Stane's expression was pained. In a low voice, he said, "Can you turn him off? All the way?"

"Spin down, Jarvis," said Tony, who had already removed the letter from the envelope. He scanned it and the further he went, the higher his eyebrows arched. He looked up, surprised. "Your resignation?"

Stane nodded and said, as if making a confession, "You were right. It's not my company. Not my name on the building. We were a great team, but I guess this is where our paths diverge."

Tony was about to reply when he heard a blip from the phone system. The name "Pepper Potts" appeared in digital form on the LCD. "Pepper. I should take that."

"Tony. Please." His tone was pleading. Tony had never seen Stane like this. He actually seemed . . . vulnerable. "I'll be out of here in a minute."

Slowly Tony nodded and then pushed the button on the phone, kicking the message straight to voice mail. When he did, Stane put a hand on his shoulder. His expression was kindly, his voice fatherly. This was the Stane that Tony had known for so long, the one on whom not only Tony but also Howard Stark had depended. "We have too much history to part on bad terms. I'd like your blessing."

Tony was about to respond, but suddenly his body was shot through with paralyzing pain. His first instinct was that Pepper was right, he should have gone to the hospital, because he was having a heart attack or stroke. Then he saw the demented smile on Stane's face and spotted what appeared to be some sort of electronic filter in his ear. It was at that moment that he remembered the sonic taser that he had designed for undercover police officers, reasoning that undercover cops should be able to carry some sort of small but devastating weapon that would elude routine searches.

Now the weapon was coursing through him, shutting

down his entire nervous system exactly as it was supposed to do. Tony sank down in a chair, staring straight ahead, twitching spasmodically but otherwise unable to move.

Stane placed the taser down on the table and then crouched in front of Tony as if he were a friend talking him through some sort of an attack. "Easy now. Try to breathe." Tony's eyes widened as Stane slowly, methodically, began to unbutton his shirt. "You can't mess with progress, Tony," he said as if he were incredibly regretful about the way in which things were turning out. "It's an insult to the gods. You created your greatest weapon ever, but you think that means it belongs to you. It belongs to the world."

Stane pulled open Tony's shirt and smiled. The glow from the miniature in Tony's chest highlighted his face. He looked almost satanic smiling down at Tony in that manner. His eyes wide with pain, Tony remained unable to move. He was screaming inside his own head, deafening to himself, inaudible to anyone else. All he could do was gasp and gurgle as Stane began removing the chest piece from its socket. "Your heart will be the seed of the next generation of weapons. They'll help us steer the world back in the right direction—put the balance of power back in our hands. The right hands." Like a doctor delivering a child, he pulled loose the reactor and held it high. "By the time you die, my prototype will be operational. It's not as . . . conservative . . . as yours."

He carefully removed a cloth from his pocket and wrapped it around the reactor. He held it close, sighing happily, a child with his fondest birthday wish clutched in his greedy hands. Then he stood, pocketing the sonic taser. Tony rolled off the chair and hit the floor, staring up at the ceiling. He thought he could actually feel the metal shards, no longer held back by magnetics, beginning to inch their way toward his heart. Yinsen had never told him how much time he would have had without mechanical intervention. Hours? Minutes?

Stane was looking down at him with what actually seemed to be sympathy. "The sad thing is, we're both the good guys."

Like hell. Like hell we both are, you bastard . . .

Naturally Stane didn't hear his response. Instead, he calmly turned off the light, leaving Tony Stark in darkness. Tony lay there, unmoving, and he heard the door click softly, indicating that Stane had departed.

The words "I am invincible" seemed a lifetime ago.

"What do you mean, he paid to have Tony killed?" Rhodey said to Pepper over her cell phone. "Slow down. Why would Obadiah—?"

"Because he wants it all! He saw his chance and he took it! That's why!" As Pepper spoke, she was hurrying across the pavement of an underground parking lot, the clacking of her heels reverberating through the structure. Coulson and five men were running alongside her. "I just got done showing some Feds the proof!"

"Where is Tony now?"

"I don't know, he's not answering his phone. Will you just go over there and check on him?"

"Why, where are you? Aren't you—?"

"We're heading over to the office to round up Stane. So can you—?"

"Of course. I'm on it."

"Thanks, Rhodey."

She snapped shut her cell phone as the agents clambered into their Crown Victorias. Coulson held open the door for her. Instead Pepper made a beeline for her parked Audi, which one of the agents had driven over to their headquarters while they'd been questioning her. "I know a shortcut," she said briskly as she clambered into her car.

"I'll ride with her," Coulson called, climbing into the passenger's side.

The Audi tore out of the garage. Coulson grabbed the sides of his seat, trying to look as if he wasn't suddenly regretting not riding with the other agents. He glanced behind them and saw that the Crown Vics were keeping up, but just barely.

In a low, angry voice, while never taking her eyes from the road, Pepper said, "If anything happens to Tony because you were busy playing twenty questions with me, so help me God, I'll kill you."

"Threatening a federal agent is a crime."

She looked away from the road long enough to lance him with a glare. "Do I look like I give a damn?"

"No. No, you don't," admitted Coulson, who was suddenly glad he had a gun to provide self-defense just in case Pepper lived up to her threat . . . which, he suspected, she might well do.

The elevator doors that led into Tony Stark's workshop slid open and Tony fell out. He lay there for a moment, gasping, every breath labored. The metal hadn't penetrated his heart yet, but as the shrapnel pressed closer and closer in, it placed increased strain on his chest and made breathing nearly impossible. His entire torso felt as if it were on fire.

He was running on fumes as he clawed and crawled his way across the floor toward the workbench. His pulse was thudding in his ears, and the world seemed to be developing a reddish tint.

There, on his workbench, was his target: the original chest piece that Pepper had mounted in Lucite. It sat there and glowed at him, simultaneously inviting and contemptuous. *Come crawling back, have you?* Tony could have sworn he heard it saying, mocking him. *Why would you have need of me? I'm old. I'm antiquated. I'm yesterday's news, remember? You have your nice, pretty new model, oh, wait. Lookee there. You don't. Now isn't that just too, too unfortunate.*

He reached for the chest piece but didn't have close to the strength required to haul himself to it. He thought grimly, *Okay. Fine. If Muhammad can't make it to the mountain,* and yanked on the workbench as hard as he could. The entire structure tilted, and then the chest piece tumbled off the desk and clattered to the floor.

The Lucite kept it intact. Several other tools had fallen from the workbench, including a screwdriver. Tony grabbed it and half-crawled, half-threw himself over to the reactor lying on the floor. Within seconds he had managed to pry the reactor out of the Lucite. He lifted it and looked at it with pure joy. He'd never thought he would be so proud to see something that was obsolete.

Keep on shining. Keep it going so that we can beam the flood of justice on Obadiah Stane.

He considered what he had just thought and decided it was so puerile that it was probably one of those declarations best kept to oneself. He also couldn't help but think that, if he survived this, Pepper—who had preserved the chest piece when he'd been ready to dump it—was never going to let him hear the end of it.

In the subbasement pipe room, Obadiah Stane perched atop a stepladder in front of the massive armored suit. He held the glowing miniature reactor carefully as he inserted it into the chest of the armor. It took him a moment to find the correct position, but after a bit of experimentation he was able to make it click properly into place.

For a moment nothing happened, and Stane believed

he was about to experience another crushing disappointment. But then the eyes of the armor began to glimmer softly in the dimness.

Stane sighed gratefully as if welcoming an old friend. He fought the impulse to cry out, *It lives! It lives!* Instead he simply said, "Hello, Iron Monger."

The Iron Monger did not respond except that the eyes shone even more brightly as power flooded into the armor.

The door to Tony Stark's living room trembled for a moment, and then burst open, shards of wood flying everywhere. Rhodey staggered in, rubbing his shoulder where he had driven it full force into the door. He looked around frantically when he saw furniture overturned and, worse, no sign of Tony Stark.

"Tony! Tony! Where are you?"

He ran to the stairs that led down into the workshop. When he got there, he stopped, shocked, his gaze playing over what could only be termed a hall of armor. There was the suit that Rhodey recognized from the pursuit of the Raptors, still battle scarred with bullet dents and scorch marks. And Tony clearly hadn't stopped there. There were components everywhere for another model: helmets, gloves, boots, and prototypes for future developments. It was at that moment that Rhodey realized Tony Stark's mind never, ever shut down.

But Tony's body was as human as anyone else's, and if Stane had managed to shut that down, then Rhodey was personally going to tear off Stane's head and shove it right up his—

Then he thought he heard a movement from elsewhere in the workshop, something lurking in the shadows. "Tony?" he said cautiously.

The body in the shadows slumped forward. It was indeed Tony Stark, lying on the floor, looking like he'd been given mouth to mouth by a vampire.

Rhodey ran to him, dropped next to him on the floor while shouting his name. His hands reflexively hovered over Tony's chest, about to administer CPR, and then he stared down at the miniature Arc generator. For all he knew if he pushed down on the thing, he'd blow up the entire neighborhood.

So he grabbed Tony by the shoulders, shaking him violently while continuing to shout his name. For long moments there was no response, and then Tony's eyelids flickered. "Oh great . . . an earthquake," he muttered.

"Tony! God, I thought you were—"

"I almost was. I may yet be," said Stark as he sat up with a low grunt.

"What the hell happened?"

"Obadiah," he said, "tried to kill me."

"Yeah, well his trying-to-kill days are done."

Tony looked around. "Wait. What are you doing here? Where's Pepper?"

"That's what I'm trying to tell you. She called me, told me to come here. She was worried about you . . . with good reason, obviously. She's with five Feds. They're going to arrest Obadiah."

Tony Stark slowly shook his head. "That's not going to be enough."

Coulson had tried to talk Pepper out of descending into the subbasement with them, but she wouldn't hear of it. "No one knows that maze of tunnels the way I do," she had told them. "Even the diagrams on Stane's computer aren't entirely accurate." None of that was true: She only had a passing familiarity with them, and the specs were in fact 100 percent right. She just wanted to be damned sure she was there when Obadiah Stane got his.

Their entry into Stane's lair was thwarted by the locked door into the subbasement. Pepper's access key failed to trip it, indicating that Stane had overridden it. This slowed the agents only for as long as it took them to lay down detonator cord around the door hinges. "Clear!" shouted Coulson as everyone sought cover. When they were secured, Coulson hit the detonator, and the door was blown clear off its hinges.

"Impressive," said Pepper.

Coulson flashed a grim smile. "Your tax dollars at work."

Stane heard an explosion. Some unwanted visitors were forcing their way in. He glanced at a security monitor and saw exactly what he expected to see.

"Guests," he said softly, and the last "s" hung in the air as if enunciated by a snake.

He prepared to greet them.

In Tony Stark's lab, there was a soft clanking and Tony stepped from around a bank of machinery. Rhodey's eyes widened in awe.

Tony was clad in red and gold armor and was holding a helmet in his hands. In all his years in the army, of all the weapons he'd witnessed in action, Rhodey had never seen anything quite as terrifying as the sight before him now. And that wasn't even because of the powerful-looking armor that Tony was wearing. It was because of the fierce determination on Tony's face.

"What's the plan?" said Rhodey.

"I'm going after Stane. I'm betting he's back at the office."

"Betting you're right. I'm right behind you," said Rhodey.

"I'm counting on it."

Tony lowered the helmet over his head and it clicked

into place. The eyes lit up and there was the sound of energy building. Rhodey took a step back, as much from being intimidated by what he was seeing as from concern over some sort of explosive charge that was about to be generated. Tony looked upward and Rhodey wondered why. Two seconds later he received his answer: The boots ignited and Tony blasted straight up through the ceiling, sending debris raining down. Rhodey shielded his face from it even as he thought, *So that's where the holes in the ceiling have been coming from.*

Rhodey stared after his friend, impressed. Then he noticed that the earlier version of the armor was still there. It was battered, yes, but perhaps it was still functioning. He yanked off his jacket as he made a beeline for it, grabbed the helmet, and pulled it down over his head.

Or at least tried to.

Unfortunately he wasn't able to get it over his nose, and it felt as if it was crushing his forehead. The thing was too small.

"Damn."

He had cabbed over from Edwards, unwilling to take the time to requisition a jeep. The cab hadn't waited around, so his only option was to delve into Tony's car collection. He suspected Stark wouldn't mind. Looking them over, he decided on the silver Audi R8. He jumped in. The key was in the ignition. He fired it up and the engine roared. "A V-8," he said, pleased with his choice. "Sweet." He gunned it and screeched out after Tony.

xxii.

Pepper led them toward the subbasement pipe room. Coulson wasn't letting her take point, however; he was right next to her, his gun out. The other agents followed in a "V" formation.

"What the hell?" Coulson said softly as they moved through the pipe room. "It looks like a morgue for the Transformers." Pepper couldn't blame him for his reaction. They were moving through a metal jungle of vats, machines, armored limbs, and metal guts hanging from tethers. Utility pipes lined the walls, like oversized metal veins.

"Wait," said Pepper, and the others automatically stopped. She had stopped in front of a large metal scaffolding. She stared at it, unease poking at her.

"What? There's nothing here," said Coulson.

"I know. What worries me is that maybe there was before."

Coulson's lips thinned. He turned and said, "Okay, I want you to fan ou—" He stopped.

"What's wrong?" said Pepper.

"Where's Colan? Colan!"

The others turned and now Pepper saw that there were only four men following. One had vanished.

"Colan! Report!"

No answer.

Coulson turned to Pepper and said, "Get out. Now. Back the way we came. Go."

"But—"

"Now!" he said sharply and chambered a round in his gun, his gaze sweeping the perimeter. The other agents closed ranks, and Coulson roughly shoved Pepper back in the direction of the exit.

As they moved away from Pepper, she flattened against the wall and pulled out her cell phone. No signal. She put it away, turned back to the agents, and suddenly saw something in the darkness: a pair of glowing eyes. The agents didn't see it. They happened to be looking everywhere except that particular direction.

"There!" shouted Pepper, and then her outcry was drowned by the whirring of hydraulics and grinding metal.

The agents opened fire. The bullets ricocheted, striking the pipes lining the wall and sending blasts of steam into the tight hallways. There was a deafening clanking, like a bulldozer with legs, and suddenly there was a scream as another agent was yanked from view, vanishing into the steaming murk. Pepper spun, tried to run from the scene, and banged her head against one of the lower pipes. She staggered and fell, and there was more screaming, bullets being fired to no avail. One ricocheted off the wall mere inches from her head and embedded itself in the cement wall to her right.

Another one of the agents staggered out of the mist, shouting into his radio, "Agents down! Agents down!" He spotted Pepper and gestured angrily to her. "Get out of here!"

He yanked her to her feet and practically threw her toward the exit. She staggered, nearly fell, and then caught herself on the railing for the stairwell that led up to the exit. She was partway up the stairs when they began to shake violently under her feet. *Don't look back don't look back for God's sake don't look back.*

She looked back.

She remembered the diagrams that had said "Iron

Monger" in the files, and now something of that general shape and form was barreling down the corridor at her, with an ominous and familiar glow emanating from its chest. She couldn't make out the details, and had no desire to be close enough to do so. She sprinted up the stairwell, a different means of access to the pipe room than the one the agents had used. She took the steps two at a time, and she was almost to the top when the Iron Monger reached the bottom. But it was too wide for the stairwell and wound up crashing into it, sending up a shower of debris. There was an angry whine and then a roar of hydraulics, and even as she tried to tell herself that this couldn't be Obadiah, that even he couldn't be this far gone, a voice bellowed from the armor, distorted but still recognizable. *"Get back here!"*

Oh my God. It's him. As the Iron Monger furiously started tearing at the cement, grinding against the stairwell to get after her, Pepper shoved open the door at the top of the stairs and stumbled through.

She slammed the door behind her and turned to see where she was. As it turned out, she was in the main reactor room, with the long-dormant Arc reactor sitting not ten feet away.

She tried to catch her breath, but it wasn't easy. There was no sound from behind her, but she knew that that wasn't going to last. Stane would be after her. He wasn't going to let this go. He'd gone power mad, tromping around in the Iron Monger armor and annihilating everyone and anyone who was in his way. He wasn't going to hesitate to dispose of Pepper Potts if he'd been willing to kill federal agents and plan for the murder of Tony Stark.

Tony . . .

She pulled out her cell phone and started dialing frantically, thinking all the while that if she got punted to voice mail yet again, and she survived this whole thing, and Tony was still alive, then she was definitely going to kill him for getting her into this mess.

Tony hurtles through the air, wishing to hell that he had somehow managed to invent a matter transporter device so that he could just magically appear where he was needed. Despite the speed with which he is moving, it's like every passing second is a nail being hammered into Pepper's coffin.

Worse, he feels as if the armor is actually beginning to slow. He checks the HUD and discovers that he's not imagining it; he's lost about five knots off his airspeed. He knows he's not responsible for it. "Jarvis, what the hell! This is no time to shift me into low gear!"

"'Time' is actually the consideration, sir. It is not something that you have in abundance, not with your earlier model generator in place. I am merely endeavoring to conserve energy."

"All the conservation of energy isn't going to mean a thing if I get there too late to help Pepper!"

"If you arrive deceased, you'll hardly be in a position to help anyone."

"Give me the velocity I need, Jarvis. Once I get there, I'll make it short and sweet and won't come anywhere close to the generator's limits."

"That sounds akin to wishful thinking, sir," Jarvis says, but the speed picks up nonetheless.

He hopes it is fast enough.

Pepper's heart sank as the cell phone continued to ring and she knew that, yet again, she was going to be sent straight to voice mail. Every time she was, she became more and more convinced that it wasn't a case of Tony ignoring her calls; it was because he was lying dead somewhere, courtesy of—

"Pepper." It was Tony's voice; he'd picked up, and obviously caller ID had done the rest.

"Tony!" She sagged in relief against the wall. "Thank God, I got hold of you. Listen to me. Obadiah went crazy! He's got a big suit. It's kind of like yours. He calls it the Iron Monger."

It was hard for her to hear him. He sounded as if he were speaking from inside a wind tunnel. "Where are you?"

There was a *thump* from below her that caused her to lose her balance. Before she could pull herself together, the floor cracked. She looked down in horror and backed away as there was another *thump*, and another. The Iron Monger, unable to navigate the steps, was below her, pounding his way up. Before she could give it enough distance, the concrete cracked wide beneath her feet, sending her sprawling. The cell phone skidded away as one of the Iron Monger's fists came right through the floor.

Looking for all the world like a hatching dinosaur, the Iron Monger pushed away the concrete and steel, pulling himself out of the ground. No, not a dinosaur: It was like witnessing the birth of a god.

Finally he rose to his full height, ten feet tall, and he loomed over Pepper like a skyscraper. She was a gnat compared to this dull gray leviathan.

"Obadiah," she gasped.

Whatever remained of the occasionally avuncular Obadiah Stane she'd known for so long was nowhere evident in the creature standing before her, with its steel face and body and dead eyes. She had managed to get to her feet and now she was backing up as the Iron Monger slowly advanced on her. He took his time. No reason not to; she had nowhere to go.

Suddenly her foot bumped up against her cell phone. She grabbed it up and shrieked "Tony!" into it. Her back bumped up against the Plexiglas that comprised the outer shield of the Arc reactor.

"Pepper," came Tony's voice, "I have one thing I need to say to you: *Duck!*"

She didn't waste time looking around. Instead, she hit the ground, covering her head. The Iron Monger paused and then jerked his head upward, just in time to see another armored figure dive-bombing straight toward him, through the upper story. Repulsor rays blazing, the iron-clad form of Tony Stark smashed into the Iron Monger, sending the two of them crashing back down into the hole from which the Iron Monger had just pulled himself.

Pepper stared dumbfounded at where the two gladiators had just gone. Before she could think of what to do, alarm klaxons suddenly began to fill the air. She looked around for the reason, and to her horror spotted it almost immediately. The atrium glass of the Arc reactor had ruptured outward from the underground impact.

Even though the Arc reactor had been generating only minimal output, catastrophic damage to the unit could still cause equally catastrophic results. That was the case now as the impact from both Stane's entrance and his abrupt and very loud exit cracked the reactor housing. Pepper darted behind a large steel wall for protection, but as the alarms escalated and as she heard an ominous hissing, she wondered just how much protection the wall was going to provide.

He falls through to the subbasement, pounding on the far larger Iron Monger, hoping to find a flaw and end this quickly. But it's not going to be that easy. The Iron Monger strikes a grating below and crashes through. Tony ricochets off along the floor and rolls out of control, slamming up against a far wall. He shakes it off, clambers to his feet, and starts to go in pursuit of the crazed Obadiah Stane. Then he stops, looks around, sees the ruptured pipes, the leaking steam. Except it's not just steam: It's the coolant which keeps the Arc reactor within safety levels.

He activates the comm-link in his armor, which he had been using to speak to Pepper. An ordinary cell phone wouldn't have signal where he is, but the comm-link is more sophisticated. "Pepper."

"Tony!" her relieved voice comes back at him. "Are you okay?"

He has no time for such concerns. "Listen to me. We've got big problems: The Arc reactor is melting down."

"I know. It just blew up."

"No." He shakes his head. "It didn't. When it blows up, it's going to take the whole city with it."

"That makes me feel better," she says dourly.

His mind races, trying to find an easy solution—hell, any solution. "The only way to prevent a meltdown is to overload the reactor and discharge the excess power."

"How are you going to do that?"

"You're going to do it."

"You're going to do it."

Pepper suddenly couldn't breathe. Her vocal cords were closing up on her. "Me?" she barely managed to squeak out. Her cell phone was pressed hard against her ear in order to hear it over the warning bells.

"Yes. I want you to go to the central panel . . ."

She looked in pure terror at the central control room where the central panel was situated, deep in the heart of the Arc reactor station. Her voice went up an octave. "You want me to go in *there*?"

"Yes. Go to the panel and close all the low-voltage relays. Then I need you to go to the east wall and close all the 800-amp breakers."

She was trying to retain everything he was telling her while endeavoring not to panic. It wasn't a good combination. "I don't know what you're talking about!" she said in exasperation.

All things considered, his voice was remaining remarkably calm. "Pepper, just turn on all of the little switches, then turn on all of the big switches. You can handle it; I have to find Stane."

"Wait—turn them on? I thought you wanted me to close them? Tony? *Tony*? You want me to close them or turn them on?"

No answer.

Instinctively, she knew why.

"It's miraculous, Tony. It's your Ninth Symphony."
Stane's mechanized voice floats from all around him as he makes his way through the pipe room. It's impossible to get a sense of where he is, although obviously he's managed to make his way up from below. Tony sweeps the steel maze with his infrared, but the perforated pipes and the blasts of steam, casting red plumes and confusing shadows everywhere, are making it impossible for him to lock in on Stane's location.

"Trying to rid the world of weapons," continues Stane, *"you gave it its best one ever."*

"This wasn't meant for the world."

"How can you be so selfish?" He sounds disappointed, as if Tony had brought home a test paper with a failing grade on it. *"Do you understand what you've created? This will put the balance of power back in our hands for decades. Your country needs this."*

"What kind of world will it be when everybody's got one?"

"Your father helped give us the bomb. What kind of world would it be if he'd failed us?"

Tony is about to reply that it would be a much safer

one, but he doesn't have the opportunity, as he realizes a hair too late that the Iron Monger has emerged from behind some machinery and girders and is coming at him like a bullet train. The Iron Monger's viselike grip catches him up, yanks him off his feet, and together they smash right through one of the restraining walls that separates the sub-basement—elevated on its concrete island—from the highway outside.

They smash into a tractor trailer, annihilating the back of the rig, and keep going. They clang to the asphalt, bouncing once, twice, three times. The air is filled with the screeching of tires and the collision of cars. A hydrogen-powered bus jackknifes, skidding to a halt through the herculean efforts of a driver who never gives up trying to maintain control of his vehicle. Car doors are opening everywhere and people are running like mad. No one is hanging around to see how this bizarre fight that's playing like something out of a Michael Bay movie is going to turn out. They just want to put as much distance between themselves and it as possible.

Unfortunately Tony is aware of something that they are not: If Pepper cannot shut down the reactor, there's not going to be anywhere they can run.

Pepper wasn't sure what she had expected once she finished doing everything that Tony had told her to do, although she certainly hoped that a cessation of the klaxon would be forthcoming. No such luck. Alarms continued to sound, and she was terrified that the reason was because she had done something wrong. It wouldn't have surprised her if she had; she'd taken her best guess at shutting down and turning on what she was supposed to shut down and turn on, but there was always the chance she'd screwed it up.

"Tony," she said into her cell phone. "I need some

help here. I closed all the . . ." She gestured helplessly and vaguely in the direction of the control boards, ". . . the things."

Tony sounded stressed. "Go to the TR1 box and hit the red button!"

"Did you find Obadiah?" she said as she spotted a circuit box labeled TR1 and ran toward it.

"You could say that . . ."

She got to the box, flipped open the panel, and prepared to hit the red button.

There was an array of eighteen red buttons, all flashing.

"Thanks, Tony," she said with a moan.

Tony watches in horror as the Iron Monger raises a Volvo station wagon over his head. A terrified mother and her children are inside, trapped. The children are screaming, the mother white-knuckling the steering wheel in panic.

"Don't," he calls, jacking up the volume so he can make himself heard over the honking of trapped cars and the screams of the mother and children. "This is our fight!"

"People are always going to die, Tony," the Iron Monger informs him, as detached as if he were teaching a lesson on the art of war. "Part of the chess game."

Tony tries to bring his Repulsors to bear. Nothing. He designed the armor to be powered by his latest-model chest reactor, not the more primitive version he has been forced to employ. Consequently, everything is taking twice as long to power up, especially after it has been discharged.

"Emergency power!"

"Sir," Jarvis's voice cautions, "you'll drain the—"

"Now!"

The Iron Monger is about to heave the car at him

when the Repulsor rays surge from Tony's gauntlets and slam into Stane. The Iron Monger is knocked backward, flipping the car in Tony's direction at the last second. Tony catches it, grunting under the weight. He tries to set it down, but the leverage is wrong. The armor's gyros are unable to compensate, Tony's knees buckle, and he goes down under the car. The good news is that he cushions the impact with his body so that no one in the car is injured. The bad news is that he is pinned under the car.

The HUD informs him "Power Critical: Recharging."

Jarvis's voice sounds in his helmet. "How is the short and sweet strategy proceeding, sir?"

"Not now, Jarvis."

"At current power levels, you may not have a later, sir."

He hears a thundering footfall approach, like a T. rex. The Iron Monger is heading his way. Then, over the thudding of the approaching armored figure, Tony hears the thin, terrified voice of the boy from within the car shouting, "Go, Mom! Go!"

Oh crap, he thinks.

Before he can disengage himself from the car, the wheels spin and catch, and the car peels out. Tony is dragged along as the Volvo speeds away from the Iron Monger as fast as it can go, heading back the way it came. A shower of sparks blasts out from under him where his armored back is being dragged along the street. The Volvo weaves from side to side, dodging crashed cars and people who are trying to get out of its way. The thundering footsteps continue, except now they're interspersed with crunches of metal. Without seeing, he knows what's happening: The Iron Monger is using stopped cars like stepping stones.

He tries to think of a day that's sucked worse than this one. He's unable to come up with any, and that's even taking into account the day he was captured by terrorists. At least the terrorists never claimed to be his friend or brought him pizza.

Rhodey drove the Audi R8 like a madman. He barreled around slower cars and sped along on the shoulder of the road, honking constantly and flashing his lights. People might have thought he was an ambulance as he blew past them. Taillights flashed past him like tracer bullets as he sped past tight traffic.

Then he noticed something ominous: There was no traffic coming from the other direction. None. Which meant something had closed it off.

He hoped that, whatever it was, it had nothing to do with Tony.

He also had the funny feeling that he was destined to be disappointed on that score.

Tony finally manages to push the car off himself. It speeds away, heading the wrong way up an entrance ramp, with three gaping children staring at the back. They'll probably have some serious stories to tell at school tomorrow, provided school hasn't been blown off the map.

He staggers, trying to regain his footing, as the Iron Monger bounds off the hood of a car and lands only a few yards away.

Power levels are still only at 50 percent according to his HUD. Barely enough for proper maintenance of life support, let alone less offensive weaponry. Much more and he's going to be tapping into the life support power as well, and that could kill him before the Iron Monger gets the opportunity.

A biker, thinking he's going to thread his way through stopped traffic, weaves around a truck and nearly collides with the Iron Monger. The biker realizes his mis-

take, but too late. Seeing a weapon, the Iron Monger grabs the motorbike, sending the biker flying, as he whips the cycle around and slams it into Tony, knocking him backward. His head rings inside his helmet as he's sent crashing backward. Thank God it was only a rice burner, is the only thing that Tony can think.

He skids to a halt, landing in front of the stopped hydrogen bus. As he does so, Pepper's voice sounds in his ear: "Tony, it's not looking good. On this central panel, the monitors are showing the red bars rising."

He doesn't respond immediately. He can't; he's busy catching his breath. People are still scrambling to get out of the way. The Iron Monger stomps toward him, ground shaking so fiercely that Tony can't help but wonder if the Iron Monger could inadvertently trigger a fault line, because all the day needs is an earthquake to be truly complete. Tony once again tries to bring the Repulsors online and once again they're not ready to be fired. And this time there's no emergency power from which to draw. It's just going to have to recharge, and he doesn't have that kind of time, especially since the Iron Monger has just landed next to him and slammed his booted foot down atop Tony. Tony struggles to dislodge him and can't even begin to do so.

"The Arc reactor has been damaged, Obadiah," he says, a desperate appeal to reason. "It's going to blow up. A lot of people are going to die."

For all the reaction he gets from the man in the Iron Monger mask, he might as well not have said anything. "It didn't have to end like this, Tony. You were down; you should have stayed down."

He starts to apply pressure. He clearly intends to crack Tony's armor like a rotten coconut, and he has enough power to do it.

* * *

Rhodey barreled through the breakdown lane, weaving wildly around fleeing people, who scattered frantically to get out of his way. He redlined the engine, popped the clutch, and used every cylinder in the V-8 engine. The Audi surged forward like a rocket.

He blew around a stopped truck and right there in front of him were two armored figures, one on the ground, the other towering over him. Rhodey didn't even slow down. Instead, he opened it up all the way and the Audi rammed the taller figure's leg. The car didn't come close to surviving the impact; the front end crumpled like aluminum foil and the vehicle spun away, the engine screeching in protest.

Tony is uncertain at first what just happened. He hadn't seen it clearly; he had heard the rev of a familiar engine, a crash, and suddenly the Iron Monger was staggering.

Propping himself up on one elbow, Tony watches in astonishment as the Iron Monger lurches, out of control, his vast height working to his disadvantage for the first time. The Iron Monger almost manages to regain his balance, but then loses it, and crashes into the jackknifed abandoned hydrogen bus, perforating it. Struggling to free himself, the Iron Monger instead only manages to exacerbate the situation as his groping metal fingers create sparks by scraping across the metal ruins of the bus. The sparks ignite the bus, and a massive fireball erupts, enveloping the Iron Monger.

Through the filters covering his eyes, Tony sees that the flames have reached the sports car, which has crashed up against the median divider. Propelled with fresh urgency, he gets to his feet and staggers to the car. He rips it open and a stunned Rhodey is still inside. He yanks Rhodey out, snapping the seat belt as if it were limp spaghetti, and pulls him clear. Then he turns his back to the car, clutching Rhodey to his chest, as flames lick at the leaking tank of the Audi. Seconds later the sports car goes up in flame.

"You had to take my car," Tony says in annoyance.

Nothing is emerging from the conflagration that was the bus. It could well be that Stane is dead, but Tony wouldn't put money on it, and he was someone who— once upon a time—was willing to put millions of dollars on a roll of the roulette wheel. The problem is that he's got bigger concerns than Obadiah Stane right now.

"Get this area evacuated. There's going to be a melt-down." It's probably a lost cause with the safety of all Los Angeles in the balance, but if Tony somehow manages to localize the damage, then better to have no one local.

He ignites his boosters and hurtles skyward as Rhodey shouts from below, "You could have said thank you!"

xxiii.

"Pepper? How's it going?" came Tony's voice.

Pepper stood at the central console, feeling like a mental pygmy, while the entire area *thrummed* with an energy buildup that did not bode well. "It's not looking good, Tony," she said, trying to sound casual, as if she were giving him an update on a losing Dodgers game in the bottom of the ninth. "I did everything you told me but it says 'circuit not complete.' "

"I've got to get to the roof. Sit tight."

"Sit tight," she muttered. "Wonderful." She shook her head. "There damned well better be a major bonus in my envelope come Christmas, that's all I'm saying."

As he barrels toward the reactor building, he sees waves of energy coming off it, like the shimmering of a mirage, except this is no optical illusion. The clear roof, made from unbreakable Plexiglas, is lined with satellite dishes, intended to channel the reactor's energy to orbital receiving stations once the reactor became fully functional. The reactor never reached that level of development and so the dishes sat useless, waiting to be pressed into service. But Tony is going to be able to make use of them now. Landing on the roof, he paces it, using his HUD to guide himself to a key length of cable, which he tears up from beneath his feet. Below him the reactor is going insane, heading toward a cataclysmic buildup.

"Power at forty percent and dropping, sir," says Jarvis. *"You need to stop moving entirely for at least half an hour to have any hope of sufficient recharging."*

"Not happening, Jarvis."

He rips the cable in half, yanking one end with him. He attaches the cable to one of the satellite dishes. Power is pulsing through it with an urgency that will not be ignored.

"Pepper, I'm about to complete the circuit. Once I do, it's going to discharge all the power and channel it up through the roof. Get ready to push the Emergency Master Bypass. But not until I'm off the roof. It's going to fry everything up here."

He disengages his gauntlet and leaves it affixed to the antenna to hold the cable in place.

"Circuit complete, Tony!" comes Pepper's excited voice. *"The screen on the reactor says 'circuit complete'!"*

"Pepper, wait till I get clear, then hit the button."

There is a thud behind him. He turns and the Iron Monger is right there, right in front of him, flame licking off his blackened armor.

"Tony, what was that noise?" says Pepper.

"Thirty-five percent, sir," Jarvis says.

Great, *he thinks.*

He has no time to move before the Iron Monger nails him with a huge roundhouse punch. Tony skids across the rooftop. He quickly recovers, bounding to his feet and igniting his boots. He hurtles toward the Iron Monger. Despite everything else that's been going on, he's managed to devote a section of his brain to discerning the weaknesses in his opponent's armor. He believes he has it now as he comes in close and grabs for the hydraulic lines that he has identified as essential for the Iron Monger suit to function. He knows it is a *calculated risk, getting this close, but he sees no other way.*

He takes the risk and loses as the Iron Monger intercepts the thrust and throws his arms around Tony in a massive bear hug. The pressure on Tony is murderous. His armor starts to crack under the pressure. He struggles to maintain consciousness as his HUD begins to splinter and break apart.

"Twenty-five percent, sir," Jarvis says.

Think of something . . . think of anything . . .

He discharges the chaff that he had used to confuse the missiles. It distracts the Iron Monger only for a moment, but it's enough for Tony to reach down and disengage discs he has attached on either hip. They are explosives, and their detonation lets loose a mass of smoke and flame that causes the Iron Monger to lose his grip on Tony. The Iron Monger waves the smoke away, steps out of it, and tries to find where Tony has gone.

He doesn't react nearly quickly enough as Tony leaps onto his back. The Iron Monger makes his first tactical mistake: Instead of throwing himself backward, slamming Tony to the ground like a wrestler, he instinctively tries to reach around and grab at him. It's his undoing as Tony reaches down and rips loose the hydraulics, pulling a long cable out of the Iron Monger's spine as if he were ripping open the side of a Jiffy envelope.

The Iron Monger staggers. He's clearly losing power, and Tony doesn't let up. He continues to pummel him. The Iron Monger, making one last desperate effort, manages to grab Tony by the head and whip him around. He sends Tony flying. The air whips past Tony's face and he realizes that the Iron Monger has his helmet.

He has lost his HUD and Jarvis's advising him how much time he has left before his generator shuts down completely and the shrapnel has an unobstructed path to his heart.

＊   ＊   ＊

"Tony? Tony, where'd you go?"

Pepper was starting to get extremely concerned. What the hell was he waiting for? What was going on up on the roof? She heard stomping around, sounds of a . . .

"Oh lord, no," she said in realization. "Obadiah."

Tony lands on the roof, facing his massive opponent. The Iron Monger crushes Tony's helmet in his oversized hand and then tosses the scrap metal aside. He stomps across the roof toward him, stretching out his arm, and Tony sees a massive Gatling gun snap into view. If he still had his full armor, it wouldn't be a problem; without his helmet, he's vulnerable. He leaps to one side as Stane opens fire, but the damaged hydraulics have ruined his ability to manipulate his weaponry properly. Bullets spray everywhere, cracking the Plexiglas rooftop. The plexi was designed to withstand stress, but this is beyond anything conceived for it. It cracks in a spiderweb pattern and then shatters, sending Tony tumbling down toward the reactor, which is bubbling like a cauldron. He reaches out desperately and catches a metal girder. Plexiglas rains down, and from the corner of his eye he sees Pepper down there, covering her head and trying to avoid the shards coming down all around her.

The Iron Monger, still on the roof, looks down through the hole and brings his Gatling gun to bear once more. Tony quickly ignites his boots and they propel him back up onto the roof before the Iron Monger starts shooting. The last things he needs are bullets ricocheting around down there.

Landing on the far side of the hole, he shouts, "Pepper, hit the button!"

＊   ＊   ＊

Pepper's hand hesitated over the button. She screamed over the cacophony of the klaxon, "You said not to!"

"*Just do it!*"

"Are you off the roof?"

"*Pepper, we don't have a choice,*" Tony's voice came from overhead. "*We have to stop him! Do it now!*"

Pepper hit all the switches, praying that she hadn't just killed her boss, and then dove under the consoles for cover as the world went steel blue.

Tony braces himself for it, and then it comes: an electromagnetic pulse, flashing upward along the reactor. The searing flash of the EMP is momentarily halted between the satellite dishes. Then it surges outward, turning both Tony and the Iron Monger into statues as the pulse knocks out both their power and electronics. The blast continues, unstoppable, radiating concentrically outward, rendering everything dark in its wake. The roof, unable to withstand the incredible heat generated by the surge, buckles, its center sagging. Tony is completely paralyzed. Everything is offline, even his chest reactor. The metal is back to seeking out his heart. My God, just how many ticking clocks am I supposed to deal with?

The Iron Monger, closest to the collapsing section of the roof, topples over. His dead fingers catch on a seam and he lies there precariously on the edge of the slope.

"I guess this is a draw," *says Stane.* "The genie is out of the bottle. We've done our part. We've brought a great gift to the world and now it is time to go. That is the law of nature, Tony."

Then the roof gives way completely and Stane tumbles down, down into the bubbling purple miasma that is the Arc reactor. He disappears into it. There is no scream.

Tony, still paralyzed, watches him go. He waits to feel something—disgust, triumph, anger . . . anything.

Instead he feels nothing, even as the reactor that will save his heart reboots and comes back online.

"And that is the law of gravity," he says.

xxiv.

"You've all received the official statement of what occurred at the Stark Industries facility last night."

Rhodey was standing in the lobby of the Stark Industries building, delivering a prepared text to an assemblage of reporters who had shown up at the front doors and would not back off until they had their story. In his office upstairs, Tony kept glancing at the television that was carrying the live feed.

Rhodey continued: "There have been unconfirmed reports that a robotic prototype malfunctioned and caused damage to the Arc reactor. Fortunately, a member of Tony Stark's personal security staff was able to neutralize that situation utilizing classified Stark technology. We are also investigating the Arc reactor breach and are happy to report that, although some disruption to the Howard Stark Parkway occurred, no civilians were injured. It is now confirmed that ninety percent of the power has been restored in the surrounding area. Regarding the specifics of the events as they transpired, I urge all of you not to jump to conclusions and to wait for the facts as they unfold."

A copy of the *Los Angeles Times* lay on Tony's desk. A grainy newspaper photo from the freeway battle adorned the front, and above it was a full-column headline which blared the question, Who is Iron Man? Tony smiled and wondered which headline writer at the *Times* was a Black Sabbath fan.

Then he winced. "Careful," he said.

"Don't be a baby," said Pepper, relentlessly touching up his facial wounds with dabs of alcohol. Once she was satisfied, she began using makeup to hide them from intrusive TV cameras.

On the other side of the room, Agent Coulson was scanning a set of note cards he had in his hand.

"Iron Man," said Tony, glancing once more at the headline. He remembered when the terrorists had shouted that name in fear upon first seeing him storm into their midst like a juggernaut. Apparently it was a recurring theme . . . and besides, Man of Steel was already taken. "I like that. It's not technically accurate—the suit is a gold-titanium alloy—but I like the ring of it. I like the imagery. Plus, you know, you have to love Ozzy. *I am Iron Man*," he intoned.

"No. You're not," said Coulson firmly. "And to prove it, here's your alibis." He handed Tony the set of cards. "You were on your yacht. We have port papers that put you in Avalon all night, and sworn statements from fifty of your guests."

"Maybe it was just Pepper and me."

"This is what happened. Read it word for word."

He glanced through the cards in a perfunctory manner. "There's nothing here about Obadiah Stane."

"That's being handled. He's on vacation. Small jets have such a poor safety record," Coulson said sarcastically.

"Is this going to work?"

"This isn't my first rodeo, Mr. Stark. Just stick to the official statement and this will all be behind you." He nodded to Pepper and then said, "We'll be in touch."

"I know," said Pepper. "The Strategic Homeland Intervention, Enforcement, and Logistics Division."

"Just call us SHIELD."

"Much better," said Tony.

Coulson nodded once and then walked out the door,

leaving the two of them alone. Tony continued to thumb through the cards. "I have to admit, this is pretty good. Even I don't think I'm Iron Man."

"You're not Iron Man."

"You know, if I *was* Iron Man," he said slowly, "I'd have this girlfriend who knows my secret identity and is always worried that something bad is going to happen to me—but at the same time is so proud that I'm out there saving the world. She's conflicted and that only makes her crazier about me."

He waited for her to say something. Instead, she didn't reply, and an awkward silence grew between them. He cleared his throat uncomfortably. "You ever think about that night?"

"What night?" Her face was the picture of innocence.

"That night on the balcony."

"You mean that night that I had too much to drink and had a lapse in judgment that will never, ever happen again? You mean that night?" Having finished the makeup job, she gave it one final inspection, then reached to his neck and straightened his tie.

He got it, of course. The long look she gave him made it abundantly clear. It was too much for her. The thought of him running around in an armored suit, risking his life—too much. Too much emotion, too many roiling feelings that she simply couldn't stand to deal with. If this—this suit—was going to be a part of his life . . . then she was going to have to limit the part of his life that she was willing to share. It was the only way she would be able to survive.

"Will that be all, Mr. Stark?"

"That will be all, Miss Potts."

And then she was gone as well.

He was alone.

* * *

"*And now, Mr. Stark has prepared a statement. He won't be taking any questions.*"

Tony steps up to a podium that's been set up. The reporters, including Christine Everhart, of course, are gathered, waiting. Questions start to bubble up and he promptly puts up a hand to silence them. The cards are arrayed on the lectern.

"*I'm just going to stick with the cards this time,*" he says a bit haltingly. "*Because last time . . .*" He pauses. "*There has been speculation that I was involved in the events that took place.*"

"*Do you honestly expect us to believe,*" says Christine, "*that you now have a bodyguard who nobody has ever seen or heard of before, who has conveniently appeared despite the fact that you historically disdain bodyguards?*"

"*Yes,*" he says, hurrying back to the cards. "*Some have gone so far to actually suggest that . . .*"

Everhart is relentless. Hell hath no fury. "*And this mysterious bodyguard was somehow equipped with an undisclosed 'Stark high-tech powered battle armor prototype'?*"

"*See, I'm getting to that. Some have gone so far to actually suggest that I was actually the guy in the suit—*"

"*I'm a little confused,*" says Christine. "*Is the story that they were both bodyguards in high-tech powered battle armor, or that one was a bodyguard and the other was a giant robot that was fighting the bodyguard in high-tech powered battle armor?*"

"*I know it is confusing. I—*"

He stops.

He looks at them, really looks at them. At their faces, at the questions on their faces.

He thinks about how lying and deceit from others has brought him to this pass. He has sworn to put an end to that sort of thing, to do away with underhandedness

*and double-dealing. With the sort of mind-set that re-
sulted in weapons being secretly sold to enemies and de-
stroying lives.*

The words of Obadiah Stane resound in his head: We
are iron mongers. *Except they've been more than that.
They've been fear mongers, adding more fear to a world
that already has a bellyful of it. Fear of weapons. Fear of
death and destruction. And the greatest fear of all: fear
of the unknown.*

People don't really know what happened last night.
More questions will be raised, and more. There has to be
an end to fear, and an end to secrecy, or otherwise this
wreck of a world is going to be the best they've got and
it's only going to get worse.

And the honesty, the transforming of the unknown
into the known, the upfront dealings with people . . . it
has to start somewhere.

"I am going to drop the cards," he says, and he
knows that somewhere Agent Coulson is about to have
a fit. He puts the cards down carefully, folds his hands.
"The truth is, I'm not the heroic type. I've had a lot of
indiscretions in my days. I've made a lot of mistakes.
Some of you know more about that than others," he
says pointedly in Christine's direction.

"But the fact of the matter is, in all honesty . . ."

Black Sabbath howls in his head. He smiles and says
the sentence that will be plastered all over tomorrow's
newspaper with his picture accompanying it:

"I am Iron Man."

With those four words, Anthony Stark knows he will
never be bored again.